RETURN TO THE WILD

SEEKERS

THE LONGEST DAY

SEEKERS

RETURN TO THE WILD

MANGA

Also by Erin Hunter

WARRIORS

THE NEW PROPHECY

Book One: Midnight

Book Two: Moonrise

Book Three: Dawn

Book Four: Starlight

Book Five: Twilight

Book Six: Sunset

POWER OF THREE

Book One: The Sight

Book Two: Dark River

Book Three: Outcast

Book Four: Eclipse

Book Five: Long Shadows

Book Six: Sunrise

OMEN OF THE STARS

Book One: The Fourth Apprentice

Book Two: Fading Echoes

Book Three: Night Whispers

Book Four: Sign of the Moon

Book Five: The Forgotten Warrior

Book Six: The Last Hope

DAWN OF THE CLANS

Book One: The Sun Trail

Book Two: Thunder Rising

Book Three: The First Battle

Book Four: The Blazing Star

Book Five: A Forest Divided

Book Six: Path of Stars

EXPLORE THE WARRIORS WORLD

Ravenpaw's Path #1: Shattered Peace
Ravenpaw's Path #2: A Clan in Need
Ravenpaw's Path #3: The Heart of a Warrior
SkyClan and the Stranger #1: The Rescue
SkyClan and the Stranger #2: Beyond the Code
SkyClan and the Stranger #3: After the Flood

NOVELLAS

Hollyleaf's Story
Mistystar's Omen
Cloudstar's Journey
Tigerclaw's Fury
Leafpool's Wish
Dovewing's Silence
Mapleshade's Vengeance
Goosefeather's Curse
Ravenpaw's Farewell

SURVIVORS

Book One: The Empty City
Book Two: A Hidden Enemy
Book Three: Darkness Falls
Book Four: The Broken Path
Book Five: The Endless Lake
Book Six: Storm of Dogs

THE GATHERING DARKNESS

Book One: A Pack Divided

Survivors: Tales from the Packs

NOVELLAS
Alpha's Tale
Sweet's Journey
Moon's Choice

RETURN TO THE WILD

SEEKERS

THE LONGEST DAY

ERIN HUNTER

HARPER

AN IMPRINT OF HARPERCOLLINS*PUBLISHERS*

Special thanks to Kate Cary

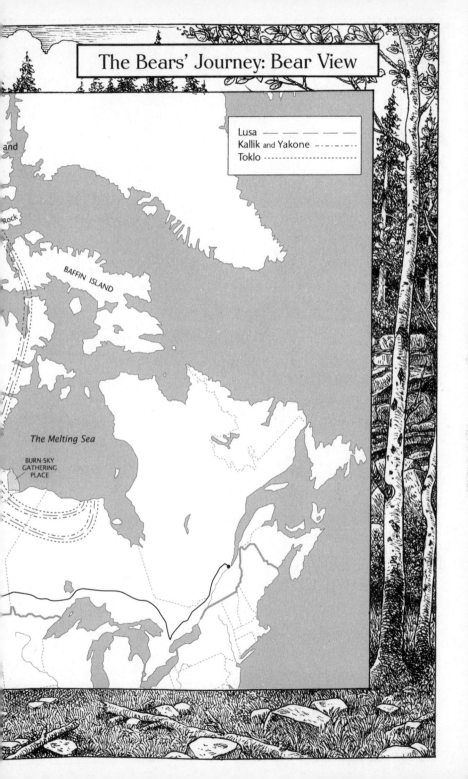

The Bears' Journey: Bear View

Lusa — — — — —
Kallik and Yakone ––·––·––·
Toklo ·······················

BAFFIN ISLAND

Rock

and

The Melting Sea

BURN-SKY
GATHERING
PLACE

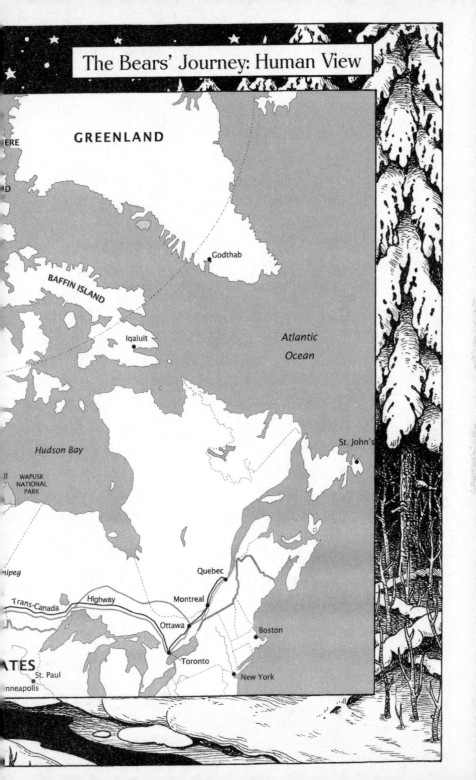

CHAPTER ONE

Lusa

Sunshine scorched Lusa's back. Hot wind whisked around her paws. From up on the hilltop, she could see across the top of the pines, and beyond them, at the foot of the slope, the lake glittered like stars.

Great Bear Lake. Lusa had forgotten how big it was. It stretched all the way to the horizon, reaching long, shimmering paws into wooded valleys on either side.

"Look at all those bears!" Yakone's gasp snapped Lusa from her thoughts. Beside her, the white bear was staring at the shore, where a group of brown bears moved across the stones. *They look so small from here!* Lusa thought. Farther along, white bears lay at the water's edge, clearly limp in the heat.

The bears were gathering for the Longest Day. *There aren't as many as last year.* Then Lusa realized that they must be among the first arrivals for the gathering. *We're early!*

On the far shore, a white bear plunged into the water. Nearer, a brown bear lounged on a rock. Lusa's heart quickened. *Where are the black bears?* She strained to see along the shore. *They must be among the trees.* Excitement tingled in her paws. Would Miki be there? Chula? Or any of the other black bears she'd met here a suncircle ago?

It was hard to believe that so many moons had passed since they were here. Lusa glanced at Toklo and Kallik. They'd grown. *So have I!* And that wasn't the only thing that had changed. Last time, Ujurak had been with them. Grief tugged at Lusa's heart. Was he watching them now?

Of course he's still with us. She knew his spirit traveled with them. *And now we have Yakone, too.* She glanced fondly at the broad-shouldered white bear. He was standing close to Kallik, his eyes wide.

"Why aren't they fighting?" Yakone's gaze flicked to Toklo. "I thought brown bears didn't like sharing territory, especially not with white bears."

"The white bears, brown bears, and black bears keep to their own parts of the shore," Toklo explained.

"There is peace between everyone during the Longest Day gathering," Kallik explained. "We come to honor our spirits."

Not always! Lusa scowled, remembering last time they were here. Kallik's brother, Taqqiq, and his friends had tried to take over the black bears' territory. "Let's hope that there's nothing to fight over this time," she muttered.

"Come on!" Toklo began to head down the slope.

Lusa stiffened. "Wait!"

"What's wrong?" Kallik must have heard the alarm in Lusa's bark.

"We can't just go down there!" Lusa blinked at Toklo.

Didn't he want to say good-bye before he joined his own kind?

Toklo misunderstood. "You're right. I guess it would look strange for a brown bear, a black bear, and two white bears to arrive together."

"We should go down separately," Kallik agreed.

"Do you think they'd really mind?" Yakone was watching the groups on the shore.

Lusa struck the ground with her forepaw. "That's not what I meant!" She remembered last night with a pang; the berries Yakone had brought her as they shared prey one last time. She could still taste the juice on her tongue. *Our final meal together.* Didn't this moment mean anything to them? They had journeyed farther than any other bears at the lake. They had protected one another over forest, mountain, and ice. "Is this the end of our friendship?" she whispered, looking from Toklo to Kallik and Yakone.

Kallik's eyes widened. "Of course not!"

"We'll see each other before we leave the lake." Toklo padded over and rested his muzzle on top of Lusa's head. "We'll always be friends."

Yakone gazed at her gently. "We came here for you, Lusa," he reminded her. "So you could meet other black bears and find a real home."

"Like I've found mine." Toklo had already staked out his territory in the mountains where he had been born. He would return there after the Longest Day was over.

"And we know where we'll find ours." Kallik glanced affectionately at Yakone. The two white bears would be traveling together to Yakone's island on the Endless Ice.

Lusa's eyes felt hot.

Kallik touched her nose to Lusa's ear. "We can't keep traveling forever, little one."

Kallik's right. This was why they'd come. Lusa looked down at the shore, imagining the black bears waiting in the trees. She remembered the deep longing she'd felt in the cave on Star Island all those moons ago as she stared at the picture of herself marked on the cave wall; the longing to go *home*—not to the Bear Bowl, but to a place where she would truly belong, with trees and sunlight and berries and grubs, and *other black bears*.

She pushed away her sadness. She'd already proved she could live beyond the Bear Bowl. This was her chance to have a life like a real black bear, among bears who knew what it was like to find the juiciest root and relish the taste of leaftime berries. Yakone and Kallik could feast on seal fat. Toklo could chase deer through the forest. They all had so much to look forward to.

Lusa lifted her snout, forcing her eyes to brighten. "Then what are we waiting for?" Breaking into a run, she slipped past Toklo and plunged down the grassy slope.

As she reached the pines, cool shadows swallowed her.

Kallik's call sounded behind her. "Good luck, Lusa!"

Lusa ran on. *Where are the black bears?* The sharp scent of sap filled her nose. Pine needles crunched beneath her paws. As the slope steepened, she veered sideways, racing along it, her ears pricked. She remembered from last time where the black bears made their temporary home for the Longest Day. If she followed the woods around the shore, tracing the curve of the lake, she would find them at the point where pines gave way to birch, spruce, and rowan.

She quickened her pace. Through the trees, she could hear the rippling of the lake against the shore. Heavy paws crunched on pebbles. Bears muttered gruffly to one another. She must be skirting the brown bears' gathering place. Toklo would be on his way there now. She glanced up at the trees, searching for black pelts among the branches. As the pines thinned and pale birch bark showed among the dark trunks, Lusa's heart leaped. This was the place!

Sun dappled the forest floor. The scent of freshly dug earth washed her muzzle. She hurried past a patch of uprooted ferns. A black bear had been foraging here recently. She could smell his scent. She scanned the forest ahead, happiness surging in her chest as she spotted black pelts moving between the trunks. Craning her neck, she saw bears clinging to branches overhead. A furry black face stared down at her, gnawing on a pawful of leaves.

Lusa slowed to clamber over a tangle of tree roots that crossed her path. A bramble bush swished beside her, and she turned to see a black bear peering curiously at her over the top. Two more bears were digging at the base of a spruce, scooping out pawfuls of wriggling grubs.

Lusa halted and gazed around. Brilliant shards of sunlight sliced through the branches. Black bears moved through them, their pelts gleaming. Lusa gasped. It was strange to be surrounded by bears her own size. She'd been a cub last time she was here, and she'd spent so long traveling with bears so much bigger than her. Suddenly she felt like a giant!

"Dustu!" A happy grunt sounded through the trees. A female bear scrambled down the slope, her gaze fixed on a grizzled black male who was ambling across a clearing.

The male bear looked up. He narrowed his eyes as though trying to see into the shadow. "Dena? Is that you?"

"Yes!" Dena chuffed as Dustu hurried to greet her. "How was your journey?"

"Long." Dustu shook one hindpaw, then another as though shaking away stiffness. His pelt glowed red in the dappled sunlight, betraying his age. Lusa wondered how many times he'd made this trip to the lake. He must know every bear here. "Is Leotie with you?"

Dena nodded. "She's picking berries. Have you seen Chula yet?"

Lusa tilted her head to listen. Chula had been here with her brother Ossi and their mother last suncircle. "Excuse me, did you say Chula?" She hurried forward. "Is she coming?"

Dustu and Dena stared at her.

"Do you know her?" Dena asked.

"I met her at the last gathering." Lusa stopped in front of them, her gaze flicking beyond them as she searched for familiar faces.

Dustu tipped his head. "I remember you," he grunted, his face softening. "You're the one who saved Miki from the white bears."

A young male bear crossed the clearing toward them.

"Lusa?" he called. "You came! Welcome!"

Lusa frowned. The bear's face was familiar. His name came to her in a rush. "Pokkoli!" He was a friend of Miki. "How are you?"

"Great, thanks."

"How's Miki?" Lusa asked. "Is he here?"

"Not yet. But he'll be here soon." Pokkoli swung his snout toward a group of black bears foraging farther up the slope. "Come and join us." He bounded toward them.

"It's nice seeing you again!" Lusa called to Dustu and Dena as she hurried after Pokkoli.

Ossi! She recognized the young male bear from the distinctive patch of white fur on his chest. He was sitting on the ground, chewing a fern root. Pokkoli had stopped to scratch his hindquarters against a tree. Two other bears were nibbling cloudberries from a bush while a female dozed in the sunshine.

Lusa suddenly felt shy. Would she remember how to act like a black bear? Would they notice she was different?

"Lusa!" Ossi scrambled to his paws. "It's good to see you again!" He was much taller and his voice was deeper than it had been last suncircle. He strode toward Lusa and butted her shoulder affectionately.

She staggered, surprised by his strength.

He huffed with amusement. "You've grown."

"So have you!" Lusa looked into his wide, open face. Happiness shone in his eyes.

"Isn't it great to be back?" Ossi stretched, rolling his shoulders.

"Is Chula with you?" Lusa couldn't see Ossi's sister among the others. "And your mother?"

"My mother stayed at home this year," Ossi told her. "Chula's traveling with Sheena and her cubs. They were planning to meet up with Miki. I came ahead with Pokkoli."

Pokkoli swallowed a berry and grimaced at the sharpness. "So, Lusa, what have you been doing since last leaftime?"

"Just traveling," Lusa told him.

Ossi looked surprised. "Alone?"

"With some friends." Lusa shifted her paws.

"Are they here?" Pokkoli looked around.

"Not exactly," Lusa mumbled.

Ossi frowned.

"They're with the brown bears and the white bears." Lusa peered through the trees. She could just make out the lake sparkling between the trunks.

"What are they doing *there*?" Pokkoli grunted.

"They're with their own kind."

"Their *own* kind?"

"Kallik and Yakone are white bears, and Toklo's a brown bear."

"You've been traveling with white bears?" Suspicion clouded Pokkoli's gaze.

"And a *grizzly*?" Ossi's frown deepened.

Lusa's fur prickled. She changed the subject. "Is Hashi here?" Hashi was the gruff old male who had seemed to be in charge of the black bears last time.

"Not yet." Pokkoli was still staring at Lusa.

Ossi scratched his flank with a large paw. "He's too ancient to walk fast."

"He might have met up with Chula and the others," Pokkoli suggested.

"If he's traveling with Chula, he'll never get here," Ossi chuffed. "Chula has to stop for food so often, she's slower than a two-legged coyote."

Pokkoli sat down. "And if Hashi stops to inspect every tree for a bear spirit, they won't be here until cold-earth."

"Poor Hashi. He's worried his ancestors might say something important when he's not listening," Ossi joked.

Lusa crept toward the cloudberry bush. Her belly was rumbling with hunger. She was relieved that Ossi and Pokkoli had stopped asking her about Kallik and the others. "Is it okay to share these?" she asked two bears who were reaching between the branches, plucking the swollen red berries.

"Help yourself." One of the foraging bears nodded toward the far side of the bush. His jaws were sticky with berry juice. "There's plenty over there."

Lusa sat down and tugged a berry from the bush with her teeth. The juice bathed her tongue, as sweet as honey. "Do you want some?" she asked Ossi.

Ossi shook his head. "No, thanks. I've just had a heap of fern roots."

When she was full, Lusa sat back on her haunches. The berries had made her thirsty. She stood up and headed through the forest toward the lake.

"Where are you going?" Ossi called.

"To get a drink."

"Watch where you go!" Ossi hurried after her with Pokkoli at his heels. They steered her onto a trail of trampled ferns. "You don't want to cross into the brown bears' territory."

Lusa sniffed. "They won't hurt us."

"I wouldn't be so sure." Pokkoli nosed past Ossi. "The brown bears are even grouchier than usual this year."

"Why?" Lusa walked out of the trees and hopped down a sandy ledge onto the pebbled beach. She glanced toward where the brown bears were gathered, beyond a rocky outcrop that jutted into the lake.

Ossi jumped down after her. "Oogrook's not here this time."

"Oogrook's their leader," Pokkoli explained as they reached the water's edge. "He settles arguments and makes them behave."

Lusa scanned the brown bears, her heart lifting as she spotted Toklo among them. He was as big as the others now, no longer a cub. "But Oogrook will arrive soon, won't he? Just like Hashi." She swished through the shallows and leaned down to drink. The water was cold on her tongue.

"No, he's dead." Ossi waded in beside her.

"Dead?" Lusa jerked up her head, her muzzle dripping.

"He was old." Ossi shrugged and took a drink.

Pokkoli hung back at the water's edge, his gaze on the brown bears. "The brown bears will have to decide who their new leader will be."

Ossi's ears twitched. "Brown bears can never decide anything without fighting. You'd best stay away from them until it's been settled," he grunted.

Lusa tried to catch Toklo's eye. Did he know about Oogrook's death yet? But he hadn't noticed her. *Please, Arcturus, watch over him.* They'd seen too many fights on their journey. *Don't let him walk into another.*

CHAPTER TWO

Toklo

Toklo broke from the trees and stopped at the edge of the shore. He could see Pawprint Island shimmering in the middle of the lake. The ancient story, repeated by every generation of bears, rang in his mind. *Arcturus strode across this lake, and where he set his paw, an island sprang up. Fish thronged around it and he ate his fill before he journeyed on.*

Pride swelled in Toklo's chest. *Did I really swim that far?* He'd only been a cub at the last gathering, and yet the other bears had chosen him to make the journey. Fish had been scarce and the bears had decided that one bear's swim to the island would be an offering of respect to Arcturus.

Toklo remembered the spirits of Oka and Tobi swimming beside him, his mother and brother boosting him up against the currents and urging him on as exhaustion dragged at his fur. As he'd swum back from the island, Toklo had caught a huge salmon and carried it to the others. They'd greeted him enthusiastically, knowing the salmon was a sign that their bellies would be full once more.

The breeze lifted Toklo's fur, and he felt strangely peaceful. *I belong here as much as I belong in my own territory. I will come to the gathering every suncircle,* he silently promised Arcturus.

He headed toward the gathering of brown bears. They seemed agitated. A single bear lounged on a cluster of rocks, but the others moved as they talked, shifting restlessly from paw to paw.

Curiosity sparked beneath Toklo's pelt. Had something happened? He quickened his pace. *Will they remember me?*

"Toklo!" A sturdy, coarse-furred bear nosed his way from the crowd. "You came!"

Toklo broke into a run, pebbles swishing beneath his paws. As he reached the bear at the edge of the group, he chuffed happily. "Shesh! It's good to see you!"

Shesh wrinkled his graying snout. "You smell like you've traveled far. Is that mountain scent in your fur?"

"Yes. And forest scent and sea scent and river scent," Toklo told him proudly. He examined Shesh. No new scars marked his pelt, and he was fatter than last burn-sky. "You look like you've had a good season."

Before Shesh could answer, angry snarls erupted behind him.

An old male swiped a paw at a younger bear. "You know nothing about where to hunt!"

"I know better than *you!*" the young bear snapped back. "Only a cloud-brain thinks that pine forests are good for hunting."

"The prey is rich there."

"But what bear can run through such thick forest?"

"You must be clumsy!"

"Any bear is clumsy compared with a deer."

The two bears glared angrily at each other.

Toklo looked around for Oogrook. The wise old bear could put a stop to the argument before it turned nasty.

But Oogrook wasn't here.

Toklo lifted his muzzle. "*All* forest is good for hunting. We should thank Arcturus for the prey it brings us."

Shesh nodded. "Toklo's right, Tuari." He caught the young male's eye before glancing at the older bear. "Holata, you should be *teaching* Tuari instead of arguing with him."

Holata dropped onto all fours, grunting. "It's impossible to teach a young bear anything." His gaze flashed to Toklo. "They think they know everything already."

"And *you* don't?" Tuari sank grumpily onto his front paws.

The other bears shifted around them, pelts twitching uneasily.

"Where's Oogrook?" Toklo asked.

Shesh looked down at his paws. "Oogrook died."

Toklo blinked. "How?"

Shesh shrugged. "He was old. He didn't wake up from his long sleep."

Toklo didn't want to believe it. He wanted to tell Oogrook about his journey. The old bear would understand how brave he'd been, how much he'd lost, and how much he'd achieved. With Ujurak, Kallik, and Lusa, Toklo had brought the spirits back so the wild would be safe. He'd helped Ujurak return to his home among the stars. Oogrook would have realized that he'd been right to put his faith in the young cub who had swum to Pawprint Island and carried a salmon back to shore.

Sadness pierced Toklo's belly. "Are you sure he's dead?"

"Wenona saw his body. She lives in the territory beside his." Shesh beckoned Toklo with a jerk of his muzzle. "Come, we have laid a tribute to him."

Toklo followed Shesh through the bears. They stopped near the spot at the lake's edge where Oogrook used to sit. Water lapped at a small pile of rocks and sticks, placed there deliberately. "His spirit runs with the currents now," Shesh murmured.

As Toklo stared at the ripples, he heard a friendly growl. "Are you the bear who swam to Pawprint Island?"

Tuari had followed them to the pile of stones. Two cubs peered from behind his wide haunches; they looked so similar that Toklo guessed they were denmates.

"He can't be! He's too young!" the she-cub huffed.

"That's what made it so special," her brother chuffed.

"Elki! Elsu! Be quiet!" Holata lumbered over and scolded the cubs.

"We're only talking to Toklo!" protested the she-cub.

"They're not bothering me—" Toklo began.

Holata cut him off. "Come away," he snapped. Elki and Elsu trotted obediently over to him.

Tuari stayed where he was, gazing at Toklo. "*You* made the fish come back!"

A she-bear hurried closer. "That's what I heard, too! You

made Arcturus send them back to the rivers and the lakes."

More bears gathered around him. Toklo's pelt twitched self-consciously as they stared at him.

"Thanks to you, I've had a full belly since last fishleap!" Tuari barked.

Toklo backed toward the water, his hindpaw grazing Oogrook's memorial of sticks and stones.

"Don't be shy." Shesh nudged his shoulder. "We're grateful to you. You were a brave cub."

Toklo was proud, but the gaze of so many bears felt hotter than the burn-sky sun. "I was happy I could do it," he mumbled. "I just wanted to help—" His voice trailed away as he caught sight of a huge brown bear with glossy fur the color of bark. Toklo recognized him at once, and his heart sank.

"You wanted to prove you were better than anyone else!" Hattack snarled, his black eyes glittering with dislike. "*I was* going to swim to the island, but you butted in before I could offer."

"That's not true!" Toklo growled. Hattack had claimed he couldn't swim to Pawprint Island because he had cramps in his legs. He'd been the bears' strongest swimmer, but he'd let Toklo take his place.

A she-bear pushed in beside Hattack and glared at Toklo. "You came to show off at the last gathering, and now you're here to show off again!"

"He's not showing off, Wenona!" Tuari objected.

Anger surged through Toklo's pelt. Why would he show off? He'd been scared half to death on the swim to Pawprint

Island, and he hadn't asked anyone to thank him for it now.

He felt Shesh shift beside him. "It's too hot to argue. Let's hunt instead." The old bear nodded toward the trees. "We can find out if Holata is right about pine forests being the best place for prey."

Holata snapped his head around as he heard his name. He narrowed his eyes warily.

Toklo didn't like the tension that swirled around the gathering, as stifling as the hot wind whisking down from the hills. *Oogrook should be here.* He guessed that more than one of the bears was silently hoping to take the old leader's place.

He said out loud, "That's a good idea, Shesh. Let's hunt." Chasing prey might ease the bears' hunger—for food *and* for leadership. At least it would take their minds off it for a while.

Toklo let Hattack, Holata, and Wenona take the lead, and walked between Shesh and Tuari as they climbed the shore and pushed their way into the ferns. Coolness swept over his pelt as he padded beneath the pines.

"Holata!" A young bear's call sounded from behind. Elki and Elsu were scrambling through the ferns, their eyes shining with excitement.

"Go back to your mother!" Holata snapped. "We're busy."

"But you promised you'd teach us to hunt when we reached the lake!" Elsu protested.

Elki pushed past him and gazed at her father in dismay. "You said *as soon as* we reached the lake."

"I said go back!" Holata sounded frustrated.

Hattack stopped. "Let them come! You can teach them

how to catch rabbits while *we* catch some *real* prey."

Holata scowled. "Go back to Muna!" he told the cubs.

Their eyes clouded with disappointment. Swapping glances, they turned and trudged back to the shore.

Shesh sighed. "If Hattack and Wenona weren't trying to make this a competition, Holata would have let them come," he murmured.

"Holata can teach his cubs to hunt anytime." Tuari shrugged and followed Hattack deeper into the forest.

Toklo swallowed back a growl. "I wish Oogrook was here," he grunted.

Shesh walked beside him. "Things change, Toklo."

Toklo thought he'd seen enough change over the past sun-circle to last his whole lifetime. He'd found friends and lost them. He'd hardly slept in the same den for more than a few nights. *For once, I'd like everything to stay the same!*

Ahead, the swish of ferns caught his eye. A red pelt flashed between the trees. *Deer!*

Wenona must have seen it, too. She charged forward, Hattack at her heels. Toklo watched them barge through the undergrowth, each struggling to get ahead. Hattack swerved into Wenona, sending the she-bear off balance. Wenona barked with anger and pushed back. The deer sprang over a fallen tree and pelted away. The two bears thundered after it, shoulder to shoulder. Toklo winced. Couldn't they see the trees narrowing ahead of them? With a thump, Hattack's flank hit a trunk. Needles showered down as he stumbled and fell. Reaching out, he caught Wenona's hind leg with his front paw. Wenona lost her footing and tumbled over. Just in front of them, the deer disappeared through a swathe of brambles.

Toklo felt a rush of frustration. The bears would do better if they worked together instead of competing.

Shesh grunted. "Perhaps we should hunt alone."

"Is that how it's going to be?" Toklo grumbled. "Each bear hunting alone because we can't cooperate without a leader?"

"Once in a suncircle, we share territory with each other," Shesh reminded him. "The spirits don't ask any more than that."

"Why not?" Toklo thought of his long journey with Lusa, Kallik, and Yakone. They would never have survived alone.

Toklo caught the sound of running water and headed toward it, relieved to have an excuse to be by himself. "I'm going to get a drink," he told Shesh. "I'll catch up to you."

"No rush." Shesh started to amble after the others. "By the time Wenona and Hattack have crashed into every tree in the forest," he called over his shoulder, "there will be nothing left to hunt."

Toklo followed a stale deer track through a thick patch of ferns, sniffing for the scent of a stream. As he smelled it, earthy and fresh, his thirst seemed to grow. Hurrying closer, he nearly tumbled into the narrow channel that opened in front of him. He dipped his snout into the cool water and drank deeply.

Pawsteps sounded upslope. He looked up and saw Hattack heading toward him. Toklo stiffened. "What are you doing here?" he growled.

Hattack sniffed. "I'll never catch anything with that great lump, Wenona," he grumbled. "So I thought I'd join you. You look like you know how to hunt." His gaze flickered over Toklo's well-muscled shoulders.

Toklo shook the water from his muzzle. Why was Hattack being friendly now? Did he just want a hunting partner?

"Let's try this way." Hattack nodded toward a patch of woodland where the trees opened up enough to let a little sunlight through. The undergrowth was lusher there. "Where there are good leaves, there's good prey."

"I promised Shesh I'd catch up to him," Toklo protested.

"You don't want to hunt with him," Hattack snorted. "He's so old, he'll have you doing all the running."

I don't mind. Before Toklo could argue, Hattack headed between the trees.

"Come on," the other grizzly called. "Unless you're scared that you're not good enough to hunt with me?"

Toklo lifted his chin, annoyed with Hattack for challenging him, and annoyed with himself for being so easily goaded. Reluctantly he followed the other brown bear through the forest.

"Look!" Toklo saw a pale pelt race along the ground. "A weasel."

"A weasel!" Hattack snorted. "We're taking something better than *that* back to the shore." He marched on, ignoring the rustle of leaves as the weasel disappeared into a patch of ferns.

Toklo followed, slowing expectantly each time he heard the call of a grouse or scented a raccoon. But Hattack seemed determined to lead them deeper and deeper into the forest, until the glimmer of the lake disappeared behind them and the pines closed around them. Toklo slowed, his paws growing heavy with apprehension. Was Hattack even *looking* for prey? Why was he leading them so far away from the others?

"Hattack," he ventured. "We should head back. I don't think there'll be much deer here." He could see spruce and birch among the trees ahead. "Besides, I think we're getting near the black bears' territory."

Hattack turned, his gaze suddenly malicious.

Toklo tensed. Had Hattack led him here to fight? "We're supposed to be hunting." He held his ground as Hattack walked slowly toward him. Hattack had grown since the last gathering. Muscles bulked out his flanks, and the scars on his nose showed that he was used to fighting. "Come on," Toklo reasoned. "Let's head back and find a deer."

Hattack narrowed his eyes. "You think you can just come here and proclaim yourself leader of the bears?" Anger rumbled in his growl.

"I haven't!" Toklo shifted his paws, flustered. "That's not why I came!"

But Hattack wasn't listening. "Reminding everyone that it was you who swam to the island and caught the salmon." He stopped a muzzle-length from Toklo. His eyes bored into Toklo's, and his meaty breath bathed Toklo's snout.

Toklo fought back anger. "I came to honor the spirits, and meet with brown bears, just like you did."

"Really? Is that because you're *so* devoted to your ancestors?"

Hattack sneered. "And *so* loyal to your own kind?"

"Of course I am!" Toklo snapped.

"So why have you been living with black bears and white bears?" Hattack pushed past him, striding away through the undergrowth. He called over his shoulder, "Who wants a leader who prefers bears who live on ice or hide up trees? I'll make sure everyone knows who you really are."

Toklo stared after him. His paws were shaking, half with shock, half with rage. He'd only been here for one day and he'd already made an enemy! Why did Hattack assume he wanted to be leader of the brown bears? That wasn't his plan! That wasn't his plan *at all*!

CHAPTER THREE

Kallik

Kallik followed Yakone along the ridge above the water, feeling the sunshine burn into her pelt. She couldn't wait to get to the lake and drench herself.

Yakone paused and looked over his shoulder. "Are you okay?"

"Yes." Kallik realized she'd been lagging behind. She trotted to catch up. "I'm fine."

Yakone tipped his head to one side. "Are you worried about leaving Toklo and Lusa?"

Kallik blinked. "Will we ever see them again?" The thought had been nagging in her belly like homesickness.

"Of course." Yakone turned to head down onto softer ground. Around them, stunted bushes and spiky grass covered the sandy earth. They were nearing the shoreline, where white bears lay in the shade of a stand of pines.

"Lusa and Toklo would never leave you without a proper good-bye," Yakone murmured, his flank brushing hers.

Kallik hoped it was true. The brown bears looked small

from here. Would they allow a white bear to wander onto their stretch of shore? She couldn't see Toklo among the others, and by now Lusa would be lost in the shelter of the forest with the other black bears.

They slithered down a steep slope and crossed a marshy pool. Muddy water sloshed around Kallik's legs. Instinctively she glanced at Yakone's injured paw. The wound from the flat-face trap, which had ripped away two of his toes, had healed now, but the scar was still delicate.

Yakone caught her eye. "It's not hurting," he grunted, reading her thoughts.

"I just like to make sure you're okay."

He splashed water at her playfully. "I can look after myself, you know."

Kallik lifted her muzzle. "Of course you can. But you like that I care." As she climbed onto harder ground, she felt her spirits lift. They were finally here! Which familiar faces would they see? Anticipation sparked beneath her pelt, and she quickened her pace.

Their path took them close to a strange flat-face construction, a tall thin tower built of white stone. *This is where my journey began!* Kallik had first met the others here, when Lusa had rescued a black bear cub from Taqqiq and his friends. Brambles had grown around the tower since last suncircle. Kallik couldn't make out the hole that led into the hollowed-out stone.

A whole suncircle of traveling! The journey had taken her farther than she could ever have imagined; it had led her to

Yakone. And now she was back, with Yakone still at her side. "Come on!" She broke into a run.

Crossing the stones, Kallik splashed into the lake and sank joyfully into the water. It flooded over her flanks, quenching the heat in her fur. Yakone waded in after her and flopped down in the shallows. Kallik rolled over, rubbing her dusty pelt among the pebbles and feeling the grit float free. Water flooded into her nose and eyes as she dipped her head underneath.

"Yakone? Is that you?"

A voice from the shore made her sit up. Her fur streaming, she blinked at the white bear calling from the edge of the lake.

Yakone heaved himself to his paws. "Illa?" he barked in disbelief. "What are you doing here? The Star Island bears haven't been to the Longest Day gathering for suncircles!"

Kallik pushed herself up. Yakone and Illa had lived together on Star Island, before Kallik had met them. And Tunerq was with her.

Yakone gazed at the young male. "You've grown!"

"We've eaten well since you taught us how to hunt musk ox," Tunerq answered.

"Great!" Yakone's gaze slid past Tunerq. "Is Unalaq here?"

Kallik felt her heart sink. Unalaq was Yakone's brother. He had objected to everything she, Toklo, and Lusa had suggested when they'd tried to help the bears of Star Island. He'd even fought with Toklo.

She felt secretly relieved when Illa shook her head. "He stayed with Aga. She said that she was far too old for such a journey, and Unalaq decided that she shouldn't be left alone. Of course, Aga objected and said she could look after herself, but you know how stubborn Unalaq can be."

Yakone snorted. "I remember. But Aga's stubborn, too. They're probably quarreling right now about the best ice hole to fish at." He paused. "Is Aga well?"

"She's fine," Illa assured him. "She told me which route to follow to find the lake. We didn't get lost once."

Yakone gazed at her proudly. "I'm so pleased you came. There have been times when I wondered if I'd ever see you again."

Kallik shivered, the coldness of the water reaching through her pelt. Was Yakone thinking of the times when he'd nearly died on the journey? Injured and bleeding, he'd faked death to lure out the coyotes that were tracking them. And the injury itself had almost killed him.

Kallik pulled her thoughts back and scanned the shore. Was Taqqiq here? She wanted to see her brother and know he was well. Her gaze flicked from one bear to another. Taqqiq wasn't the only familiar face she was hoping to see again. Kallik pictured a young cub gazing trustingly up at her. *No,* she told herself. *He's too young to have made the journey.* But even as she thought it, she saw a young bear bounding from the shade of the pines. Her heart soared. She could hardly believe her eyes. *Kissimi* was racing toward her.

Kissimi's eyes lit up as he saw Kallik. He charged past Illa and splashed into the shallows. Barking excitedly, he ran to meet her, rubbing his muzzle against hers. "Kallik! You came!"

Affection flooded Kallik's heart. "Oh, Kissimi! I'm so happy to see you!" She nuzzled him fiercely. He'd been a new-born cub—hardly bigger than a seal—when she'd found him beside his dead mother on Star Island. Kallik had *so* wanted to look after him. She knew what it was like to lose a mother, and she couldn't let Kissimi feel as alone as she had.

But a cub could never have made the journey that lay ahead of her. Reluctantly, Kallik had given him to Illa, his mother's sister. Leaving Kissimi behind had been heartbreaking, but she knew Illa would take good care of him, and as he snuffled happily against her cheek now, as strong and healthy as any cub, she knew she'd made the right decision.

Kallik drew back and looked at him proudly. "You have traveled so far! You must be very brave!"

"I bet *you've* traveled farther!" Kissimi bounced around her.

Kallik glanced at Yakone. "We've been a long way," she huffed as they moved into the shallower water by the bank, Kissimi following.

Illa and Tunerq spilled over with questions.

"Where have you been?" Illa asked.

Tunerq shifted from paw to paw. "How far did you go?"

"We've been to the Melting Sea," Yakone told them. "We've crossed mountains and forests and ridden on the back of a firesnake."

Tunerq tilted his head. "A firesnake? What's that?"

"It's like a great trail of firebeasts that races across the land on endless silver lines. It breathes smoke and growls louder than thunder."

Kissimi's eyes were huge. "You rode on its back?"

Yakone nodded as he joined Kissimi in climbing up onto the bank. "That's right."

As the shallow water washed around her paws, Kallik saw how happy Yakone looked as he shared his news with old friends. Anxiety clawed at her belly. Would she ever feel as close to these bears as Yakone did? She shook her pelt. What did it matter? As long as she was with Yakone, she would be happy.

Lost in thought, she hardly noticed Yakone lean over the water to snuffle her ear. "Come and join us," he murmured. "It's not just me they're happy to see."

Kallik climbed up onto dry land, and she dipped her head in greeting to the Star Island bears.

Kissimi immediately pressed against her. "I take seal blubber to where you buried Ujurak," he told her. "I know he can't eat anymore, but I thought his spirit would be happy that we still remember him."

Kallik was surprised to feel her eyes sting with grief. At once, she was back on Star Island, her heart breaking as Toklo kicked snow over Ujurak's battered body. Ujurak had moved a rock to protect them from the avalanche that had killed him. "That's really kind of you," Kallik whispered to the little cub.

"We see him every night in the stars," Kissimi told her.

The bears farther up the beach were shifting, making the stones crunch. As fresh scents wafted over Kallik, she looked toward the rocky ridge at the top of the shore. Three bears were stumbling wearily over the boulders. *Taqqiq*! Kallik recognized her brother at once. Shila and Tonraq—Shila's younger brother—were with him. Kallik scanned the ridge, expecting to see Salik, Iqaluk, and Manik. They had been Taqqiq's friends once. Kallik didn't like them, and she still blamed them for leading Taqqiq astray at the previous Longest Day. But it seemed as if her brother had traveled without them this time.

She ran up the shore to greet him. "Taqqiq! How are you?"

"Kallik!" Tiredness seemed to lift from her brother's shoulders. "I hoped you'd be here." He lowered his head—he was taller than her now, and much broader across his shoulders—to nuzzle her ears.

Kallik sighed with relief. *He's happy to see me!* Too many times in the past, Taqqiq had met her with hostility.

Shila dipped her head as Yakone joined them. "I hope your journey was easier than ours." She glanced teasingly at Taqqiq. "We got lost three times and had to hide from wolves."

"We weren't hiding," Taqqiq huffed. "We just chose a different route."

Shila rested her shoulder against his. "If you say so," she murmured.

There was a closeness between the two bears that Kallik recognized. She shot a questioning look at Yakone. Had he seen it, too? Were Taqqiq and Shila mates?

Yakone was watching Tonraq as the young male lumbered down the beach toward them. "Is Pakak with you?" he asked. "And Sakari?"

"My mother didn't want to make the long journey," Tonraq told him.

"And Pakak stayed with her," Shila added.

What about Salik, Manik, and Iqaluk? Kallik swallowed back the question.

Taqqiq stared at the lake. "I'm so hot!" He nudged past Kallik and stormed into the water. As soon as it was deep enough, he plunged beneath the surface.

Tonraq eyed the water hungrily. "I'm hot, too."

Shila snorted. "Go on, then! You don't need my permission." As Tonraq hurried away, she rolled her eyes. "One day they'll learn to think for themselves."

Kallik gave an amused grunt. "Taqqiq seems happy. You must be a good influence."

"It's not me," Shila told her. "He's just back to his old self, that's all. Without Salik and the others around, he doesn't need to act tough." Her gaze softened as she watched Taqqiq wallow in the lake. "He's sweet. I'm glad I have him."

As she spoke, Taqqiq called from the water. "Come on, Shila. Let's catch fish!"

Shila caught Kallik's eye. "We'll catch up later, okay?" She raced to the water's edge and waded in.

Kallik leaned happily against Yakone. "I glad they came."

Yakone rubbed his muzzle against her ear. "Me too. Let's go fish with them. I'm hungry."

Kallik followed him into the lake. Ducking under the surface, the bears headed for the deeper water. Above them, the sparkling surface grew dim. Kallik could see the pale shapes of Taqqiq, Shila, and Tonraq a few bearlengths ahead. A trout flitted past her nose, and she swung a paw toward it. She missed, but Yakone turned and, stretching out his head, snapped it between his jaws. He lifted his muzzle and pushed up toward the surface.

Kallik swam after him, her lungs tight. It was a long time since they'd been in such deep water. She'd forgotten the pleasure of its weight pressing around her. She couldn't wait till they reached the Endless Ice, where there'd be seawater to swim in. Salt water felt thicker than lake water; it pulled at her pelt with a reassuring heaviness.

As she broke the surface, she saw Yakone floating on his back with the trout between his jaws. Taqqiq popped up a bearlength away, Shila and Tonraq surfacing beside him.

"Get back to your side of the water!"

An angry bark took Kallik by surprise. Four brown heads were bobbing behind Taqqiq. *Grizzlies!* Kallik glanced back at the shore, surprised they'd swum so far. And yet they weren't that close to the brown bears' beach. These grizzlies were a long way out.

"The lake's big enough to share!" she called back. It felt strange to be arguing with a brown bear after so many moons hunting beside Toklo.

In response, one of the grizzlies pushed through the water toward Shila, Tonraq, and Taqqiq. Shila had a large salmon between her jaws, and Kallik saw the grizzly's gaze fix on it as he plowed closer. The other three brown bears swam in his wake.

Yakone dropped his trout and flipped onto his front. Kallik dove to catch it. As she surfaced, she saw Yakone heading toward Taqqiq. Tonraq and Taqqiq were facing the grizzlies, growling.

Tonraq slapped a paw hard on the lake's surface, sending water spraying toward the brown bears. "No brown bear tells us where to hunt!" he snarled.

Taqqiq swam sideways, blocking the gap between the grizzlies and Shila. "You have the forest to hunt in!" he shouted.

"The fish here are ours!" The grizzly who had spoken before was now swimming in place, his lip curled. "Get back to your own side."

"Or what?" Tonraq growled.

Taqqiq snorted, slapping the water again. "Don't threaten a white bear when he's swimming! You can hardly keep your head above water. Go back to the shallows. Your paws are only fit for land."

The other brown bears lined up beside the first. One snapped his jaws, the wet fur around his neck spiking.

Kallik dropped the trout into her paws. "Come on!" she called to Taqqiq. "Let's leave them to fish."

Tonraq spun around, spraying water, and hissed at her. "Have you forgotten where your loyalties lie?"

"But we're all *bears*!" Kallik glanced toward Taqqiq and Yakone, hoping one of them would back her up. But they both kept their gaze fixed on the brown bears.

Frustrated, Kallik looked at Shila. Did she think this was a battle worth fighting? Shila was struggling to keep hold of the salmon thrashing in her jaws. "Let's take our catch back to shore," Kallik urged her. If she could get Shila away, the others might follow. She placed the trout back between her jaws, before turning away from the blustering males and swimming back toward the white bears' beach. As she felt the lake bed rise to meet her paws, she glanced back.

Shila was following, but Yakone and the others were still exchanging splashes and snarls with the brown bears. At least none of them were within striking distance; perhaps this would be a show of strength rather than a fight with teeth and claws.

Kallik climbed up the sloping shelf of rock onto the shore. Shila padded beside her, pelt streaming. They dropped their catch as they passed the waterline.

"Those dumb brown bears." Shila stared angrily across the water. "If I wasn't holding a fish, I'd have shown them who was trespassing!"

At last, Yakone, Taqqiq, and Tonraq were swimming for shore. The brown bears had turned away and were diving for fish.

"What was that about?" Illa hurried over the stones toward Kallik and Shila. "What were those grizzlies doing?"

Before Kallik could answer, a gruff bark came from farther up the shore. "They were on our side of the water!" She recognized it at once.

Taqqiq's former friend Salik was staring across the lake, fury in his eyes. Manik and Iqaluk stood beside him, their pelts spiked with anger. Kallik's heart sank. They must have just arrived, and they were already stirring up trouble.

Then she saw Anarteq amble from beneath the pines. The old white bear would soon sort this out. Kallik felt a tremor of concern as she studied him. He looked smaller than last suncircle. And so old! His white fur had yellowed and his snout was grizzled.

Yakone splashed from the water. Kallik jerked her head in the direction of the old bear. "Look, Anarteq has shrunk!"

"*You've* grown," he reminded her.

"But he looks so old."

"He *is* old."

"Not too old to stop this silly argument." Kallik looked hopefully toward Anarteq.

Salik was already circling the old bear. "Are you going to tell those brown bears that they're trespassing?"

Shila growled. "We can't let them get too close—not unless we want them to start thinking they can fish in *our* part of the lake."

Grunts of agreement sounded from the other bears gathered on the shore.

Kunik, an old male whom Kallik remembered from the last gathering, turned his cloudy gaze toward the brown bears' stretch of shore. "Perhaps we should send a group to discuss a boundary within the lake."

Anarteq followed his gaze, not speaking.

Salik tossed his head impatiently. "Well?"

To Kallik's surprise, Anarteq shrugged. "What does it matter?" he muttered. "Fish will go where they like, as will bears."

"Is that *it*?" Salik spluttered.

Illa looked puzzled. "But what if they come into our part of the lake?"

Anarteq blinked. "If you want to fight, then fight. If you want to fish, then fish. Whatever you do, the world will still keep melting around us." He lumbered back into the shade and lay down stiffly on the pine needles.

Sympathy for the old bear washed over Kallik. *He must be weary after the long journey here.*

"Is that all he's going to say?" Illa protested.

Yakone pawed the trout toward her. "Here, at least we caught something. And I don't think those brown bears will be in a hurry to come too close to us again."

Kallik shifted her paws uneasily. Yakone had slipped back into the ways of the white bears so easily—hurrying to defend Taqqiq and Tonraq; untroubled by the tension that had already sprung up between the white bears and the brown bears. Hadn't his journey with Toklo and Lusa changed him at all? *Perhaps it changed me too much.* Guilt stabbed Kallik's belly. She looked back toward the brown bears' shore. The grizzly and his friends were clambering out of the water. Other bears clustered around them, and Kallik felt sure they were throwing glances toward the white bears. Were they muttering angrily among themselves just like Salik, Iqaluk, and Manik?

"Brown bears are too greedy," Salik complained.

"They think they own the water *and* the woods," Manik snarled.

Yakone nudged a piece of trout toward Kallik. "Eat," he murmured.

She lapped up the pale meat and chewed, hardly tasting it. Why couldn't the bears find a way to be peaceful? *Is everyone just looking for a reason to fight?*

CHAPTER FOUR

Lusa

Lusa brushed dried leaves into the dip where she'd made a nest with Ossi. Pokkoli was already sleeping, tucked into a crook in the tree above them. She could hear his gentle snores and just make out his shape, little more than a shadow among the branches. The sun had been slowly setting and, at last, had dropped below the horizon. It would still be a while before dark, and Lusa remembered with a pang of affection the long leaftime evenings in the Bear Bowl, when she had played with Yogi in the twilight.

Ossi slid into the dip, sending the leaves fluttering. Curling up at the bottom, he yawned. "I'm so sleepy."

"Me too." Lusa hesitated at the edge. Around her, the other black bears were settling in for the night. Dustu had tucked himself beneath a cloudberry bush. Dena was sharing a nest beside a fallen tree with two other she-bears. More bears clung dozily to the branches around the camp, letting the breeze rock them gently to sleep. *No sign of Miki or Chula.* Lusa turned around, scanning the woods one more time.

A she-cub was moving beneath the trees. She stopped beside a swirl in the bark of a birch tree and whispered, "Spirit? Are you there?"

Lusa watched her, remembering when she'd found Chenoa's spirit. Chenoa was a black bear who had traveled with them for a while. But the friendly she-bear had died when the river had swept her over a waterfall. Grief twisted Lusa's heart. Was this she-cub searching for a lost friend, too?

Two young bears bounded up the slope toward the cub. They looked so alike that Lusa guessed they were brothers. "Are you still looking for bear spirits?" the larger bear asked.

"Mother says you have to come back to the nest," the other told her.

The she-cub stared at them crossly. "I'm not coming until I've found one. There must be lots here."

Lusa glanced at the trees. What a lovely thought! To be surrounded by black bear spirits as she slept.

The larger bear rolled his eyes. "It's getting dark. Even if there are spirits, they won't be able to see you."

The she-cub dug her paws into the earth. "I'm not coming yet."

The smaller brother started back down the slope. "Let's leave her."

"But we're supposed to be fetching her."

The smaller bear kept walking. "Let her stay out all night. So what if a brown bear eats her, or a white bear steals her?"

The she-cub squeaked in alarm. "That won't happen!"

The bigger bear swapped a knowing look with his brother. "I suppose the spirits will look after you," he told her casually. "But I'm not sure about the brown bear spirits or the white bear spirits. Once it's dark, who knows what they will do to a tiny cub lost in the woods?"

Lusa saw fear spark in the she-cub's eyes. "But I *have* to find more spirits in the bark!"

"Oh well." Her brother turned to leave. "Good luck."

Lusa's heart lurched. "You can't abandon her!" Hurrying from her nest, she ran over to the she-cub. "You can look for bear spirits again in the morning," she suggested. "I'll help you if you want."

The cub blinked at her. "I want to find one before I go to sleep."

Lusa rubbed her chin on the top of the little bear's head. "I once found a tree spirit when I woke up. I opened my eyes and there it was, in the bark right beside me."

"Really?" The cub opened her eyes wide.

Lusa nudged her gently toward her bothers. "Sometimes it's easier to find things after a good night's sleep."

The cub let herself be steered away. "Perhaps our mother will let me sleep in a tree."

"Let's hurry back so you can ask her." One of the cub's brothers nodded to Lusa. "Thanks."

As the young bears headed away, Ossi called from the nest. "Are you coming to sleep, Lusa?"

"Yes." She hopped down beside him. "Do you think Miki

and Chula will get here tomorrow?"

"Probably." Ossi snuggled deeper into the leaves and closed his eyes.

Lusa curled up beside him. Above them, Pokkoli's snores were growing louder. Breathing the musty scent of earth and dried leaves, Lusa closed her eyes.

Around her, the forest slipped away, leaving her on a wide plain, alone beneath a starry sky. Looking up, Lusa saw the dazzling outline of Ursa. She seemed to blaze brighter than the other stars, except for her son Ujurak. Lusa shivered. Star-Ujurak was staring straight at her. She felt it deep in her fur.

"Ujurak?" Her voice sounded tiny. "What's wrong?" Lusa raised her voice. "Tell me what to do!" She longed for Ujurak to spiral down from the sky and become a real bear again, warm and furry and close to her. But he remained still and distant in the crow-black sky.

Lusa pricked her ears. The air around her seemed to quiver. A rumble like thunder sounded in the distance, growing louder as it swept toward her. Fear lurched through Lusa as the earth shook beneath her paws. She dug in her claws to steady herself, but the ground shuddered harder and the thunder filled her ears. Numb with terror, Lusa flung herself to the ground and buried her nose beneath her paws. "Ujurak, help me! Arcturus! Please!"

Yelps of pain split the air. Were other bears here? Lusa lifted her head. "Where are you? Are you hurt?" A shriek of anguish sounded on one side of her, then the other. Lusa jumped up. Suffering bears surrounded her in the darkness. She could hear them! "Where are you?"

Dust swirled around her, blinding her. Lusa staggered forward, trying to keep her balance on the quaking ground, flattening her ears against the roar. "I'll help you!" Her eyes stung and tears streamed down her snout. An agonized bark screeched through the shadows. "I'm coming!" Lusa wailed.

A paw grabbed her shoulder and shook it.

"Lusa?"

Ujurak! Relief swept through Lusa. He'd come to help her save the bears. She opened her eyes, surprised to find she was in the forest. Early morning sunshine dappled the nest, warming her pelt.

Ossi stood over her, his paw on her flank. "You were dreaming."

Lusa stared up at him, still trembling. "Is everyone okay?"

Ossi glanced around. "As far as I know."

"Was anyone calling out in pain?" Lusa couldn't shake the feeling that something terrible had happened. She heaved herself up, shaking off Ossi's paw.

"No." Ossi looked puzzled. "Everyone's getting ready to go for the dawn forage."

Leaves showered over them as Pokkoli slithered down the trunk. "Did someone say forage?" He sat back on his haunches and rubbed his belly. "I hope so. I'm starving."

"Lusa had a bad dream," Ossi told him.

"I have bad dreams when I'm hungry." Pokkoli glanced at a family of bears as they ambled past. More black shapes flickered between the trees. They were heading upslope. "Come on."

Lusa hung back as Pokkoli and Ossi followed the others. "It wasn't hunger that gave me a bad dream," she called. "It was something else." *Ujurak was trying to warn me about something.*

Ossi glanced back at her. "Come and eat anyway," he urged. "The berries higher up are really sweet. They'll help you forget your dream."

Lusa climbed out of the dip and shook the dried leaves from her fur. She wasn't sure she wanted to forget her dream. It had frightened her, but what if Ujurak *was* trying to warn her? She followed Ossi and Pokkoli through the woods, spruce and birch giving way to aspen and beech so sparse that sunlight streamed through the canopy. A she-bear was guiding a group of cubs toward an old beech tree. Its thick roots arched up off the ground.

"Watch." The bear began digging at the soft soil.

One of the cubs leaned forward in delight as white creatures wriggled at the bottom of the hole. "Grubs!"

The she-bear stepped away. "Try digging for yourselves now. There'll be enough grubs for everyone."

The cubs began scrabbling in the dirt, shouting each time they unearthed a new writhing nest.

Two older bears had stopped beside a patch of ferns and were hauling fronds from the earth and gnawing on the sweet roots. Another bear joined them, while two young males charged deeper into the forest.

"There are blueberries this way," called one. "I can smell them!"

Others began to follow them, swiping their tongues around their jaws.

Lusa called to Ossi. "Should we go with them?"

"No." Ossi glanced over his shoulder. "Pokkoli knows where there's a cloudberry patch."

"Cloudberries?" Dustu's rasping growl sounded behind Lusa.

She turned and saw the grizzled old bear ambling after her. "Do you want to join us?" she asked.

Dustu's eyes sparkled. "Yes, please."

Lusa let him pass as she watched the black bears foraging around her. She'd never hunted like this. She was used to Toklo, Yakone, and Kallik racing away after deer or chasing down elk. She'd helped where she could. She'd even learned to catch fish and rabbits. But it felt good to be part of a group that hunted for food the same way she did. She could help the cubs dig up grubs, or search for roots with the older bears. Or she could follow Pokkoli and Ossi to a patch of juicy cloudberries.

A bear's roar echoed in the distance. The cubs rooting around the beech looked up, fear darkening their eyes.

"Don't worry," the she-bear reassured them. "It's just the brown bears showing off."

Dustu snorted beside Lusa. "They're all roar and no claw."

That's not true, Lusa thought. Toklo was the bravest bear she knew. She wondered how he was. Had he met bears he knew from the last gathering? Was he lonely without her? Did he miss Yakone and Kallik?

Her dream flashed in her thoughts, and she wondered if Ujurak had been trying to warn her that her friends were in danger. *I would have known if they had been calling to me, surely?*

Ossi and Pokkoli were heading away through the woods. Dustu hurried to catch up with them. Lusa trailed after them, her pelt tingling with anxiety. *It was just a dream,* she told herself. *It didn't mean anything.* As she struggled to push away her worries, the scent of cloudberries touched her nose. Ossi had broken into a run. Sunshine pierced a clearing ahead of him, and Lusa saw berries glowing on the forest floor.

She stopped and pulled at one with her paw, lifting the stem so that the berries dangled in front of her snout. Their tangy scent made her mouth water. "How did you know they were here?" she called to Pokkoli.

Pokkoli was already stuffing berries into his mouth. "I remembered them from last suncircle!"

Lusa took a mouthful of the fat, juicy fruit. With sunshine warming her pelt, she ate until her belly was full. Then she leaned against a tree trunk. Drowsy with food, she slipped back into her dream. The dust storm swallowed her at once. Bellows of pain surrounded her while the ground shook and thunder battered her ears. Flashes of starlight glimmered through the choking air.

Ujurak? Was he trying to reach her through the chaos? She strained to see his starry shape. Then a voice Lusa recognized sounded beside her ear. "Help me! I'm trapped!"

She awoke with a start. "Chula!"

"Chula?" Ossi jerked his snout toward her. "Is she here?"

He began scanning the trees.

"No!" Lusa stared at him, her thoughts tumbling. "She's in trouble! We have to find her."

Pokkoli frowned. "How do you know she's in trouble?"

"Did you hear something?" Dustu asked, his mouth full of berries.

"I just *know*!" Lusa's panic hardened to rage. How could she explain to these bears that her dream was a sign? Chula needed help. She stared at Ossi. "Which route would Chula take to reach the lake?"

"The same one as me and Pokkoli, I guess."

"You have to show me." Lusa ran to the edge of the clearing. "Come on! We need to find her as soon as we can." Miki and Sheena were traveling with her—and possibly Hashi, too. And Sheena's cubs! If Chula was in danger, they might be, too! Lusa raced up the slope, swerving between the trees.

Glancing over her shoulder, she saw Ossi following. Her shoulder thumped into a trunk and she staggered sideways.

Ossi overtook her. "This way."

Lusa silently thanked Ossi for not asking questions. As she ran, she searched for movement in the undergrowth. She expected Ujurak to appear at any moment—as a moose, or a hare—anything that might guide them.

Brambles shivered to one side and a bird exploded from between the stems. *Ujurak?* It fluttered up toward the canopy, disappearing among the branches.

Just an ordinary bird! They must have startled it from its cover.

Ossi scrambled up a rise. Lusa was panting when they reached the top. She drew in a gasping breath as she looked down the other side, hoping to catch a glimpse of Chula and the others. But only dense forest lay ahead, the pale leafy trees giving way to tight rows of pines.

"Is this definitely the way you came?" she asked Ossi.

He gazed around. "We definitely traveled through pine trees," he told her. "But one pine looks the same as the other. I'm not sure which way to go from here."

"Is there *anything* you remember?" Lusa's heart was pounding. "Did you stop to gather berries? Was there a clearing? Did you cross a river?"

"A BlackPath," he told her suddenly. "We crossed a Black-Path."

"Where?"

Ossi tilted his head on one side. "I'm not sure!"

Lusa began to pace. "You *must* remember. It was only two sunrises ago! *Think!*"

Suddenly Ossi leaned forward. "There!" he barked.

Lusa followed his gaze. She could see only trunks and shadows.

"The stream!" Ossi plunged down the slope. "We drank there."

As Lusa followed, she saw a sparkle between the trees where water reflected a shaft of sunlight. Ossi swerved between the trees, Lusa at his heels. He skidded to a halt as he neared the stream. Lusa slid past him, her paws slithering on the pine needles. "Which way now?"

"Upstream," Ossi told her. He turned and followed the stream up a rise that lifted toward daylight. Lusa could see sunshine flooding into the forest where the trees ended.

A rumble sounded from the gap. Lusa's pelt tingled with fear. *A firebeast.* She recognized the sound too well. They were getting close to the BlackPath. At least they were heading in the right direction. Another rumble sounded, as loud as thunder. Lusa's breath caught in her throat. *That's the noise from my dream!*

Brambles blocked their path, but Ossi forced his way through, and Lusa squeezed through the gap he'd made. Sunlight splashed across her face as she burst out the far side.

The BlackPath lay in front of them, stretching far into the distance in one direction and disappearing around a curve in the other. Ossi stopped at the edge and stared into the forest on the far side. Fresh rumbling rolled toward them, and Lusa saw a massive firebeast approaching around the curve. It raced nearer, eyes flashing on its orange head and along its flanks. Slain trees were lying on its back, and Lusa shuddered.

A second roar sounded from the other direction. A blue firebeast appeared, hurtling along the BlackPath toward the orange beast.

Lusa pressed close to Ossi. "Are they going to fight?" Perhaps they should go into the woods until it was over.

"Wait." Ossi leaned backward. The blue firebeast was howling, splitting the air with a shriek that made birds fly up from the trees behind Lusa. The orange firebeast howled in reply, and both began to slow. Pulling toward the far side of the BlackPath, they rumbled to a halt, snout to snout, then fell silent.

Lusa realized she was trembling. "We should go around them." They couldn't let the firebeasts get in the way of saving Chula. She started to head along the shoulder, keeping to the shadow of the pines.

"Look!" Ossi hissed.

The side of the blue firebeast's head swung open. A flat-face climbed out, pulling a limp, bleeding flat-face after him. A moment later, the side of the orange firebeast's head opened and another flat-face jumped out. It raced to help. Together, they half dragged, half carried the injured flat-face to the orange firebeast's head, then pushed him inside. Climbing in, they pulled the opening shut. Smoke billowed from the firebeast's tail as it rumbled to life. With a shudder, it jolted forward, its massive head rolling straight for the bears.

Ossi backed toward the brambles. Lusa leaped alongside him as the firebeast lurched toward them, the three flat-faces locked inside. Crashing over bushes, snapping branches with its shoulders and haunches, the firebeast slowly turned itself around. It churned mud from the edges of the BlackPath as it straightened up and headed back the way it had come.

"That flat-face was hurt!" Lusa yelped. The sight of blood had unnerved her. Chula might be bleeding, too.

Ossi was crossing the BlackPath, his snout twitching as he approached the abandoned firebeast. Lusa followed him reluctantly. When he reached the firebeast, Ossi reared up on his hind legs, pawing at the trees stacked on its back. Lusa heard him whimper, and felt a stab of pity. The swirls in the bark of the trees showed the countless spirits of black bears, helplessly taken from the final resting places they had chosen for themselves.

"We can't save them," Lusa whispered. "But we can help Chula."

Ossi swung his head toward her, his paws still resting on the side of the firebeast. "We can't just leave them!"

"We have to!" Lusa insisted. "Chula needs us *now*!" She grabbed Ossi's scruff between her teeth and hauled him down. "You have to help me." She turned away, not giving him time to argue, and began to run along the shoulder in the direction the firebeast with the injured flat-face had come from. She glanced over her shoulder. Ossi was lumbering after her, his eyes glittering with grief.

Beyond the curve in the BlackPath, Lusa glimpsed the shiny skin of another firebeast. She skidded to a halt, confused. It wasn't roaring. It wasn't even on the BlackPath. It had rolled onto its side and lay helpless on the shoulder, black paws hanging in the air. Split trees spilled from its back.

Ossi pulled up beside her, a wail rumbling in his throat. "Oh, those poor spirits," he rasped, staring at the jumble of logs crisscrossing the ground. "I can hear them crying."

Lusa pricked her ears. He was right. Moans drifted from the cut trunks, wails of pain and terror. *Just like my dream.* Had Ujurak sent her here to witness the suffering of the tree spirits?

Then Lusa smelled blood. She stiffened. There was the

scent of death, too, and more fear than she'd ever smelled before. "That's not the crying of spirits," she breathed. "That's the sound of *real* bears." She stopped, feeling sick as she glimpsed black fur showing between the spilled trees. "Ossi! There are bears trapped under the logs!"

CHAPTER FIVE

Lusa

"Help!" The thin cries were getting louder.

Lusa raced forward. Ossi pounded after her. She spotted Chula at the edge of the spilled trees, lying in the long grass with a log crushing her hind leg. Lusa's heart lurched. But as she reached the injured bear, she noticed a rock jammed beneath the trunk, lifting some of the weight.

Chula's eyes rolled with pain and fear. "I can't get free!"

Ossi was already pushing his paws beneath the tree, grunting as he tried to heave it away from his sister's leg. Lusa dug her claws into the bark and tried to help. The tree didn't budge. "We're not strong enough!" she hissed to Ossi. *Chula must be in agony.* Even with the rock supporting the log, she could see Chula's leg was squashed tight between wood and earth.

Lusa broke away, roaring with frustration. She froze as she saw fur shimmering between the trees. Was that a brown bear? Would he help? Rearing onto her hind legs to see better, she recognized Ujurak's face among the shadows. Lusa felt a surge of hope. She waited for him to bound forward, or transform into a moose and help roll the log away. But he stayed where he was, watching her.

Anger welled in Lusa's belly. "Help us!" she roared.

Ujurak's voice sounded faintly in her mind, as though he were a long way off. "I can't do anything, not this time."

Ossi glanced up at her. "What are you bellowing at?"

"Hush!" Lusa waved at him to be quiet. She had to hear Ujurak.

"You know what to do," Ujurak went on. "Take a breath. Stay calm. Trust yourself."

The reassuring tone washed through Lusa like a cooling breeze. Her thoughts slowed. She looked down. There was a gap beneath the log where the rock pushed it up. Lusa's paws pricked. "I have an idea!" Scrambling past Ossi, she crashed through the ferns and raced into the trees. She scanned the ground for sticks, inspecting them carefully until she found what she was looking for: a solid branch, newly fallen and still strong. She grasped one end between her teeth and heaved it into the sunlight. Hauling it past Chula, she dropped it beside the log.

Ossi looked puzzled, but as Lusa began to thread the thickest end of the stick through the gap beneath the log, his eyes brightened with understanding. "We can lever the trunk off!"

She nodded. "If we're careful, the trunk will roll away without hurting Chula."

Once the stick was firmly beneath the log, she hurried to the other end and heaved it up with her forepaws. She wanted to pry the log away from Chula's leg. It creaked as she pushed upward, but she could feel strength in the wood. *Please hold!* Ossi grabbed the branch and heaved, too. Between them, Ossi and Lusa lifted it high enough off the ground for Ossi to dive underneath and push up with his powerful shoulders. Groaning with the effort, he forced the branch higher while Lusa pushed with all her might.

The tree trunk shifted. One more heave, and the log lifted a paw's width from the rock.

Lusa's heart leaped. "We're doing it."

Ossi grunted beside her, his eyes tightly shut as he strained at the branch. Chula whimpered with fear.

"Can you pull yourself free?" Lusa called to her.

Chula winced as she dragged herself forward. "Yes!" Her hind leg slid from beneath the trunk.

The moment it was clear, Lusa barked at Ossi. "Get out!" she warned. "I'm going to let go."

As Ossi ducked free, Lusa jumped away from the branch. It slammed onto the ground, and the log rocked back into place.

Lusa rushed to Chula and ran a paw over her leg. It felt stiff and swollen, and heat pulsed from it.

Ossi leaned in beside her. "How bad is it?"

"I don't know." Lusa looked at Chula. "Can you move it?"

Chula grimaced as she strained. But her hind leg didn't move.

"Does that mean it's broken?" Ossi asked.

Lusa shook her head. "I don't know. It might be. But there's a lot of swelling. We won't know until that eases."

Ossi snuffled his sister's cheek. "Don't worry, Chula. We'll look after you."

"What about the others?" Chula grunted. "Are they okay?"

"Who was with you?" Lusa asked.

"Hashi and Rudi," Chula rasped. Lusa guessed she must be in a lot of pain. But they had to know who else needed to be rescued. "Sheena and her cubs, Tibik and Hala."

"And Miki?" Lusa asked.

Chula nodded. "Miki, too."

"Is that all?"

Chula nodded, her eyes clouding with pain.

"I'll find you some herbs," Lusa promised. "But first we have to look for the others." As she spoke, a growl sounded from the log pile. Lusa ran toward it, picking her way over the mess of strewn trunks.

"Under here!" Ossi had squeezed through a gap where the logs rested against the fallen firebeast.

Lusa clambered toward him. "It's Sheena," Ossi told her as she reached him.

Lusa peered into the shadows. Sheena was cowering in a space between the firebeast and the logs. "Are you trapped?"

Sheena blinked at Lusa as if she hadn't heard. "My cubs?" she croaked. "Are my cubs safe?"

"We haven't found them yet," Lusa told her. "But we've freed Chula. She's hurt. Can you come and help her?" She softened her voice, hoping to coax the shocked bear from beneath the logs.

Sheena grunted with effort as she hauled herself forward. Lusa backed away to make space, relieved that Sheena didn't seem to be pinned by the logs. But the she-bear was badly scratched and bruised. Her fur stood out in clumps, her cheek was swollen, and she smelled of blood.

As Sheena emerged into the sunshine, Lusa sniffed her pelt, checking for serious wounds. "Just cuts and swelling." Relieved, she nodded to Ossi.

Sheena narrowed her eyes against the brightness. "Tibik?" she called, fear tightening her voice. "Hala?"

"Go sit with Chula," Lusa ordered gently. "We'll find your cubs."

Sheena stared at her. "When I saw the firebeast begin to fall, I told them to run," she whispered. "It was going too fast and it lost its balance. I could see it was going to roll onto the shoulder, and I shouted to Tibik and Hala to run into the woods." She stared helplessly at the pines. "I knew they'd be safe there."

"You did well," Lusa reassured her. She glanced toward the woods, praying that the cubs had had time to make it to the shelter of the trees.

Ossi scrambled over a log. "I'll find them," he called over his shoulder.

"Go to Chula," Lusa told Sheena again. Hopefully, the two shocked bears could comfort each other while she looked for the rest of the group.

As Sheena padded heavily away, a husky shout sounded behind Lusa.

"Help!"

She turned, scanning the logs spilling from the firebeast's back. "Where are you?" she called when she saw nothing but bark and shadow.

"Here!" The call was gruff with age.

Lusa picked her way over the logs, her heart pounding. What if she set the trees rolling? She might crush a bear beneath them. Testing each pawstep, she crept forward.

"I'm down here!" The gruff voice sounded underneath her.

Lusa peered down through a gap between the logs. Sunlight sliced through, showing black fur tinged red with age. The fur shifted and black eyes shone up at her. It was a male bear. Lusa could smell his scent now, tainted by blood. She recalled the names Chula had told her. She wouldn't have recognized Tibik's or Miki's scent, but this bear was old, so she knew it couldn't be either of them. And it definitely wasn't Hashi, whose scent she did know. She guessed it was Rudi,

"Are you hurt, Rudi?" she called through the gap.

"Just a bit battered," he told her. "A few cuts."

"Are the logs squashing you?" Lusa could hardly believe he wasn't crushed beneath the pile.

"They're resting on the firebeast," the bear told her. "I have just enough space to move, but there's no way out."

"I'm Lusa," she barked. "I'm going to help you."

"How? The logs are too heavy to move," Rudi growled.

Lusa looked down. Of course they were. She was standing on a trunk thick enough to take the weight of a *brown* bear. "I'll get help." If she could gather enough black bears, they could work together to shift the wood. She turned toward Chula and Sheena. "Someone needs to go back to the camp!" she called.

Sheena looked up anxiously. "Have you found my cubs?"

"It's Rudi," Lusa explained. "He's trapped beneath the logs. We need more bears to move them. You must get help."

Sheena's eyes widened with distress. "I'm not leaving until I find my cubs!"

Lusa hesitated. They needed help, but how could she send Sheena away now? "Let's wait for Ossi to get back," she decided. If he'd found the cubs, Sheena could leave. If not, Ossi could go.

"Is Rudi hurt?" Chula called.

"Not badly," Lusa replied.

"Are the others okay?" Rudi growled below her.

"We're still looking for Hashi, Tibik, Hala, and Miki," she told him. "Chula's hurt her hind leg, but Sheena's safe."

"I saw Tibik heading into the woods," Rudi rasped.

"Ossi's there now, searching." *Rudi sounds parched. He needs water.* Lusa looked at Sheena, who was scanning the forest, her eyes glistening with worry.

"Search the forest for some moss," she ordered. "Find a stream and soak it. Rudi is thirsty. Chula must need water, too." She glanced at Chula. The she-bear's eyes were dull with pain.

Sheena blinked at her. "But what about my cubs?"

"Ossi is searching for them!" Lusa told her sharply. Perhaps keeping Sheena busy was the best way to help her. "Rudi and Chula need water now!"

"Okay." Sheena stumbled to her paws and headed for the trees.

Lusa wondered if she should leave Rudi and continue her

search for the others. Before she could decide, she saw Sheena freeze at the edge of the trees. The fur rippled along the she-bear's back. "Hashi?"

Lusa followed her gaze. Sheena was staring at a lump of black fur beneath a swathe of ferns. Lusa jumped from the logs and raced to Sheena's side. "Go find that moss," she urged. "I'll see to Hashi."

As Sheena disappeared into the woods, Lusa parted the ferns. Her nose twitched when she smelled blood. Pushing back the overhanging fronds with a paw, she saw the ancient black bear lying on the ground. His eyes were closed and blood glistened along his flank. Lusa crouched beside him and laid her ear against his chest. Relief swamped her as she heard his rasping breath. *He's alive!*

She sniffed Hashi's wound, shocked to see how deep the gash ran. Blood oozed from it, dripping from his fur and staining the grass. Panic fluttered at the edge of Lusa's thoughts. She fought it away. *What would Ujurak do?*

He'd stop the bleeding.

How?

She listened for Ujurak's voice, but heard only her own. "Pack the wound with moss." Lusa straightened up and scanned the shadows beyond the ferns. Pushing through the fronds, past Hashi, she headed into the woods.

Moss grew thickly among the roots of the trees. It was sodden near the earth, but drier where it reached up the trunk. Lusa peeled away pawfuls of the driest moss and hurried back to Hashi. As she pressed moss into his wound, blood seeped through and she pressed harder, relieved that the old bear was unconscious. At last the bleeding eased.

Hashi's flank twitched beneath her paws. Lusa stiffened as his eyes flickered open. "Are the others safe?" he croaked.

"Sheena isn't hurt, but Rudi's got some cuts, and Chula has an injured leg. We're still looking for the rest," Lusa told him.

Hashi's rheumy gaze rested on her for a moment. "You were at the last gathering," he mumbled thickly.

Lusa nodded. "Try not to move," she urged. "I need to stop this bleeding."

If only she had some of those yellow flowers Ujurak used to keep the wound from turning sour. The moss was soaked with blood, but Lusa kept pressing, hoping that she wasn't causing Hashi too much pain.

Hashi grunted softly. "Take care of the others."

"I will," Lusa promised. As she spoke, she heard pawsteps in the woods. *Ossi? Are Sheena's cubs with him?*

Ossi raced from the trees, a small male cub chasing after him.

"Sheena!" Lusa barked. "Tibik's here!"

Sheena burst from a wall of ferns, dripping moss in her jaws. She dropped it and raced for Tibik.

"Take the moss to Rudi and Chula," Lusa told Ossi quickly, still pressing Hashi's wound.

As Ossi hurried for the moss, Sheena nuzzled her cub. Tibik reared up and clung to his mother's head with his front paws, gnawing at her ears. "I ran just like you told me!" he chuffed. "I was superfast! Did you see?"

Sheena lifted her snout, shaking Tibik off. "Where's Hala? Did she run away with you?"

Tibik hesitated. "I—I thought she was following me."

"Did you see her in the woods?" Sheena prompted.

"No, I didn't." The cub's voice was very small.

Ossi had pushed dripping moss through the logs to Rudi and now dropped the last piece beside Chula. "She probably ran in a different direction. I'll go back and find her."

"Wait!" Lusa called to him. She could hear firebeasts rumbling in the distance. Flat-faces might be coming to rescue this one. She had to free Rudi and find Miki and Hala. But her paws were full with Hashi. "Come and hold this moss in place!"

Ossi's eyes widened as he caught sight of the old bear leader. "Hashi! Will he be okay?"

Lusa ignored the question. How could she know? "Keep this moss on his wound," she ordered. "We have to stop the bleeding."

Hashi moved his head weakly. "See to the others first," he croaked.

"We will." As Ossi's paws replaced hers, Lusa leaped up and rushed to Sheena. Her ears twitched as she heard the distant firebeasts rumbling. "You *have* to get help," she told her. She couldn't risk sending Ossi. He was the only other bear who wasn't injured. She needed him here.

Sheena stared at her. "What about Hala?"

"We'll find her," Lusa promised. "And Miki."

Tibik looked up at his mother. "I'll help them," he barked.

"I know Hala's scent better than anyone. I bet I can find where she ran."

Sheena glanced at him uncertainly.

Lusa willed Sheena to understand. "We *have* to get Rudi free before flat-faces come. We can't do it alone. We'll look for Hala. You bring help." She stared into Sheena's eyes.

Slowly, the she-bear nodded. "Okay," she agreed. "I'll go." She glanced at Tibik. "Be careful."

"Don't worry!" Tibik lifted his snout. "I'll be fine."

Relief washed Lusa's pelt as Sheena turned and headed across the BlackPath at a trot. She turned back to Hashi.

Ossi was leaning over him. "He's hardly breathing."

Lusa recalled Ujurak telling her about a purple flower that could speed up a bear's breathing. Would that help a bear who was so close to death? "Wait there." She charged into the woods.

"What should I do?" Tibik called after her.

"Find your sister's scent," Lusa barked back. She charged between the pines, searching for patches of sunlight where flowers might grow. A clump of furry leaves sprouted between the roots of a pine. *They'll help Chula.* But there was no time to collect them now. She needed flowers to keep Hashi alive. Lusa's heart leaped as she spotted a splash of purple among the trunks. Skidding to a halt beside the plant, she plucked a mouthful of petals and held them gently between her teeth as she raced back to Ossi.

Tibik was sniffing among the spilled logs. *Won't Hala's scent be in the forest?* The thought flashed through Lusa's mind for a moment before she reached Hashi. Hooking the petals from her mouth with her claws, she worked them between Hashi's teeth. The old bear had lost consciousness again. Easing his mouth open, Lusa tucked the flowers beneath his tongue. She looked at Ossi. "Has the bleeding stopped?"

Ossi nodded toward the wound. "Almost." His paws were scarlet.

Suddenly Hashi gasped, his chest heaving. Lusa froze. Were the petals working, or was he getting worse? She put her paw to the old bear's chest, hollow with fear as she felt him shudder. Froth bubbled at his lips.

Have I poisoned him?

In a heartbeat the old bear relaxed. His chest began to rise and fall in a slow, steady rhythm. Lusa put her ear to his flank and heard his heart beating away. *I did it, Ujurak!* She listened for the rumble of firebeasts. They were still far away.

"Can you keep holding the wound while I check on Chula?" Lusa asked. She remembered the wide, soft leaves she'd seen. They would ease the pain in Chula's crushed leg if she wrapped them around it.

Ossi glanced at Tibik, who was sniffing more frantically among the logs. "What about Hala?"

"We'll find her once I've seen to Chula." There was so much to do! But someone had to press Hashi's wound, and Chula was in pain. Surely a lost cub could wait a few more moments?

Lusa plunged back into the woods, heading for the patch of soft green leaves. She tore off as many as she could carry in her jaws and ran back to Chula. "How are you feeling?" she asked gently, dropping the leaves beside the she-bear.

Chula was sitting up with her injured hindleg sticking out awkwardly. "I'm okay," she grunted.

Working carefully, Lusa wrapped wide leaves around her leg, making a thick dressing. Then she reached for the wet moss that Ossi had left beside Chula and squeezed it over the leaves. Lusa hoped that the leaves would give out their healing sap faster if they were damp. "It should start to feel better soon," she promised.

Chula's gaze was on Hashi. "He hasn't moved," she murmured.

Lusa didn't know what to say. The old black bear was badly wounded.

"Hala!" Tibik's bark made her turn. The cub was scrabbling at the logs, his pelt ruffled with panic. "Hala!"

Lusa raced toward him. As she neared, she saw black fur beneath the pile. "I thought she was in the woods!" she gasped.

"She didn't run!" Tibik wailed, tugging at a piece of wood. "I thought she was behind me, but she never ran!"

Lusa shoved her paws beneath the narrow trunk and helped Tibik heave it clear. They began working at another. The logs here were hardly more than branches, slender enough to lift, and they hauled a second piece away. Clearing log after log, they made a space in the pile.

Lusa stared into it and felt her heart shatter.

"Hala!" Tibik jumped into the gap and crouched beside the crushed body of his sister. "Hala! Wake up!"

Lusa could see that the she-cub was dead. There was already

stiffness in her small paws. Her dull eyes stared blankly at the logs that had killed her.

"Tibik," she whispered. "There's nothing we can do for her now."

"She can't be dead!" Tibik looked up at Lusa, panic-stricken. "She was alive just now! We shared blueberries and played chase." His gaze clouded. "What will my mother say? I should have made sure Hala was with me!"

"This is not your fault," Lusa told him. "Firebeasts move quicker than bears. You did well to escape. Your mother will understand that. She will be thankful she still has you."

"Tibik!" Ossi called to the cub from Hashi's side. "Come here. I need your help."

"Help?" Tibik stared at Ossi, bewildered.

"We need to help Hashi now," Ossi told him.

Tibik glanced from Ossi to Lusa. "But what about Hala?"

Before Lusa could find an answer, Ossi barked again. "Hurry, Tibik! I need you." He caught Lusa's eye. She guessed he was trying to distract the cub from his grief. She dipped her head to him. They could grieve later. Right now, they had to take care of the living. And free Rudi before the flat-faces returned.

As Tibik bounded toward Ossi, Lusa pricked her ears, relieved to hear that the firebeast rumble was still distant. Perhaps she was just hearing a faraway BlackPath. Perhaps the flat-faces weren't coming after all.

"I need you to go into the forest and find fresh moss," Ossi told Tibik.

Tibik nodded and headed into the trees.

"Bring as much as you can carry!" Ossi called after him.

"I'll go with him." Lusa glanced again at the dead she-cub, her heart twisting, and then followed Tibik into the forest. *Ujurak? Are you still watching?* As Lusa slipped into the shadow of the pines after Tibik, she felt fear close around her. Hashi was badly injured. Could moss and petals really save him? What about Chula's leg? Could lame bears survive in the wild? Where was Miki? If they dug deeper beneath the logs, would they find his body like they'd found Hala's? Lusa's breath stopped in her throat and she stumbled to a halt.

"Lusa! Quick!" Ossi's growl distracted her. He sounded alarmed. Had the flat-faces come?

"Stay with me!" Lusa called to Tibik as she whirled around. Crashing through the ferns, she broke from the trees.

She stopped dead in surprise when she saw Yakone and Kallik lumbering across the BlackPath on the heels of Sheena. Lusa raced toward them, relief bursting through her like sunshine. "What are you doing here?"

"We were in the forest looking for you," Kallik panted.

"We wanted to see if you had found the black bears' camp," Yakone explained. "We met Sheena and she told us what happened."

Chula crouched down, her eyes wide with fear. "White bears?" She glared at Sheena. "Why did you bring *white* bears?"

"They said they could move the logs," Sheena replied. "It was quicker to bring them here than go all the way back to the camp."

Lusa led Kallik and Yakone around the firebeast and nodded toward the slipped logs. "Rudi's trapped under there. Hashi's wounded. Chula's leg is injured." Lusa glanced at Sheena, her heart sinking. How was she going to tell the she-bear that her daughter was dead?

Sheena was staring at Tibik. He was standing at the edge of the forest, moss dangling from his mouth. Lusa watched grief spread from his gaze to Sheena's. She tried to move, to explain, but her paws seemed to have taken root and the words dried on her tongue.

"Hala?" Sheena's growl was husky with horror.

Tibik turned his head and stared at the space among the logs where Hala's body lay. Sheena walked slowly toward it, her shoulders stiff. Tibik dropped the moss beside Ossi and hurried after his mother. "I thought she was running behind me," he told her, his voice cracking.

Sheena stared into the gap, her eyes clouding.

"If I'd known she wasn't running, I'd have stayed with her." Tibik sounded desperate. He watched his mother lean over his sister's unmoving body. "I'm sorry," he croaked. "I should have saved her."

Sheena swung her head toward him. "*How?*" Anguish glittered in her eyes. "How could you have saved her from this?" She swung her nose toward the fallen firebeast, her gaze flashing over the spilled logs. "How could *any bear* save her from this?"

Tibik flinched. Sheena looked at him, a sob shuddering through her, then she swept him close with a paw and sheltered him beneath her belly. "I'm glad you aren't hurt," she murmured thickly. "We'll take Hala back to camp and give her a proper burial where her spirit will be safe."

Lusa heard more firebeasts. This time, it was not the distant, steady rumbling. Their growling was getting louder. They were coming this way. "We must hurry," she told Yakone. "We have to get everyone away from here."

Kallik pricked her ears. "Firebeasts?"

"They'll be coming to collect this one," Lusa guessed.

Sheena leaned into the gap and gently picked up Hala's body, then walked slowly toward the trees, Tibik pressing against her, and laid the dead cub—hardly more than a bloody scrap of fur—on the grass.

"Rudi's over here." Lusa ignored the pain twisting in her heart. They didn't have much time. She climbed the log pile and poked her paw between the logs that trapped the old bear.

Yakone sniffed around the edge of the pile, his gaze flicking over the trunks. "If we move this one first," he told Kallik, "the others should stay where they are."

Kallik nodded. "Then we can move the two underneath," she suggested. "It should make a big enough gap for him to squeeze out." She turned to Lusa. "Is he wounded?"

"Just a few scratches, I think." Lusa hoped it was true. The firebeasts were rumbling closer, and she hadn't even found Miki. Her heart lurched. They had to get these bears away from here first.

She went over to Ossi. "How's Hashi?" The fresh moss was

already stained with the old bear's blood. Ossi's face was stiff with worry.

Behind Lusa, wood creaked as Yakone and Kallik began to shift the logs. Kallik grunted with effort. Yakone called through gritted teeth, "One more heave!"

The log clattered noisily as it rolled away from the pile. Lusa spun around, alarmed. But the white bears had pushed it safely away from the group of dazed and injured black bears. Yakone reached a massive paw between two logs and began to heave away a second trunk.

The firebeast's growling grew louder.

"How is Chula going to make the journey?" Lusa looked at the injured she-bear, whose leg still stuck out stiffly.

"I'll carry her," Ossi growled.

"What about Hashi?" Lusa fretted. "He can't walk."

Ossi nodded toward Yakone and Kallik as they moved the last log clear. "Would your white bear friends carry him?" Was that an edge in his growl? Did Ossi resent their help? Lusa's pelt prickled. But she held her tongue. Getting everyone away safely was more important than how Ossi felt about white bears.

"Rudi!" Chula gasped with relief as the old bear hauled himself out from the logs. Shakily, he limped from the pile and slithered onto the grass.

Lusa ran over to him. "Where are you hurt?"

"Where *aren't* I hurt?" Rudi grunted, shaking out his pelt. His eye was swollen and tufts of fur stuck out along his flanks. He lifted a paw and shook it, then limped toward Chula. "Are you okay?" He sniffed at the leaves wrapping her leg. "What's all this?"

"Lusa did it," Chula explained. "It's helped to ease the pain."

Yakone lifted his snout. "The firebeasts are close," he warned. "We should leave."

Ossi left Hashi and hurried to Chula's side. "Come on." He crouched down. "Climb on my back."

"Are you sure you can carry me?"

"As long as you haven't been gorging on berries all the way here."

Grunting, Chula heaved herself onto her brother's back and clung there like an oversized cub.

Kallik padded toward Hashi and sniffed his wound. "This one can't walk."

Yakone joined her. "Can you lift him onto my back?" Kallik nodded. She gently grabbed Hashi's scruff and heaved him up onto Yakone's shoulder. Draping him over the larger bear's back, she steadied him with a paw. "Walk steadily," she told Yakone.

Yakone shifted his weight from one paw to the other until Hashi fitted snugly between his shoulders.

Lusa looked at Sheena. "Are you ready to leave?"

"Yes." Sheena leaned down and picked up Hala's body and headed for the BlackPath. Tibik followed, his head down. Yakone and Kallik walked in their wake.

Lusa looked anxiously along the trail. The firebeasts were roaring closer. The hard stone trembled beneath her paws. Quickening her step, she guided Rudi after the others. Ossi plodded heavily behind her, Chula gripping on tight to her brother's fur.

"What about Miki?" Tibik stopped and turned toward Lusa. "We never found Miki!"

"He wasn't under the logs. He must have run into the trees like you did." Guilt swirled in Lusa's belly, and she prayed to all the spirits that she was right. She felt as if she was abandoning Miki, choosing to save his friends over him. But what else could she do? The firebeast was clearly visible on the long stretch of BlackPath now, roaring closer.

She nosed Tibik forward. "Quick!"

Kallik and Yakone disappeared into the pine trees on the far side; Sheena hustled Tibik after them, Hala's body dangling like limp prey from her teeth. Lusa moved aside to let Ossi carry Chula into the shadowy woods. As Rudi shambled after them, Lusa glanced back at the stricken firebeast. *I hope Miki ran clear before it fell.*

The ground started to shake as the living firebeast bellowed toward its friend. Heart lurching, Lusa darted between the pines.

Rudi was glancing nervously over his shoulder.

"If we keep walking, we'll be okay," Lusa promised him. She noticed the old bear was limping. "Kallik, can you carry Rudi?" she called.

Kallik looked back. "Of course."

Rudi snorted. "No white bear's going to carry me." He glanced at Hashi with a flash of disapproval in his eyes.

Lusa felt a rush of anger. "Would you rather we left Hashi

for the flat-faces to find?" she snapped.

Tibik tugged Lusa's fur. "Can Kallik carry *me*?" he whispered.

Lusa blinked at the little cub. His shoulders drooped with exhaustion. She glanced questioningly at Sheena. "Tibik's tired," Lusa told her. "May Kallik carry him?"

Sheena stared at her blankly. Hala swung from her jaws, and grief welled in her eyes.

Lusa decided not to wait for an answer. "Come on, Tibik." She led him over to Kallik and dug her snout beneath his hindquarters to boost him up. Tibik snuggled into Kallik's fur. The white she-bear nodded to Lusa and began to walk gently forward.

Yakone was several bearlengths ahead. Lusa quickened her step to catch up. Unease flowed through her pelt as she reached him. The white bear's flank was red with Hashi's blood.

Yakone turned his head and looked at her. "I think he's gone," he whispered.

Lusa lifted her muzzle toward the old bear and sniffed his leg as it dangled against Yakone's side. It hung stiff and strange, no longer the leg of a living bear. Sadness tightened Lusa's throat. Unable to speak, she met Yakone's gaze.

"Let's not tell the others until we reach camp," he murmured.

Lusa glanced back at the bedraggled group. They needed encouragement now, not more grief. She nodded at Yakone.

The trek to the camp seemed endless. Lusa stayed close to

Yakone, glancing anxiously at Hashi, fearful that the others might notice how limply the old bear lay upon Yakone's back. The sun began to sink behind the distant hills. Its dying light flared through the forest like flame, and Lusa lowered her gaze to avoid its glare.

Her thoughts strayed back to the BlackPath. Where was Miki? Was he alive? Was he injured? She pictured him hurt and bleeding, alone among the pines. Perhaps he was dazed and wandering in circles. *We haven't given up on you! I'll come back, I promise!* Lusa hoped that wherever he was, Miki knew that.

Movement among the trees ahead pulled her from her thoughts. A familiar scent washed over Lusa, and she sagged with relief. They had reached the camp.

"White bears!" A frightened wail rang through the forest. Black shapes darted between the twilit trees, barking urgently at one another.

"We're being attacked!"

"Climb the trees!"

Lusa ran forward on legs that seemed crumpled with exhaustion. "The white bears are *helping*!" She stopped at the foot of a tree where Dena was scrambling up the trunk. "There was an accident on the BlackPath. Chula is injured and Hashi—" She stopped.

Dena lowered herself gingerly down the tree, her gaze on Yakone as he stopped beside Lusa. Dena looked at the blood on his flank and lifted her head to stare at the dark shape on the white bear's shoulders. "Who is it?" Then she recoiled in horror. "He's dead!"

"Dead?" Rudi had reached them, Ossi, Sheena, and Kallik close behind. Chula was clinging wearily to Ossi's back.

Lusa faced them, wishing with all her heart that this day was over. She couldn't stand more sadness. "He died on the journey," she told them quietly.

More bears were approaching, their curiosity clearly overcoming their distrust of the strangers in their camp.

"Lusa!" Pokkoli's bark rang through the trees. "Ossi! You've been gone for ages. Did you find Chul—" He stopped when he saw Yakone and Kallik, his pelt twitching as his gaze flicked from them to the others.

Sheena stepped forward and placed Hala's body on the ground. "We must bury her," she murmured.

"No!" Tibik slithered off Kallik's back and crouched beside his sister. "She needs to stay with me."

Kallik touched Tibik's head with her muzzle. "She'll always be watching you, little one." Glancing up, she nodded toward a swirl in a trunk beside them. "I think I see her face in that tree already."

Tibik shot an angry look at the swirl. "That's not Hala!" he snapped. "She's *here*! Dead! She's not in a tree!"

Sheena wrapped herself around both her cubs, a low moan in her throat. Lusa closed her eyes. The forest seemed to spin as bears streamed around her, guiding her and the others into the camp. Suddenly weary, she fought to focus. She was dimly aware of Kallik and Yakone saying good-bye before slipping away, leaving Hashi's body lying in the center of the clearing, silvered by the darkening sky.

Lusa spotted an unused dip at the edge of the clearing, wide and shallow and already filled with dry leaves. "Ossi, put Chula here." She nodded to the other end of the dip. "Rudi, rest here. Sheena, stay beside him—I haven't checked you for cuts and bruises. I must make sure every bear's wounds are treated. The weather's warm, and they could turn sour."

There was no point checking the bears for injuries until she had collected some herbs that would help. Summoning the last dregs of energy, Lusa pushed her way out of the cluster of bears. They were all firing questions at the injured bears now, demanding to know what had happened.

Lusa felt a stab of relief as she left the chatter behind and plunged into the quiet forest. Her nose twitched as she sought out the herbs that Ujurak had shown her before. Was he watching her now, urging her toward the leaves she would need? *I'm doing my best!*

Guilt pricked her fur. Her best wasn't good enough.

Darkness settled on the forest like a heavy pelt. All around Lusa, the black bears were asleep, even the wounded. Lusa had found enough herbs for all their injuries. She'd rewrapped Chula's swollen leg. She'd even found a precious plant that would bring them sleep, despite their pain and grief. Sheena had been the last to close her eyes, insisting that Hala sleep between her and Tibik for one last night. Lusa had sat beside her, pressing close until the she-bear's breath had finally deepened into sleep. Now Lusa stared into the trees, aware that she was the only bear left awake. Her body was weary, but her mind buzzed with worry. Miki was still out there. He must be so afraid.

She pushed herself to her paws and crept out of the hollow where the injured bears slept. Ossi was snoring at the edge, his nose dangling over the rim. Chula rested against Rudi, who snuffled gently beside her.

Lusa picked her way between the nests of the other bears, treading lightly over the leaf-strewn forest floor. Through the trees, the lake was starting to gleam milky-pale, heralding the return of dawn after the short night. Lusa turned her back on the water and walked into the forest. Following the fresh-made trail, scented with the blood of her friends, she headed toward the BlackPath once more.

CHAPTER SIX

Lusa

As Lusa wove through the trees, her pelt tingled anxiously. What if she found Miki *dead*? Fear pushed back her exhaustion, and she kept moving through the forest, her gaze fixed on the trail ahead. *I have to find him.*

"Lusa?"

A soft bark made her jump.

She recognized it at once and spun around in delight. "Toklo!" She ran toward him—a dark shape between the trees—and rubbed her head along his jaw. "It's been such a terrible day!" Her throat tightened.

"I know." He rested his muzzle on her head for a moment, and then pulled away. "News traveled along the shore like wildfire. That's why I came to find you. I was scared you might be hurt."

"I'm fine. But I have to find Miki."

"Miki?" Toklo repeated the name thoughtfully. "Was he the bear you made friends with at the last gathering?"

Lusa nodded. "He was traveling with the group that was

injured today. But we couldn't find him. We had to leave without him. So I'm going back." She lifted her chin, daring Toklo to change her mind.

"I'll come with you."

Lusa blinked. She thought he would try to persuade her to wait until morning.

Toklo went on. "I know what it's like when a friend goes missing. We nearly lost you, remember?"

"I couldn't forget." Lusa's thoughts flitted back to the final part of their journey. Mules had stampeded through their group and kicked her in the head. Dazed, she'd wandered in the forest until flat-faces had found her and taken her away in a firebeast. It had taken nearly a moon for her friends to find her again. Was that what had happened to Miki?

She stared wide-eyed at Toklo. "I don't know what would have happened if you'd stopped looking for me!"

Toklo met her gaze. "We would *never* have stopped looking for you." He straightened up and looked around. "Which way do we go?"

"This way." Lusa began to lead him along the blood-scented trail.

Toklo's nose twitched. "I can smell Kallik and Yakone."

"They came to help," Lusa explained. "They moved the logs we couldn't shift by ourselves."

"I wish I'd been there to help, too." Was that jealousy edging Toklo's growl?

Lusa glanced at him. "So do I." Beside them, the undergrowth rustled as a weasel scurried along the ground. An owl hooted in the distance, and down by the lake, a snipe began to chirp. "How are you getting on with the brown bears?"

"Okay, I guess." Toklo sounded unsure. "Oogrook died during earthsleep."

Lusa remembered Pokkoli's warning about the tension among the brown bears. Was it because of Oogrook's death?

Toklo went on. "It's strange that the black bears have lost their leader as well."

"But they're only leaders during the Longest Day gathering," Lusa pointed out. "Do we really need a leader to help us share with the spirits? They'll hear us anyway, won't they?"

Toklo grunted. "It's not the sharing with spirits I'm worried about. We need a strong bear to keep peace among the others. It feels like everyone is arguing, trying to prove who's the best."

Lusa nudged him. "But surely you're the best bear," she teased. "Shouldn't *you* be the leader?" She was only half joking. Toklo was young, but he was as strong and brave as any bear she'd ever known. And good-hearted, too. He'd make a great leader.

Toklo snorted and pushed through a web of broken branches. Lusa slid through after him, ducking to stop the twigs from flicking her muzzle. "Toklo?" Her mouth felt numb with tiredness. "Slow down."

"You must be worn out." He hurried back to her. "Lean on me."

Relieved, she rested against his shoulder and they moved on, walking more slowly. The warmth of Toklo's pelt seeped into hers, making her drowsy; but she didn't mind, so long as she had him to lean against.

"Can you follow the scents?" she asked.

"Of course," he answered. "I'd recognize Kallik's and Yakone's scents anywhere."

Drowsily, Lusa let him lead the way until light glowed through the forest ahead. They were nearing the end of the trees. They had reached the BlackPath.

Shaking sleepiness from her pelt, Lusa ran out of the forest and looked up at the dove-gray sky. A few stars shone faintly, but she couldn't make out Ursa or Ujurak. The BlackPath was silent. Only the calls of night birds broke the still air. Lusa gazed toward the place on the shoulder where the firebeast had fallen. The great creature had gone, leaving gouges in the grass. The logs had been stacked into a neat, straight pile.

Lusa trotted across the BlackPath, which felt cool against her paws.

Toklo was lingering on the shoulder, staring up at the sky.

"Hurry up!" Lusa called.

He crossed the path toward her, a question in his eyes. "Did Ujurak help you today?"

"I saw him," Lusa confessed. "He was among the trees. But he didn't do anything except tell me to stay calm." She looked sadly at Toklo. "I thought he might turn into a moose and move the logs, but he didn't."

"But Kallik and Yakone came," Toklo reminded her. "Perhaps Ujurak knows that we don't need him so much now." He padded around the stacked logs. "Do you know Miki's scent?"

"No," Lusa admitted. It had been a whole suncircle since she'd seen him. "But I know the scents of the others, so I could spot a different one." She sniffed the crushed grass where the logs had been. Had Miki been trapped among them? She smelled only the fear scents of Chula and Rudi—and Hala's blood. Grief seared Lusa's heart once more as she thought of the dead she-cub. She pushed it away. "He must have run into the woods," she called to Toklo. "I can only smell the others here."

"Come on." Toklo was already shouldering his way past a thicket of brambles.

Lusa hurried after him as he disappeared among the pines. Her heart sank as she saw the trees stretch into shadow on every side. The forest was huge. "He could be anywhere," she breathed.

Toklo brushed her ear with his muzzle. "He's smart—he's probably going to stay close to the BlackPath, where he last saw the others. We'll find him."

Lusa rubbed her head affectionately against his fur. "Thank you for coming with me," she murmured. "Miki must be wondering where his friends are."

Toklo didn't answer. Lusa saw him frown.

He thinks Miki might be dead. "Don't!" Lusa scolded. "We have to believe he's okay." She walked forward, then stopped and looked up at Toklo. "Did you ever think *I* was dead?" she asked. "When I was missing?"

"Sometimes," Toklo admitted. "But I never acted like you were. I vowed not to do that until I knew for sure."

Lusa started walking again. "Then that's what we'll do for

Miki," she vowed. "We brought the others home." *Even Hala and Hashi.* "We can't leave him out here alone."

"Do you think Ujurak's still watching?"

"Of course he is!" Lusa glanced up at the small snatches of sky she could glimpse through the canopy. "What else would he be doing up there?" As she spoke, a bear scent touched her nose. It wasn't Ossi's or Tibik's.

She darted forward, sniffing at the grass sprouting between the pine roots until she smelled it clear and strong. It was definitely black bear scent. "This way!" She broke into a run, stumbling over trailing brambles. Her legs were numb with tiredness, but she was so close. She had to keep going.

The ground sloped downward, and she skidded on pine needles as it dropped into a small clearing. A dark shape was slumped against a tree on the far side. In the weak dawn light, Lusa recognized Miki.

"He's here!" She raced toward Miki, her heart pounding. He wasn't moving. *Don't be dead! Oh, please don't be dead!* She braced herself for a fresh wave of grief as she scrambled to a halt beside him.

Warmth pulsed from the black bear's pelt. His flank touched Lusa's nose as it rose and fell. "He's alive!" Bright-eyed, she turned to Toklo.

Relief shone in his gaze. "Well done, Lusa!" he chuffed. "You found him!"

"I couldn't have done it without you."

"Of course you could." Toklo moved past her and nudged Miki's cheek gently with his snout.

Miki still didn't move.

Quickly, Lusa checked him for wounds. She smelled blood behind his ear and felt heat in the fur there. "He's been hit in the head."

"He might not wake for a while," Toklo warned.

"We have to get him back to the camp," Lusa insisted. "He'll be safer, and I have herbs there to treat him with." She had leaves left over from treating the others.

Toklo crouched down. "Can you heave him onto my back?"

Lusa had already grabbed Miki's scruff and was straining to lift him. Ducking lower, Toklo slid beneath the unconscious bear and jerked him onto his shoulders. He straightened up and walked carefully back across the clearing.

Lusa trotted beside him, her weariness swept away by relief. "Thank you, Toklo," she whispered.

Toklo glanced at her. "No problem. It's what friends are for."

CHAPTER SEVEN

Toklo

Toklo slowed as he neared the black bear camp. Miki lay heavily on his back. He didn't want to carry the injured bear past the brambles that marked the edge. Would Lusa want him to meet her new friends now, when they were still reeling from the firebeast disaster? She'd talked warmly of Pokkoli, Chula, Ossi, and Tibik as they'd trekked through the woods, but the black bears had more to think about now than getting to know a strange brown bear.

Sunlight was seeping between the trees, and Toklo felt an urge to get back to the brown bears' territory. With Oogrook gone, and the others jostling for leadership, he ought to be there. *It's not because I want to be their leader,* he told himself. But he didn't want to appear like an outsider to the other brown bears, not when alliances among them were already strained. "I'll leave Miki here."

Lusa looked at him, her eyes so sleepy that he wondered if she'd heard him.

"I'll leave him here, okay?" he repeated.

"Okay," she mumbled.

Toklo touched his nose to her cheek, then crouched down. "Can you grab his scruff and ease him off?" he asked her.

"I can manage." Miki's grunt took him by surprise as the black bear climbed down from his back. "Thanks for carrying me." Miki stumbled, wobbly on his paws, and Lusa came over to prop him up with her shoulder.

"You're awake! How are you?" she asked the black bear.

"My head hurts," Miki growled.

Lusa began to steer him past the brambles. "I can find some herbs that will help."

Toklo watched her wistfully. She reminded him of Ujurak— so ready to help, and so knowledgeable now.

Lusa glanced back at him. "I'll see you soon?" It sounded like a question. Was she worried they wouldn't meet again?

"Of *course*!" He might have to act like a brown bear now, but Kallik, Yakone, and Lusa would always be like family.

Lusa's eyes shone and she dipped her head, then guided Miki into the black bear camp.

Turning away, Toklo heard grunts of surprise. Paws crunched over leaves, and barks of welcome rang though the trees.

"Miki! You're safe!"

"Where did you find him, Lusa?"

With a feeling of relief, Toklo pushed his way through the ferns, heading for the shore. At the edge of the forest, he narrowed his eyes. The lake sparkled as the sun lifted above the horizon. Even this early, Toklo felt its heat through his pelt.

He could see Hattack lounging on the largest rock. *Acting*

like he's leader already. The other bears were stirring on the beach. Toklo watched a young grizzly lift his head from his nest and scan the shore. Two males were already in the water, pushing past each other as they dove for fish. A group of young bears gathered at the edge of the forest; Toklo studied their rippling pelts and the sharpness in their barks at one another. *Were they arguing over which part of the forest each would hunt in?* he wondered.

Toklo's belly rumbled, but he was too sleepy to hunt. He just wanted to lie in the shade at the top of the shore and sleep.

"Toklo!" Shesh hailed him as he clambered out of the lake, water dripping from his pelt. He shook out his fur as Toklo approached. "Where have you been?"

Tuari gave a snort. "He's probably been catching fish before those white bears can get them."

Shesh lumbered closer. "His pelt's dry."

Toklo shrugged. "I was exploring." Guilt pricked beneath his pelt. Was he ashamed of Lusa, Kallik, and Yakone? *No!* But he knew the brown bears were uncomfortable with his connection with black bears and white bears. Why stir up hostility among his own kind?

Shesh nodded toward Wenona, who was glaring at Hattack. "Wenona's been trying to persuade the others that no one should sit on the parley rock until a new leader is decided."

Toklo grunted. "It looks like Hattack doesn't agree."

Tuari kicked at the pebbly shore. "Wenona's right. That stone is for the Longest Day ceremony. It was Oogrook's stone."

Shesh glanced sideways at Toklo. "The sooner we get a new leader, the better."

That's not my problem. Toklo changed the subject. "Caught any fish today?"

"No." Shesh twitched his damp fur. "I was just in the lake to cool my pelt."

Tuari nodded to Toklo. "Do you want to come fishing with me? You can show me how you caught that salmon last gathering."

Wenona snorted. "Toklo got lucky, that's all."

A ragged male crunched across the pebbles. "That was more than just luck," he growled.

"I just want to sleep." Toklo stifled a yawn.

"It's too early to sleep!" one of the young bears by the trees called to him. "Come hunt in the forest with us!"

An old she-bear stepped forward. "We should be collecting sticks for the Longest Day gathering!"

The young bear snorted. "*You* do it! Hunting is more important."

"But it's nearly the Longest Day," the she-bear insisted. "We came to the lake to honor the spirits, not to hunt."

"I'm hungry!" Another young male lifted his snout. "The Longest Day will happen whether we pile up sticks or not."

"Why do the spirits want sticks, anyway?" Wenona put in.

The ragged male scowled at her. "It's not the sticks they want; it's our respect."

The old she-bear nodded. "Gathering sticks for the ceremony was a great honor when I was a cub!"

Wenona turned her snout toward the lake. "When you were young, there were so many fish you only had to put your paw in the lake to find one. Life is harder now. There isn't time for stick gathering."

Toklo saw the old she-bear's pelt ripple with annoyance. "We must make time to show respect to our spirits," she snapped.

"Even if it means starving?" Wenona scoffed.

Toklo stepped forward, feeling his fur crawl with tension. "There's time for hunting *and* stick gathering."

A male cub skittered to a halt in front of the old she-bear and stared earnestly up at her. "I'll help you gather sticks!"

The she-bear's gaze softened at once. "Ah, Akocha." Fondness warmed her growl. "I knew you wouldn't let me down."

Akocha's mother, Tayanita, was proudly watching her son from the other side of a smooth white boulder. "Akocha knows what's important."

Wenona huffed and walked away. Akocha puffed out his chest and bounced after the old she-bear as she lumbered toward a scattering of sticks that had been washed up close to the waterline.

"I'll help, too," Tayanita offered, following.

Shesh watched them go. "I'm glad not every young bear is only interested in hunting. Life can't only be about finding food and shelter. There must be more that we share, otherwise why come here every Longest Day?"

Toklo blinked at him, wondering whether the shady patch of sand farther up the beach would make a good place to nap.

Shesh went on. "If Oogrook were here, he'd make sure every bear knew why Great Bear Lake is so important. This was where Arcturus once traveled. I don't even think the young bears remember the story."

"They will, at the ceremony." Toklo began to pad heavily up the beach.

"But how?" Shesh followed him. "With no one to lead it?"

Toklo was only half listening. "Why don't you lead it?"

"I'm too old," Shesh answered. "I'm surprised Oogrook died before me." He quickened his pace, pulling ahead of Toklo so that he could look back at him. "Oogrook was impressed by you."

Toklo stopped as the old bear blocked his way. "Really?" *I only caught one fish.*

"Perhaps Oogrook would have asked you to lead the Longest Day ceremony if he'd lived to reach the lake."

Toklo stared at him. "Me? Why?"

"Someone needs to remind the bears that we share the same spirits." Shesh's cloudy gaze suddenly shone with urgency. "I came here from Smoke Mountain. The hunting on the journey was poor. There were too many mouths chasing too little prey. We should have worked together. We should have shared. Then no bear would have gone hungry."

"Brown bears have always competed for territory and for food," Toklo reminded him.

"That was when prey was rich." Shesh held his gaze. "Times have changed. We need a leader. Someone who can teach us to work *together* to survive."

Toklo padded around him. "I don't want to lead anyone," he grunted. "Someone will become leader soon enough. Plenty of bears want to. Just wait a little longer."

Pebbles crunched behind them. "Are you still going on about Toklo and his salmon, you old fool?"

Toklo turned to see Hattack glaring at Shesh.

Shesh squared his shoulders. "I think Toklo should be our new leader. Oogrook would have—"

"I don't *want* to be leader," Toklo interrupted.

Hattack's eyes flashed. "What kind of bear doesn't want to be leader?"

Toklo began to turn away once more.

"Are you a coward?" Hattack called after him.

Anger cut through Toklo's weariness. He faced Hattack. "I'm no coward! But there are other bears here more deserving of leadership than me."

"Of course there are," Hattack hissed. His gaze flicked around the other bears in earshot, who were turning their snouts toward Hattack, their eyes alight with interest. Hattack's eyes sparked with challenge as he looked at Toklo. "Or maybe you *want* another bear to shoulder the responsibility. After all, you'd rather travel with white and black bears than travel alone. Are you scared that you can't look after yourself?"

Toklo pressed his claws into the pebbles. "Why don't you go hunt? Lying in the sun has clearly made you grumpy."

Shesh chuffed with amusement.

Hattack bristled. Then his nose twitched. He leaned forward and sniffed Toklo's pelt. Toklo drew away, unsettled.

Why couldn't Hattack leave him alone?

"You smell of black bears," Hattack growled.

"So what?" Toklo countered.

"Traitor!" Hattack showed his teeth.

The other bears shifted uneasily.

"Are they going to fight?" Elsu whispered to Holata.

"Hush," Holata silenced him.

Hattack stuck out his chest. "Where have you been, Toklo?"

"Helping my friends!" Toklo snapped. "You must have heard about the firebeast accident! Two bears were killed on the BlackPath. I joined the search for one who was missing."

Hattack grunted. "Black bears! They can't even help themselves. They're so pathetic they don't deserve to be called bears!"

"Be quiet!" Shesh barged past Toklo, his pelt bristling with fury. He stopped a muzzle-length from Hattack and scowled up at him. "If Toklo chose to help other bears, that just shows he is a better bear than you ever will be!"

Hattack held the old bear's gaze for a moment, then jerked away. Fur rippling along his spine, he stomped down the beach and waded deep into the lake.

Shesh watched Hattack lunge beneath the water. "Let's hope that cools him off," he muttered. His gaze flashed around the watching bears. "No need to stare. There's nothing to see here."

As he spoke, the other bears turned away sheepishly. Toklo started walking toward the inviting shade at the forest's edge.

"You're a good bear," Shesh's whisper sounded in his ear.

"But you will need to learn how to be loyal."

Pelt prickling with frustration, Toklo realized that the old bear was still following him. "I *am* loyal!" *To bears that I care about.*

"You're a brown bear," Shesh murmured, his voice calm and reasonable. "It will just be easier if you stick with your own kind."

Toklo kept walking.

"My friends needed help!" How could Shesh find anything wrong with that?

"We all face problems," Shesh pressed. "Instead of worrying about black bears, you could be helping your own kind—bears who *need* you."

Toklo stifled a sigh. Was Shesh still hinting that he should lead the others? "I'm tired," he grunted. "Give me some peace."

He heard pebbles swish and fall silent as Shesh halted. Walking away from the old bear, Toklo growled under his breath. All he wanted was some rest. Couldn't everyone leave him alone?

"Toklo! Toklo!" Akocha's excited bark sounded from along the shore. The young bear was racing toward him, his paws flying over the stones. His mother Tayanita followed wearily behind. "Can we go exploring?"

"I was going to rest," Toklo told him as Akocha skidded to a stop.

"What do you need to rest for?" Akocha stared at him with round, innocent eyes. "I thought it was only old bears who needed rest." He glanced back, sympathetically, at his mother.

Tayanita looked pleadingly at Toklo. "Can you explore with

him for a while? His father is . . ."

"My father's dead," Akocha announced bluntly.

Toklo closed his eyes for a moment. He remembered begging Oka and Tobi to play with him when he was a cub. Tobi was always too sick and his mother too tired.

"Please?"

Toklo opened his eyes to see Akocha staring at him hopefully. "Okay."

Gratitude shone in Tayanita's eyes. Toklo nodded to her. Akocha was already plunging into the ferns. "Don't run too far ahead," he called.

"What's the biggest prey you've caught?" Akocha bounded toward him as Toklo ducked into the shadow of the trees.

"A moose."

"A moose?" Akocha sounded impressed. "Did you catch it by yourself?"

"My friends helped."

"What does moose taste like?" Akocha chattered. "Does it taste like deer? Or more like rabbit? I hope it didn't taste like fish. I don't like fish much. Mother says I'll get used to it, but I like furry prey, not slimy prey." The ferns rustled ahead. "Is that prey?"

By the time Toklo had caught up to him, the fronds were trampled beneath Akocha's paws.

"It must have been the wind making them rustle," Akocha decided.

Toklo sniffed the crushed leaves. Rabbit scent bathed them. "Smell this." He moved to let Akocha smell the ferns.

"What is it?"

"Don't you recognize it?" Toklo prompted. He suddenly thought of Ujurak and how helpless the young bear had been when they'd first met.

Akocha lifted his head, frowning. "Is it rabbit?" he guessed.

Toklo nodded. "It must have been hiding among the ferns. Your pawsteps were so heavy, they frightened it away."

Akocha tipped his head on one side. "Will you show me how to creep up on prey quietly?"

Toklo rolled his eyes. Was he going to have to give this energetic cub a hunting lesson as well? "We'll see." He jumped up a short, steep slope and began to climb the hill.

Akocha scrambled after him. "When Mother says 'we'll see,' it means she doesn't want to and hopes I'll forget."

Toklo felt a pang of sympathy for Tayanita. He pushed uphill, weaving between the thickly growing trees. Light showed at the top, and he wondered what lay on the other side.

"Do you want to see how fast I can run?" Akocha puffed. "I'm really fast. I collected a whole pile of sticks for the ceremony. Have you ever collected sticks for the ceremony?"

Without waiting for an answer, he charged ahead. Bounding up the hill, the cub swerved easily between the trees, his small paws making him nimble. Toklo broke into a trot. By the time he reached the hilltop, the young bear had disappeared.

Toklo scanned the trees. Ahead the land sloped steeply downward. Twisted brambles grew between the pines. Light showed through the trunks. Was it a clearing? Toklo sniffed the air but smelled nothing but pine sap. Perhaps it was a gap for a BlackPath. Toklo's heart lurched. Had Akocha gone hurtling into the path of a firebeast?

Panic flaring through his pelt, Toklo leaped down the hill. Tearing through brambles, bouncing off trees, he half skidded, half bounded down the slope, bursting from the forest hot and scared. "Akocha!"

Instead of a BlackPath, the trees gave way to a riverbank. The water swirled fast and clear, a bearlength below his paws. Had Akocha fallen in? Toklo hurried to the edge and gazed downstream.

"Toklo! Look!" Akocha's bark sounded behind him. Toklo turned and saw the young bear staring wide-eyed at a pool where the river opened up between steep banks. The pool ended in a stony cliff, twice the height of the trees around it. A sunlit waterfall poured down the cliff, making rainbows where it plunged into the pool.

"Isn't it beautiful?" Akocha shouted over the noise.

The roar of water stung Toklo's ear fur. "I thought you'd fallen in."

Akocha frowned at him. "Why would I do that?"

Toklo growled softly to himself. He should be sleeping on the shore now. And yet the river was beautiful. Enclosed by dark-green forest, it glittered in the burn-sky sunshine.

"Let's swim," Akocha suggested.

Toklo surveyed the smooth water. The pool looked cool and peaceful, despite the thundering of the falls. "Okay." Slithering down the bank, he plunged in and let the cold water fold around him.

Bubbles exploded next to him, fizzing around a small brown shape that bobbed swiftly upward, shaking droplets from its muzzle. "Let's see who can swim to the other side first!" Without waiting, Akocha struck out across the pool.

Toklo swam after him, pushing slowly through the water as Akocha raced ahead. As they neared the far bank, Akocha veered toward the falls.

"I want to swim through a rainbow!" Akocha called, paddling for the frothing water where the spray made colorful arcs in the air.

"Be careful!" Toklo warned. "Akocha, stop!" His bark was drowned by the bellow of the falls. Toklo stiffened with alarm as Akocha vanished beneath the foam. The current had sucked him under!

Gulping in a deep breath, Toklo dove beneath the churning water, eyes wide as he searched for the cub. The waterfall hit his back like a stone and pushed him down farther. Tumbling, he struck out with all four paws, fighting for calmer water. And then, as suddenly as the falls had grabbed him, they let him go. Bobbing up, he broke the surface, gasping with relief.

"Akocha!" Was the cub still swirling in the depths, pinned by the force of the falls? Toklo whipped his head around, scanning the surface. Taking another gulp of air, he prepared to dive again.

A brown head popped up beside him. "That was fun!" Spitting out water, Akocha huffed with delight. Then his eyes stretched wide. "Whoa! Look where we are!"

Toklo shook away droplets from his head and blinked

with surprise. The falls had pulled them into another world. Here, screened from the forest by the silver waterfall, a huge cave stretched deep beneath the hillside. Akocha was already swimming for a broad stone ledge at the back of the cave. He heaved himself out of the water and barked with excitement. His call echoed around the stone walls.

Toklo climbed onto the ledge beside the cub and shook his drenched pelt. The watery light that shone through the falls rippled on the sides of the cave.

"Let's explore!" Akocha darted into the shadows.

Toklo followed more slowly, sniffing the cool, wet air as the cave darkened around him. The scents of moss and stone filled his nose. "How far back does it go?" he called.

Akocha's echoing bark replied. "It stops here." He was just visible at the back of the cave, a solid black shape in the half dark.

This would have made a great den on our journey, Toklo thought. Kallik and Yakone would have loved the huge, cool space. Lusa would have stared in wonder at the falling water as it made patterns of the sunlight beyond.

"Can this be our secret place?" Akocha begged. "I don't want the other bears to know about it."

"Okay," Toklo answered absently. A breeze swirled in from one side of the falls, carrying the scent of pines. It jolted him from his memories. "We should go back to the lake," he murmured. "Your mother will be wondering where you are."

Akocha was sniffing the wall. "I don't think anybody has ever been here before us."

Toklo wondered if that was true. There were no other scents beyond wind and water here. "Come on." He walked toward a pillar of sunlight where a ledge curved around the edge of the falls and led out to the bank.

Akocha trotted after him, raising his voice as they skirted the wall of water. "We found the best place in the world!"

CHAPTER EIGHT

Kallik

Kallik slept. Dreams rushed in and out like waves lapping the shore. Black bears flashed in her thoughts, trapped and bleeding, their faces contorted with pain. Firebeasts streaked past her. The heat of their wind blasted her muzzle. She could see Lusa darting one way, then the other, eyes wild. *Ujurak!* Fear lifted her to the surface of sleep, and she broke momentarily into wakefulness before slumping back, black bears and firebeasts crowding in again. She knew Ujurak was there, skirting the edge of her dream, just out of reach.

Come and help us! As Kallik wailed out loud, she saw Lusa on the BlackPath. A firebeast thundered toward her. *Run!* Kallik tried to shriek, but no sound came out. *Lusa!*

A large, wet snout snuffled at her ear. "Kallik?"

She raised her head, shaking herself awake. Relief swamped her as she saw the barren shore sloping down to the lake. No firebeasts, no Lusa.

Yakone nudged her cheek. "A nightmare?"

"Yes." Kallik heaved herself to her paws and shook out her pelt. "I dreamed Lusa was in danger."

"Lusa's safe," Yakone soothed. "We brought her home with the injured bears, remember? She'll be curled in her nest."

"I hope so." Kallik gazed across the shore to the black bears' wooded hillside. "I'm worried she stayed up all night looking after the wounded. She seemed to be the only bear who knew what to do. She'll be exhausted."

"Lusa can take care of herself," Yakone reminded her. "She'll rest when she needs to." He nodded to the group of white bears gathered at the water's edge. Taqqiq, Iqaluk, and Salik were among them. "They're planning to swim out to that island." A small rocky hump lay a short way from the shore, hazy in the morning sunshine. "Why don't we go with them? It looks like there will be birds to catch."

Kallik gazed across the sparkling water. Gulls wheeled and fought above the island. "I can't," she told Yakone. "Lusa will need fresh herbs. I want to collect some." The forest beyond the ridge looked green and lush. She felt sure there would be plenty of useful plants growing among the trees.

Yakone's eyes rounded with sympathy. "She has other bears to help her now, Kallik. She doesn't need us anymore."

Kallik looked at him sharply. "Lusa will *always* need us! We're her best friends."

"We'll always be special to her," Yakone agreed. "But she must make her own life now."

Kallik snorted. "Maybe. But that doesn't mean we can't

help her. If you want to swim to the island with the others, then go. I can look for herbs by myself."

"No," Yakone murmured. "I'll come with you."

Kallik wasn't sure whether to feel grateful or annoyed that she'd had to persuade him to help. *Don't you care about Lusa anymore?* She brushed the thought away.

"Are you coming?" Taqqiq called.

Kallik shook her head. "We're going to the woods."

"The woods are for brown bears!" Salik called.

"And black bears!" added Iqaluk.

Taqqiq hurried up the shore toward Kallik. "What do you want to go to the woods for?" he hissed.

"We need to find herbs," Kallik told him.

Anxiety glittered in her brother's gaze. "White bears don't find herbs! They swim and hunt!" He glanced over his shoulder at Iqaluk and Salik, then looked back at Kallik. "Stop being so *different*! Please!"

"Lusa's friends were hurt in the accident," Kallik explained. "They need help."

"You're with us now!" Taqqiq snapped. "You have to forget about Lusa and Toklo."

"I can't walk away from my friends!"

"You walked away from *me*!" Taqqiq didn't give Kallik time to respond. Spinning around, he marched toward the others.

Kallik began to clamber up the ridge, feeling numb with sadness. Taqqiq was right. She had left her brother to follow her friends. Distracted, she slipped and bumped back down the jagged rock face. Landing heavily on her hindpaws, she began to scramble up again, irritated at herself for being so clumsy and at Taqqiq for making her feel guilty.

"Are you okay?" Yakone called behind her.

"I'm fine!" Kallik heaved herself up the rocks. Trees grew at the top, their trunks matted with lichen.

Yakone climbed after her. "Do you know what herbs to look for?"

She turned to face him. "Do you agree with Taqqiq?" she challenged. "Do you think I care too much about my old friends?"

Yakone calmly met her gaze. "I think you care about everyone. It's one of the things I love about you." Kallik blinked as he slid past her and began sniffing at a clump of leaves sprouting between the roots of a tree. "Are these any good?" he called.

Kallik padded to his side, feeling guilty about her temper. "I'm sorry." She didn't look at the leaves. "I shouldn't have snapped at you. You're the only bear on my side."

"There aren't any sides." Yakone looked up. "There are old friends and friends still to be made. Choosing one doesn't mean you must stop caring about the other. We are all facing the Longest Day together. It's why we're here."

Kallik dropped her gaze. She knew he was right, but she wasn't ready to agree.

By the time the sun was high in the clear blue sky, they both carried wads of fragrant green leaves. Following the forest around the lake, they skirted the stone tower and wove between mossy trees until they reached the lighter, leaf-strewn stretch where the black bears had made their camp.

"Where are you going?" A black bear blocked their path.

Kallik squinted at him, the scent from the herbs stinging her eyes.

Another black bear appeared. "This isn't your land!"

Kallik smelled fear scent; it was strong. *They're scared of me!*

Yakone laid his leaves on the ground. "We've brought herbs for Lusa."

Kallik tipped her head, hoping to look friendly.

The first bear curled his lip. "We'll make sure she gets them."

"Kallik!" Lusa's bark sounded through the trees. "Yakone? Is that you?" She pushed her way between the two males. "You brought herbs." Her eyes shone, but Kallik could see she was exhausted.

She put down her leaves and stretched forward to touch Lusa's muzzle. "Are you okay?"

"I'm fine," Lusa told her. "The swelling on Chula's leg is going down. I think it's just a sprain and not broken." She glanced at the herbs. "You found big leaves! That's great! I need lots. Oh, and we found Miki! Toklo helped."

Kallik stared at her in surprise. "Toklo?"

"He came looking for me," Lusa explained. "He was worried I'd been hurt in the accident. He searched the woods with me last night until we came across Miki."

Kallik felt a twinge of jealousy. She didn't like the idea of Toklo and Lusa having adventures without her.

Lusa went on. "Miki's had a bump on his head, but these leaves will soothe it."

"You sound worn out," Kallik told Lusa. "Have you had any rest?"

"I was going to have a nap when we got back from finding Miki, but Chula was complaining of pain and I needed to find herbs to make poultices for everyone's cuts and bruises and—"

Kallik cut her off. "Let me help." She stepped forward.

The male black bears backed away, growling.

"It's okay," Lusa told them. "Kallik and Yakone are friends."

"White bears should stick to their own side of the lake," muttered one.

Yakone dipped his head. "We can leave if you want."

"No!" Kallik shot him a look. "Not until we've helped Lusa. She's exhausted." She turned to the black bears. "Has anyone been helping her treat the injured bears?"

"We didn't know how," one growled defensively.

"We eat leaves, we don't use them for wounds," protested the other.

Kallik moved briskly past them. "Perhaps it's time you learned how."

She made her way to the dip at the edge of the clearing, relieved to smell herbs, not infection. "You've done well," she congratulated Lusa as her friend caught up, Yakone just behind her. "Tell me what I can do to help."

Chula was lying on her side, her leg wrapped in leaves. Rudi was propped against a bank of earth, his muzzle resting on his belly as he dozed. Sheena stared blankly into the trees while Tibik nestled beside her, his pelt ruffled and full of leaf scraps.

Rudi's nose twitched. He opened his eyes and looked at

Kallik, huge-eyed. "I was beginning to think I dreamed you yesterday."

A male bear sat up beside him and blinked at the white bears. His head was swathed in leaves. "Why are they here?" he asked Lusa.

"They're my friends, Miki," Lusa explained. "Do you remember the white bears I told you about?"

Miki shifted backward, his pelt bristling.

Kallik snorted. Behind her, she could hear anxious growls as the other black bears gathered to see what was going on.

"Quick! Climb a tree," a she-bear whispered.

Leaves rustled above Kallik. She looked up and saw a male cub gazing at her in terror.

Did he think she would eat him? "Lusa needs to rest," Kallik announced. "She looks like she hasn't slept in days. While she has a break, I'm going to look after the wounded bears."

Disapproving murmurs rippled behind her.

Chula shifted on her bed of leaves. "I think you should go," she told Kallik.

"No." Lusa stared wearily at Chula. "Don't you understand? Kallik and Yakone will take care of you." She turned to Kallik. "All their wounds need re-dressing. With this hot weather, they could easily turn sour." Swaying on her paws, she poked the herbs that Yakone had dropped. "These will make good poultices once you've chewed them. Save the largest leaves to wrap Chula's leg and Miki's head."

Kallik nodded. "We'll wake you when we've finished."

Lusa looked at her gratefully through bleary eyes and

stumbled away. Kallik peeled a leaf from the pile and began chewing it into a poultice. She could feel the stares of the other black bears burning through her pelt, but she ignored them. Spitting out the green goo, she nudged the rest of the pile toward Yakone. "Chew these. Save the big leaves to wrap wounds." Lapping up a tongueful of goo, she leaned down and began sniffing Rudi.

The old bear jerked away. Kallik ignored his fear scent. She was going to help him, not hurt him. If Rudi wanted to be afraid, then let him. Smelling a bloody patch of pelt, Kallik began licking sap into it. Rudi growled but held still.

As Kallik turned to fetch more leaf-pulp, she saw Ossi. He was dragging a branch, heavy with cloudberries, into the clearing.

Yakone hailed him with a jerk of his snout. His muzzle was green from chewing leaves. "Ossi!"

Ossi dropped the branch. "You came back!"

"We figured Lusa might need some help," Yakone told him.

"I was bringing her food." Ossi nodded to the berries.

Kallik grunted. "She doesn't need food, she needs help looking after these bears. There are too many injuries for one bear to take care of alone."

"Then I'll help her." Ossi glanced nervously at the others. "I really don't think you should stay here."

A she-bear stepped forward, glaring at Kallik. "Aren't there any *white* bears you could go and look after?"

"Dena, hush!" another warned. "Only a bee-brain starts a fight with a white bear."

Kallik bristled. "We didn't come here to fight. We came to help." How many times was she going to have to say it?

More black bears stepped forward, indignation sparking through their fear.

"You don't belong here."

"We can take care of our own."

The cub wailed from the tree. "Make them go away!"

Frustration welled in Kallik's chest. She only wanted to help! She glanced at Yakone. Could he say something that would calm these bears?

He returned her gaze and shrugged. "We should leave."

"What about Lusa?" Kallik protested. "How's she going to get any rest?"

"I won't get any rest with everyone fussing about you being here." Lusa was on her paws and staring wearily at Kallik. "You'd better go."

"But—" Kallik began.

"Just leave, please."

Sighing, Kallik stepped carefully over the herbs and headed between the trees. Yakone followed. She felt his flank brush hers as they picked their way along the slope, back toward the white bears' side of the water.

The black bears' fear and hostility seemed to stick in Kallik's pelt like burrs. "Why couldn't they just let us take care of them?" she growled at Yakone. "We've only ever helped them! It's not fair."

Yakone walked silently beside her.

"Taqqiq suggested that I wasn't loyal to the white bears,"

Kallik went on. "What's wrong with being loyal to all bears? Why is it better to look after a white bear than a black bear? Why can't a black bear learn to trust a white bear?"

Muttering on, she stomped back to the white bears' stretch of shore and climbed down onto the beach.

Illa was standing in the shallows, staring across the lake. She turned as Kallik approached. "Where have you been?"

Kallik met her gaze angrily. "I was trying to help the black bears! Have you got a problem with that?" Was the Star Island bear going to tell her she was wrong, too? "Not that they'd let us help," she went on. "They were too worried we were going to eat them."

Illa's gaze flicked to Yakone, and Kallik saw understanding flash between them. *They think I'm crazy.* Fury was like a fire in her chest.

"Yakone." Illa's growl was gentle. "Go fish with the others." Bears were diving near the small, rocky island.

Yakone touched Kallik's cheek with his muzzle, then waded into the water.

Illa tipped her head sympathetically. "You sound like you've had a frustrating day."

"Why can't black bears and brown bears and white bears cooperate?" Kallik sighed.

Illa beckoned her closer with a flick of her muzzle. "Come stand in the shallows. It's hard to think straight when you've got hot paws."

Kallik realized that her pelt was scorching in the burn-sky sun. She padded down the beach and waded in beside Illa.

The cold water washed comfortingly around her legs.

"It's the nature of white bears to live alone and fight for survival," Illa reminded her. "That is the way it's always been."

"But it should change," Kallik told her. "There are so many dangers now. Firebeasts and flat-faces and poisoned seals." She felt the weight of it all sweep over her. "We are only going to survive if we learn to work together."

"Perhaps that's true," Illa murmured. "But bears are not like trees or the ice. We can't change in a season."

"But they don't *want* to change," Kallik complained.

"Why should they?" Illa asked. "Not every bear has seen all you have seen. You can't expect them to understand the extraordinary experiences you've had."

"But if they don't change, they'll die!"

Illa faced Kallik. "We've survived since the beginning of time," she told her. "Times may be hard now, but if bears know one thing, it's how to survive."

The coolness of the water seemed to spread from Kallik's paws, seeping up through her pelt. "But we'll survive more easily if we help each other."

"True." Illa nodded. "Why don't we make a start now? You can help me fish." Without waiting for an answer, she waded deeper and started swimming.

Kallik wished she could be as calm as Illa. Splashing through the shallows, she followed the other bear into the deep water. *Maybe Illa's right. Maybe I can't change everything, however much I want to.*

CHAPTER NINE

Lusa

"Eat some berries."

Lusa ignored Ossi's plea. "The sooner I get these wounds re-dressed, the sooner I can rest." The cloudberries Ossi had brought smelled delicious. Perhaps they'd give her the energy she needed. But she felt too annoyed to eat. Why did the black bears have to be so hostile to her friends?

"Can't the wounds wait?" Ossi pressed. "You look exhausted."

"No, they can't wait, not in this hot weather." Lusa began to peel away the drying leaves from around Chula's leg.

Chula touched her shoulder with a paw. "Eat a berry, Lusa," she murmured. "You've worked so hard."

Ossi picked up the berry branch and dangled it under Lusa's muzzle. She shoved it away with her nose.

Miki chuffed with amusement. "Never tell a grumpy bear what to do."

"I'm not grumpy!" Lusa snapped. She paused as she saw amusement flash in Miki's eyes.

"Just eat the berries, Lusa," Chula pleaded.

Lusa's fur grew hot. She *was* being grumpy. Tibik was staring at her warily. Who wanted their wounds dressed by an angry bear? At least Rudi was dozing again and hadn't noticed. Ossi offered her the berries again.

"Careful, Ossi!" Miki backed away, pretending to be scared. "You might lose your paw."

Lusa huffed and sat down. Grunting, she snatched the branch from Ossi and began cramming the berries into her mouth. As their sweetness bathed her tongue, she felt her anger ease. Perhaps it was too much to ask the black bears to accept white bears in their camp. At the last gathering, Taqqiq, Iqaluk, and Salik had stolen their food and taken Miki. *I should be more sympathetic to my own kind.* She ignored the pang of grief that reminded her that soon all she would know was her own kind; Kallik, Yakone, and Toklo wouldn't be part of her life anymore.

She swallowed the last of the berries.

Ossi peeled a leaf from Yakone's pile. "Tell me what to do, and I can help," he offered.

"Chew the smaller leaves into pulp." Lusa got to her paws and began peeling more leaves away from Chula's leg. She ran her paw gently over the matted fur. Some of the swelling had eased, and she could feel the bone underneath. "It's not broken," she told Chula. "But you shouldn't walk on it for a few days." She looked up and saw relief on Chula's face. "Does it hurt?"

Chula nodded. "Yes, but not as much as yesterday."

"I want to let the air get to it for a while." Lusa piled leaves beneath the wounded leg and rested it on them. "I'll put a new dressing on it soon."

Ossi nudged her shoulder. "What should I do next?" His mouth was stained green, and piles of chewed leaves sat at his paws.

"Ask Rudi where his cuts are," Lusa ordered. "Lick the sap into them. Make sure you get it as deep as you can, but don't hurt him."

Ossi nodded and headed for Rudi.

Tibik looked to Lusa. "Can you give my mother some herbs that will stop her feeling sad?"

Sheena had moved her gaze from the trees. Hala's body had been taken by Pokkoli and Dena and laid beside Hashi's just outside the camp.

Lusa looked down at the cub. "She will stop feeling sad eventually. And so will you."

Rudi shifted as Ossi licked sap into a cut on his shoulder. "I'm hungry," he growled.

"I'll bring you food once we've finished," Lusa promised.

Rudi ducked away from Ossi. "I'm well enough to forage."

Lusa looked at the old bear. His fur was matted and smeared with leaf-sap, and his eyes were dull. "You should rest for another day," she advised.

"Pokkoli can organize a foraging party." Ossi sat back on his haunches and scanned the trees. "Should I go find him?"

"That's a good idea." Lusa blinked gratefully at Ossi as she pulled the dressing from Miki's head. The swelling behind his ear still looked fiery and there was a gash at the center, but the wound was clean. Lusa searched his eyes for cloudiness; they were bright and he seemed alert. "Does your head ache?" she asked.

"Like a grizzly's been stomping on it," he told her.

"Can you remember my name?" Lusa was worried his wound might affect his memory.

Miki crossed his eyes playfully. "You're Dustu, aren't you?"

Lusa nudged him. "Don't joke!" she scolded. "You've had a serious injury."

"Okay. No more jokes."

Suddenly, Sheena sat up and pricked her ears. Issa was heading toward them, her paws and chest covered in earth. "We've dug the grave." Her gaze flitted uneasily over the injured bears. "It's time to bury Hashi and Hala."

Sheena was the first on her paws, walking on trembling legs toward the trees. Tibik watched her anxiously.

Miki moved closer to the young bear. "Come on, little one. I'll take you over." He nudged Tibik out of the scoop in the ground and steered him across the clearing.

"Chula?" Ossi was blinking at his sister. "Do you want me to carry you?"

Lusa shook her head. "Chula should stay here," she warned. "The less she moves her leg, the better."

Chula leaned forward, her eyes glittering with disappointment. "But I have to be at their burial!"

"You can visit their spirit tree when your leg is better," Lusa told her. "Hashi wouldn't want you to make yourself lame for his sake."

Chula groaned in distress as Rudi climbed from the dip.

"I'll stay with you, Chula," Ossi offered.

"No." Chula shook her head. "You must be there for both of us."

Ossi nodded. "Okay."

"Promise you won't put any weight on it," Lusa told Chula. "I'll be back soon to change your bedding." The leaves and ferns lining the nest were growing musty. Fresh fronds would make everyone feel better.

Ossi fell in beside Lusa as she followed the stream of bears heading up the slope. "Chula's leg will be all right, won't it?"

"I don't know for sure," Lusa admitted. "But there's no break or cut, so there's no chance of infection. I'm sure if she rests it, she'll be able to walk on it soon."

The other bears were slowing, fanning out around the base of a towering pine. Lusa nosed her way between them and squeezed to the front. A deep hole had been scraped out among the roots of the pine. Lusa stared into it. The damp scent of churned earth filled her nose.

Hashi lay in the shadows at the bottom. Hala was curled in his paws as though she was sleeping. A moan rolled in Sheena's throat as she peered into the grave. Around her, mothers shuffled closer to their cubs.

Dustu stood with his forepaws on the edge of the hole. The sunshine filtering through the canopy showed the reddish tinge in his pelt. Sadness filled his small, round eyes. As the other bears settled into stillness, Dustu lifted his muzzle. "I remember Hashi as a young bear. He climbed to the top of this pine on his first gathering and stayed there for two days. We teased him that he was scared, but he said he could see so far across the lake that he didn't ever want to come down." Dustu's voice thickened with grief. "Hashi loved the lake. He loved the beauty of our land, and honored Arcturus for finding the wilderness we made our home."

Lusa's chest tightened. Had Hashi really once been a cub who climbed the highest trees? She glanced up, straining to see the top of the towering pine.

Dustu went on. "It is fitting that Hashi will be buried here, near the lake that he wanted to look at forever." His growl grew raspier. "His spirit will live on in this great tree, keeping watch over every Longest Day until there are no more black bears."

Sheena lifted her grief-stricken gaze. "And Hala?"

Sympathy brimmed in Dustu's eyes. "Such a young bear should not have died. But she is with Hashi, and they can look across the lake together. She will never be alone, nor Hashi. Their spirits will watch over us as one."

Sheena's shoulders slumped. Dena nuzzled her ears and Tibik nestled against her flank.

Dustu nodded, and the other bears began to push leaves into the hole. They fluttered down, covering the bodies.

"May your spirits be happy." Dustu pushed a pawful of earth over the rim.

"Watch over our land." Dena let soil sprinkle down like rain.

Sheena sent more earth showering into the grave. "Goodbye, Hala," she whispered. "Take care of her, Hashi." Eyes clouding, she turned and stumbled through the crowd with Tibik and Dena beside her.

Lusa wished she knew an herb that could ease Sheena's sadness, but she also knew that sadness, like the night, must be lived through. Dawn always came in the end.

Her pelt tingled as if someone was watching her. Lusa frowned, glancing over her shoulder. She sniffed the air, checking for strange scents. But she could smell only the trees and earth and the other bears.

I must be imagining it. The burial had unsettled her, that was all. She turned back to the grave. If only she'd managed to save Hashi. There must have been more she could have done when she'd found him beside the BlackPath. She felt Ossi shift beside her. He was pushing earth into the grave.

"Do you think I could have saved him?" she whispered in his ear.

He looked at her. "His wound was too deep."

"Perhaps I shouldn't have moved him."

"You couldn't have left him there. Flat-faces were coming."

Miki wove through the crowd toward them. "Are you okay?" He stopped beside Lusa. "You look worried."

"What if I could have saved Hashi?" she blurted out.

Miki steered her away from the others, Ossi following.

"I've tried to tell her there was nothing more she could have done," Ossi explained. "Hashi was too badly injured."

Miki halted beneath an aspen and looked at Lusa. "You did all you could," he told her quietly.

"But if I'd known more herbs, I might have saved him."

Guilt churned in Lusa's belly.

"You could learn every herb in the forest," Miki murmured. "But you can't save every bear."

Why not? Lusa knew he was right. Weariness dragged at her fur. She needed to sleep. But she'd promised to find new bedding for the injured bears. Had Ossi asked Pokkoli to find food yet? Rudi would still be hungry. She swayed on her paws, suddenly overwhelmed.

"Lusa!" Issa hurried toward her with Dena and Leotie. "You must rest."

"I promised fresh bedding and food—" she began.

Issa huffed. "The rest of us can see to that."

Dena nodded. "I'll pick ferns."

"I'll help," Leotie added.

"I'll go foraging with Pokkoli," Ossi offered.

"I'll make sure Chula and the others are comfortable," Issa promised.

Lusa gazed at them gratefully. "Are you sure?"

"Of course." Issa nudged her shoulder. "Go find a quiet place to rest beside the lake. You look like you need some fresh air."

Lusa let the kindly she-bear nose her away. She ambled from beneath the trees, feeling the earth turn to pebbles beneath her paws. A cool wind whipped off the lake and streamed through her fur, refreshing her. Lifting her muzzle, Lusa hurried toward the water. She hadn't drunk all day and suddenly realized how thirsty she was. Wading into the shallows, she dipped her muzzle into the chilly water.

A large white shape moved through the waves a few bear-lengths out. Instinctively Lusa backed away, fear flashing beneath her pelt. A white bear was swimming toward her. What was a white bear doing over here? Instantly she thought of Taqqiq and Salik and how they'd taken Miki last year.

"Lusa!"

She gasped. It was Kallik!

The white she-bear reached the shallows and began to wade from the lake. "Have you had a chance to rest?"

"Not yet," Lusa answered. "We just buried Hashi and Hala. But I've eaten. Ossi brought me berries."

Pebbles clacked along the shore. Lusa turned and saw a brown bear running toward them.

"Toklo!"

Toklo jerked his nose toward a pile of boulders farther up the shore. "Meet me there," he barked as he neared.

Lusa could see brown bears watching him from their stretch of shoreline.

Kallik must have noticed them, too. "I guess he doesn't want to be seen hanging out with us." She sounded annoyed.

Is she thinking about the way the black bears drove her out of the camp? Lusa wondered.

"Do the other white bears mind you talking to us?" Lusa asked.

Kallik rolled her eyes. "Taqqiq would call me a traitor."

Lusa squinted at the distant white bears' shore. "Come on, then. Let's get out of sight."

They reached the boulders at the same time as Toklo and

followed him into the shadows behind. Toklo nuzzled Lusa's cheek, then turned to rub his snout along Kallik's. "It's great to see you."

Kallik huffed and flopped onto the pebbles. "I've missed you both so much."

"Where's Yakone?" Lusa scanned the lake, half expecting to see another white head bobbing through the water toward them.

"He's fishing with the white bears," Kallik grunted.

Lusa frowned. Didn't he want to see them again?

"He likes being back among his own kind." Kallik rubbed her wet head against the pebbles as though scratching an itch.

Toklo propped his haunches on a boulder. "I guess he's missed the bears from Star Island."

Lusa leaned against Kallik's flank. She could almost imagine they were still on their journey. No white bears and black bears and brown bears waiting for them to return to where they should be. Just the three of them, alone.

"How's Miki?" Toklo asked.

"His head hurts," she replied. "But he'll be okay."

Toklo looked down at Kallik. "How are the white bears? I saw Salik and Iqaluk. I hope they're behaving themselves."

Kallik pushed herself into a sitting position. "As much as they ever do."

"The brown bears are restless," Toklo confided. "They need a leader."

Lusa snorted. "Why does any bear need a leader?"

Toklo glanced over the rocks toward the brown bears. "To

stop *everyone* from wanting to be the leader," he muttered. "Once we've named someone, everyone else can stop fighting."

"They're fighting?" Kallik looked shocked.

"They're just testing each other's strength," Toklo explained. "But if we don't find a leader soon, it might get vicious."

Lusa tipped her head on one side. Silhouetted against the forest, the sun lighting his thick pelt, Toklo looked strong and powerful. Did he want to be leader? Lusa tried to imagine Ossi or Miki or Pokkoli arguing over who would lead the black bears. She couldn't imagine it. They hadn't even talked about it. They had been too busy grieving Hashi's death. She frowned, remembering the accident and the burial. The brown bears were fighting and the black bears were grieving. And Yakone was too busy with his old friends to remember his new ones. Her mood suddenly darkened.

"Nothing is the way I thought it would be," she murmured. "We came here to celebrate the Longest Day. I thought it would be fun." *A special way to say good-bye.* "But it's not. My friends have been hurt and your friends are fighting."

"I wouldn't call them friends exactly," Toklo snorted.

"This is our last time together," Lusa whimpered. "It's supposed to be perfect."

Kallik gazed at her. "How could it be perfect when we're going to be leaving each other?"

Lusa's throat tightened. She stared at Kallik, then Toklo. The thought of being far away from them tore at her heart.

"Come on!" Kallik leaped to her paws. "We can't waste our last moments together being miserable. Let's go for a swim. Who cares who sees us? I'm proud that you're my friends!"

Lusa jumped up and followed Kallik and Toklo down the shore. The pebbles felt hot under her paws. Lusa welcomed the cool water as she charged into the shallows. Toklo and Kallik were already swimming farther out. Lusa followed them gingerly, tensing as the water lifted her and the lake bed disappeared from beneath her paws. She swam after Toklo and Kallik as they splashed each other, dipping under the surface before surging back up. Lusa swam around them, keeping her distance. Then Toklo vanished.

Lusa waited for him to resurface. Moments passed. "Where is he?" she called to Kallik.

Kallik ducked underwater. "I can't see him," she spluttered, bobbing back up.

Suddenly the water beside Lusa exploded. Lusa yelped as Toklo burst through the surface with a huge trout in his jaws.

Kallik's eyes lit up. "Great catch!"

Toklo headed for the shore. Lusa followed, her heart still pounding from the shock. By the time she shook the water from her pelt, Toklo had laid the trout on the stones and was sniffing it. The sun glinted on its scales.

"Let's share it!" Toklo barked.

Kallik chuffed happily. Leaning down, she ripped a mouthful of flesh from the fish. She stepped back so that Toklo could take a bite. As she watched him, Lusa noticed shapes moving at the corner of her vision. She turned and saw two brown bears padding toward them.

"Are you sharing our fish with them?" the male bear called along the shore.

Beside him the she-bear scowled. "You should be sharing it with your own kind."

"Muna! Holata!" Toklo greeted them. "Come join us. There's plenty."

"Why are you feeding other bears?" Holata growled.

"They're my friends. I can—"

Lusa cut him off. She could see rage burning in the brown bears' eyes. "Don't argue!" she hissed in Toklo's ear. "You need to stay friends with them."

Toklo glanced at her, surprised.

"Take it." Lusa rolled the fish toward Toklo with her snout. "Your *friends* must be hungry." Surely he understood?

Toklo held her gaze for a moment, then nodded. "You're right, Lusa. This is a good catch. I should share it."

Lusa watched the muscles tighten beneath his pelt. She knew he was angry. He scooped up the trout in his jaws and marched along the shore toward the brown bears. Holata and Muna followed him, casting dark looks at Lusa and Kallik as they left.

Kallik nudged Lusa's shoulder. "Well done," she murmured.

"Thanks." Sadness tugged at Lusa's heart.

"I guess I'd better get back." Kallik blinked at Lusa. "You should get some rest."

"I will," Lusa promised. She rubbed her muzzle along Kallik's jaw. "See you soon."

"Yes." Kallik gazed at her fondly, then waded into the lake and swam away.

Lusa's thoughts whirled, muddled by tiredness. Why did they have to leave? Was she really happier with her own kind of bear? She thought of Ossi and Miki and Chula. *I like them, don't I?* Heading toward the forest, she ducked into the shadow of the trees. Curling into a mossy scoop at the foot of a pine, Lusa closed her eyes. This was supposed to be the end of their journey. But she hadn't expected life with the black bears to be full of worry and grief. Already, two bears were dead. And Toklo's group was fighting among themselves.

Sleep tugged at her weary limbs. Why did life apart from her friends have to be so difficult?

CHAPTER TEN

Toklo

Toklo padded after Holata and Muna. The trout felt heavy in his jaws, its sweetness gone. His ears burned. He felt like a cub who had been scolded by his mother. How dare they treat him like this? They had probably seen nothing beyond their home territory and this lake. *Cloud-brains!* They wouldn't even know how to make friends with a black bear or a white bear.

As they neared the brown bears' territory, Elsu and Elki bounded toward them. They raced past their parents and scrambled to a halt in front of Toklo.

"Did you catch that?" Elsu stared wide-eyed at the trout. "It's huge!"

Elki fell in beside Toklo as he continued walking. "He caught the salmon last suncircle, remember?"

Elsu sniffed the fish. "It smells yummy."

Toklo stopped at the edge of the brown bears' camp and dropped the trout. "You can have it," he told Elsu and Elki. If he couldn't share it with Lusa and Kallik, he might as well let these two young bears have it. They weren't cloud-brains yet.

The other bears had gathered around Shesh beside the parley rock. Holata and Muna had already joined them, jostling for position among the others.

"We must find a bear to take Oogrook's place," Shesh growled.

Wenona was at the front of the crowd. "How do we decide?"

"The strongest bear should lead us!" Hattack reared onto his hind legs and thrust out his chest.

Toklo spotted Akocha and his mother piling up fresh sticks for the Longest Day ceremony. At least they seemed more interested in honoring the spirits than fighting over who was leader. "Come share this fish!" he called to them.

Akocha galloped toward Toklo, Tayanita following more slowly. Elsu and Elki moved aside to let them share.

As Akocha bit a lump from the fish, his mother dipped her head to Toklo. "Thank you!"

She looked so grateful that Toklo felt less sour about having to share the trout with the brown bears. "I hope you enjoy it," he grunted, and headed for the bears milling around Shesh.

Shesh was speaking again. "The Longest Day is nearly here."

Holata glanced at Toklo as he stopped at the edge of the group. "We must choose someone who knows where his loyalties lie," he growled.

Toklo sank his claws into the pebbles. *These bears have no idea what loyalty means!* He'd stuck by Kallik, Yakone, and Lusa through more than they could imagine.

"We need a leader everyone respects," Tuari called.

Wenona snorted. "That's obvious!"

A dark-brown male shifted beside her. "Why do we need a leader at all?" he barked. "I don't need to be told what to do."

A few murmurs of agreement rose from the others.

Shesh lifted his muzzle. "Someone must lead the ceremony!"

The dark-brown bear held his ground. "Anyone can lead the ceremony. It doesn't mean they lead us."

Hattack barged past him. "Of course we need a leader! Until we decide, there won't be peace among us."

Toklo held his tongue. He wanted to point out that Hattack had started most of the arguments. If they wanted peace, all they needed was to stop fighting about who should be leader. He saw Shesh's gaze fix on him. His heart sank as he guessed what the old bear would say next.

"Toklo swam to Pawprint Island and brought back the salmon," Shesh called. "That must mean something!"

"It means he's lucky!" Hattack scoffed.

"Oogrook didn't say Toklo should be leader after him," Holata pointed out.

Shesh raised a paw. "Oogrook didn't know he wouldn't be here this suncircle."

"Every bear deserves a chance to be leader!" Wenona insisted.

Muna scowled. "We can't take turns!"

Movement caught Toklo's eye. On the far side of the group, bears were breaking away, their pelts prickling. Toklo strained to see what had disturbed them. A group of bears were trekking down the beach. New arrivals! He wondered where they'd come from as he heard them bark greetings. Their voices sounded familiar.

Toklo pushed through the crowd.

"Watch where you're stepping!" An old bear tugged his paw from beneath Toklo's.

"Sorry!" He broke from the crowd. "Makya!" It was the she-bear from the Forest of Wolves. Her cubs charged forward as soon as they saw him.

"Toklo!" Flo rubbed her muzzle under his chin.

Fala bounded around him. "We hoped you'd be here!"

Makya's eyes shone. "It's good to see you again, Toklo."

Izusa was behind her with her cubs Wapi and Yas. Toklo felt a surge of hope as he searched for another face. There she was!

"Aiyanna!" he barked.

The brown she-bear joined the others from the Forest of Wolves as they crowded around Toklo.

Yas was buzzing with excitement. "We've been traveling for *moons*!"

"Wapi kept falling into things," Flo teased.

Fala huffed with amusement. "He fell into a bramble *and* a river *and* a hole."

"I did not fall!" Wapi bristled. "I jumped. It was totally on purpose."

Toklo chuffed at the cub. "I hope you didn't hurt yourself."

Wapi's pelt was dusty from the journey, but there was no sign of wounds. He nudged Flo. "They're just jealous because

I was always first to find the trail."

Yas rolled her eyes at Toklo. "Wapi's just showing off because he wants to impress Flo."

Wapi's eyes flashed with embarrassment. Flo looked at her paws.

"Go wash yourselves in the lake," Izusa told the cubs. "But stay in the shallows and watch out for currents." As the cubs hared away, she looked wearily at Toklo. "I don't know where they find the energy."

Makya shook leaf dust from her fur. "My paws are worn out."

Toklo nodded. He knew how long their journey had been. "I can show you a good place to make nests," he told her. "And help you gather ferns for bedding."

Makya glanced knowingly at Izusa. "We can sort out our own nests," she told Toklo. "Why don't you show Aiyanna around?"

Toklo snatched a look at Aiyanna before staring at his paws. "Would you like that?" he mumbled.

"Yes, please." Aiyanna sounded as awkward as he felt. Last time they'd seen each other, they'd got along fine. But now it felt as though they hardly knew each other.

"Come on, Izusa." Makya began to pad toward the trees. "I think I saw a perfect place to make nests."

"Should I stay and keep an eye on the cubs?" Izusa glanced toward the shallows, where Flo, Fala, Wapi, and Yas were splashing water at one another and barking happily.

"If they can travel this far, they can survive a bit of water,"

Makya told her. "Besides, we won't be long, and they'll be glad of fresh nests to climb into when they finally get tired."

The two she-bears ambled toward the woods.

Toklo jerked his nose along the shore without meeting Aiyanna's eye. "Let's go this way."

He brushed past the group of bears who were still arguing over the best way to choose a leader.

"It should be the best hunter!"

"The fastest runner!"

"The strongest fighter."

Toklo felt pebbles spatter his paw as Aiyanna drew up alongside him, her flank brushing his for a moment, before she jerked away.

"Sorry about the other bears," Toklo murmured, feeling embarrassed about the simmering tension in the group.

"Why are you sorry?" Aiyanna asked. "Did you start the argument?"

"No."

"Then why apologize?"

Toklo glanced at her. He liked the way Aiyanna wasn't afraid to say exactly what she was thinking. "I guess I just expected the gathering to be different."

"I heard Oogrook is dead," Aiyanna growled. "Is that why everyone's arguing?"

Toklo nodded. "They don't know how to choose a new leader."

Aiyanna shrugged. "Let's not worry about that. I want to explore! You were here last suncircle, right?"

"Yes."

"I've never seen the lake before." She stopped and stared out over the water. "It's huge!"

"Do you want to swim?"

"Sure," she told him. "But tell me about Lusa and Kallik and Yakone first. Are they here?" She scanned the long sweep of the lake, narrowing her eyes as her gaze reached the white bears' stretch of beach.

"Kallik and Yakone are over there," Toklo told her. "Lusa's in the woods with the black bears." He pointed his nose toward the patch of birch and spruce spreading among the pines.

"Can we meet them?" Aiyanna looked eager.

Toklo shifted his paws. "The other bears don't like us to mix."

"Really?" Aiyanna looked confused. "But we're all bears. And it's the Longest Day. Isn't that why we're here?"

"We're here to honor the spirits," Toklo explained uncomfortably. "Not to hang out with black bears and white bears. At least, that's what *they* say." He nodded toward the others.

Aiyanna's eyes flashed with defiance in a way that Toklo remembered well. "I'm really glad you came," he murmured.

"So am I." For the first time she met his gaze without shyness, and they stared at each other for a few moments. Aiyanna blinked first. "Show me your favorite place to fish."

Toklo turned toward the lake. "There's a stretch over there." He aimed a paw at where the water was deep blue. "The trout are huge if you swim deep enough."

"I've only ever fished in rivers," Aiyanna admitted.

"Let me show you how to fish in a lake." Toklo began to head for the water.

"Toklo!" Hattack's bark made him halt. The grizzly was trotting toward them, his gaze on Aiyanna. "Introduce me to your friend," he chuffed.

Toklo narrowed his eyes. "This is Aiyanna," he grunted warily.

Hattack stopped a bearlength from Aiyanna and dipped his head low. "How do you know Toklo?" he asked as he lifted his muzzle.

"We met in the Forest of Wolves," Aiyanna told him.

"Is that where you're from?"

"It's where we're both from," Aiyanna explained.

Toklo shifted his paws. The less Hattack knew about him, the better.

Hattack was still curious. "Is that why you came?" he prompted. "Because Toklo is here?"

Aiyanna glanced away without answering.

"I'm sorry," Hattack murmured softly. "I'm asking too many questions. You must be tired. Has Toklo shown you a good place to sleep?"

"Makya and Izusa are finding nests," Aiyanna told him.

"Can I help you hunt?" Hattack offered.

"Toklo was about to show me how to catch fish here."

Hattack nodded. "That's just like Toklo. He's a great bear. So helpful. It's good that he's here."

Toklo swallowed a growl. *He wishes I never came!*

"I'd better get back to the others," Hattack announced. "I

promised I'd teach some of the cubs how to catch deer." He turned and headed away.

"Bye!" Aiyanna called after him. "Nice meeting you!" She turned back to Toklo. "What a great bear!"

Toklo wanted to warn Aiyanna that Hattack's friendliness had been an act. But how would that sound? She might think he was mean. Or jealous. He changed the subject. "Let's fish." When Aiyanna hung back, Toklo paused. "I can show you a special place I discovered instead, if you like." *The waterfall!* She'd be impressed.

"I'm kind of tired after the journey," she admitted.

"Of course." Toklo's heart sank. Why did Hattack have to come and spoil their reunion? It had been going so well. "I'll walk you back to the others."

"Thanks." She walked beside him, her fur not quite touching his.

"Are you glad you came?" Toklo asked hesitantly.

Aiyanna glanced at him out of the corner of her eye. "Oh yes," she murmured. "Very."

CHAPTER ELEVEN

Kallik

Kallik scanned the shoreline, straining to catch a glimpse of white fur. Beside her, Shila sniffed the air, while Tonraq stalked around the rocks, nose twitching.

"I know you're there somewhere!" he called.

A stifled huff sounded from the stones ahead.

Kissimi was hiding, and Kallik, Shila, and Tonraq were playing "hunter," trying to catch him before he could dodge around them and touch the home rock a few bearlengths behind.

Yakone was sprawled on a boulder, his eyes half-closed as the sun sank toward the hilltops. He seemed to be relishing the early evening coolness, a relief after the long, hot day.

Taqqiq sauntered toward them. "Aren't you too old for this?" he grunted.

Kallik glanced at him, wondering if her brother was talking to her, but his gaze was on Shila.

Shila ignored him. She crept between the rocks, signaling to Tonraq with a jerk of her snout. As Tonraq veered toward her, Kallik saw a flash of white fur, then heard a splash. Kissimi was in the shallows, running fast. Cutting across the water, he raced for the home stone.

Kallik spun around. "Shila, I see prey!" She raced toward the stone, but Kissimi was moving swiftly, sending up spray as he dashed through the water. With a bark of delight he dove for the rock, his paws touching it before Kallik.

Kissimi lifted his chin. "I won!"

Tonraq and Shila climbed over the rocks toward him.

Tonraq was panting. "Well done!"

"Who's going to hide next?" Kissimi asked, his eyes shining.

Shila inclined her head toward Taqqiq. "He is."

Taqqiq grunted. "It's a cub's game."

"So what?" Shila tossed her head. "There's nothing wrong with acting like a cub from time to time."

Taqqiq glanced over his shoulder. The other white bears were farther along the shore, where the crags gave way to smoother stone. "Okay." He padded toward the home stone.

Kallik called to Yakone. "Why don't you play, too?"

Yakone lifted his head. "No, thanks."

"Are you worried about acting like a cub?" Kallik asked.

Yakone held up his scarred paw. Even from here, she could see the gap left by his missing toes. "I don't think I'd be very nimble on rocks," he grunted. "My grip's not what it used to be."

Kallik felt a flicker of frustration but didn't argue. Was Yakone always going to believe that his injured paw meant he wasn't as good as other bears? She'd speak to him later, when they were alone.

"I'll hide," Taqqiq announced. "Turn your backs."

Kallik turned away and listened to her brother's paws scuffing the rocks. She glanced at Shila. "Do you think he's had long enough to hide?"

Kissimi answered. "He's had *ages!*"

Kallik scanned the rocks. There was no sign of Taqqiq. She nodded to Yakone. "Did you see which way he went?"

Yakone's eyes gleamed. "I'm not helping you cheat!"

Kallik began to clamber over the craggy boulders. Pale fur moved in the distance, where forest reached all the way down to the water. Iqaluk and Salik were padding out of the trees. Kallik halted. From the direction they were coming, they'd see Taqqiq first. She crept farther along the rocks, watching them. Had Taqqiq hidden so well that they couldn't see him?

Shila's pawsteps brushed the rock beside her. "Do you think they'll give him away?"

"That's not fair!" Kissimi caught up to them. He'd seen Iqaluk and Salik, too. "They're not supposed to be looking for Taqqiq. It's not their game."

"Perhaps they won't spot him." As Kallik spoke, she saw Salik's muzzle jerk toward a tall pointed rock.

"What are you doing, Taqqiq?" Salik's bark echoed along the shore.

Kissimi hurried toward Taqqiq's hiding place. Kallik followed with Shila. As they skidded around the pointed rock, they found Taqqiq looking ruffled and unhappy.

Kissimi shook his head sympathetically at Taqqiq. "It

doesn't count," he told him. "Salik's not playing. It only counts if *we* find you."

Salik barked with amusement. "Are you playing cub games?" His eyes glinted with spite.

"Poor Taqqiq," Iqaluk growled. "Won't the grown-up bears play with you?"

Shila narrowed her eyes. "We were playing with him, and we're plenty grown up. We would ask you to join us, but we don't want the game turning as sour as your faces."

Kallik waited for Salik or Iqaluk to snap back, but they lowered their gazes. Shila had won this time. Pride warmed Kallik's pelt.

Taqqiq was watching Shila proudly. "Come on, Kissimi." He lifted his chin. "Let's find a really good hiding place. One that Kallik and Shila would never find."

Shila tipped her head toward Salik. "Why don't you make yourself useful and catch some fish? There are she-bears with cubs who haven't had a chance to hunt all day." Her gaze flicked to Iqaluk.

"I guess we could go fishing," Iqaluk muttered.

Salik shrugged. "I suppose." He headed toward the water and waded in. Iqaluk followed.

As they plunged beneath the surface, Kallik chuffed with amusement. "You certainly know how to deal with them."

"It doesn't always work," Shila confessed. "But I don't take any nonsense. They're no better than overgrown cubs."

Kallik thought of the loving way Taqqiq had gazed at the she-bear. "My brother is fond of you."

"I'm fond of him," Shila answered matter-of-factly.

"Do you plan to have cubs one day?"

Shila's eyes sparkled. "If the spirits bless us." She nodded toward Yakone, still drowsing on the rock. "What about you? Will you and Yakone have cubs?"

Kallik's heart warmed as she followed Shila's gaze. Yakone was a handsome bear, even when he was sleeping with one paw dangling from the rock. "One day."

"Kallik! Shila!" Illa's bark sounded across the rocks.

Kallik turned. Taqqiq and Kissimi were standing beside the she-bear.

"Anarteq's going to tell a story!" Illa called.

Kallik crunched over the stones toward her. She loved hearing about the ancient days when the land belonged to the bears alone. *Siqiniq told the stories at the last gathering,* she thought sadly. Siqiniq was the gentle old she-bear who had led the Longest Day ceremony. She had died a few moons ago. At this gathering, she would be among the spirits.

Anarteq was sitting on a large boulder. Age showed in his yellow-tinged fur, and as Kallik approached, she saw that his eyes were faded, as though he were staring at a distant landscape.

"A long, long time ago," Anarteq began, "before bears walked the earth, a frozen sea shattered into pieces, scattering tiny scraps of ice across the darkness of the sky."

Yakone caught up to Kallik as she sat down between Illa and Qanniq. He squeezed in beside her, his flank warm. Kissimi wriggled between them and looked up at Kallik. "Is this the story about Silaluk?" he whispered.

"Yes." Kallik nuzzled his head fondly.

Anarteq went on. "When you look at the sky, you can see a pattern of the stars in the Great Bear, Silaluk. She is running around and around the Pathway Star. It is snow-sky and she is hunting."

Kallik glanced at Taqqiq. He sat beside Shila, listening intently. Their mother Nisa had told them this story when they were cubs. Kallik wondered if Taqqiq was remembering those long-ago days in the snow-den.

"With her quick, powerful claws, she hunts seals and beluga whales. She is the greatest of all the hunters on the ice." Anarteq paused for a moment. "But then the ice melts. Silaluk can't hunt anymore. She gets hungrier and hungrier, but she has to keep running because three hunters pursue her: Robin, Chickadee, and Moose Bird. They chase her for many moons, all through the warm days, until the end of burn-sky. Then, as the warmth begins to leave the earth, they finally catch up to her."

Anarteq's growl grew dark. "The hunters gather around Silaluk and strike the fatal blow with their spears. The heart's blood of the Great Bear falls to the ground, and everywhere it falls, the leaves on the trees turn red and yellow."

Kallik shivered, just as she had done when she was a cub listening to her mother.

Anarteq went on. "But then snow-sky returns, bringing back the ice. Silaluk is reborn and the ice-hunt begins all over again, season after season."

"Tell us more!" Qanniq called.

"Yes!" Kunik, an old male, barked from the other side of the circle. "Another story!"

Anarteq sat back on his haunches, resting his forepaws on his wide belly. "I remember my first hunt," he began. "My mother and I stalked across the ice for a whole day. Each time we passed a seal hole, I begged my mother to let me dive in and catch a seal, but each time, she would tell me, 'We are catching something better than seals.' We kept walking until my belly was growling as loud as the Great Bear herself. Yet again, I begged my mother to let me catch a seal, but she was staring at a great brown shape on the ice.

"I could hardly believe my eyes. What was a brown bear doing on the ice? But when I asked my mother, she cuffed me around the ear. 'That's not a brown bear, cloud-brain. That's a walrus!'"

"You mistook a walrus for a brown bear!" Taqqiq's eyes shone with amusement.

"We were all young and foolish once," Yakone grunted.

"There's only one thing a brown bear would do on the ice," joked Kotori, a large male. "Start an argument with a seal!"

The white bears murmured in agreement, but Kallik bristled. Not all brown bears were argumentative. Toklo had been on the ice, and he had been brave and kind and wise.

Qanniq dipped her head to Anarteq. "Thank you for your stories." She blinked hopefully at him. "Will you lead the Longest Day ceremonies now that Siqiniq has gone?"

Anarteq shook his head. "I am too old. You should choose

a younger bear. One who will return next suncircle to lead the ceremony."

"He's right," Yakone grunted. "But how will we decide?"

Murmurs rippled through the crowd. Kallik scanned her companions. Would they quarrel over the leadership like the brown bears? Kallik saw Kotori's eyes flash and noticed Qanniq leaning forward. Were they hoping to lead the ceremonies?

"Shouldn't the wisest bear be chosen?" she suggested.

"What makes a bear wise?" Anarteq countered.

"Experience!" Kunik called out.

"Cleverness," Tonraq barked.

Salik snorted. "A leader doesn't need to be clever, they need to be strong." He reared onto his hind legs.

Iqaluk slapped his forepaw on a rock. "Salik is the strongest bear!"

Yakone rolled his eyes. "We want to honor the spirits, not fight them!"

Kotori nodded. "We need a bear who can think further than the next brawl."

Illa stepped forward. "We need a bear who understands the importance of the lake. One who knows how every white bear has to struggle to survive the long hungry moons of burn-sky."

"If only our ancestors were here to guide us." Anarteq looked up. Darkness was turning the sky indigo. Stars sparkled faintly, but there was no sign of the white bears' ancestors. The glowing light that rippled across the sky couldn't be seen here. Kallik wondered why their ancestors didn't make the journey to the Great Bear Lake with them.

Shila jerked her muzzle impatiently. "We can talk until the ice returns. We must *do* something to decide."

Anarteq stared at her. "Do what?"

"Let's test ourselves," Shila suggested.

Salik pricked his ears. "How?"

"We want a bear who is wise, patient, strong, and clever," Shila explained. "We can test which bear has the most of these qualities by holding contests."

Iqaluk's eyes sparked with interest. "Like who can run fastest?"

Shila nodded. "And who can catch the biggest fish."

"Who can hold their breath under water the longest," Kotori called out.

Tonraq paced forward excitedly. "Who can stalk a rabbit longest without being seen."

"Who can detect a rabbit from the farthest away!" Tartok put in.

Unease tingled in Kallik's belly. Was it a good idea to encourage this kind of rivalry? Salik and Iqaluk were already eyeing the other bears as though weighing up their skill and strength. Kallik glanced at Yakone. He was staring at his paws. Wasn't he interested in the trials? Leaning over Kissimi, she whispered in his ear. "Are you okay?"

He shrugged. "Listening to this is a waste of time," he muttered.

"Why?" Kallik was surprised. If there had to be a contest, she assumed Yakone would relish it. He was as strong and clever and patient as any bear she knew.

Yakone folded his injured paw beneath the other. "I'll never win anything with missing toes," he murmured under his breath. "The others would mock me for even trying."

Kallik felt a stab of sympathy. At the same time, knowing Yakone, she doubted he wanted to be the white bears' leader. "You don't have to take part."

He glared at her. "What will they think if I don't?" His gaze flashed to Illa and Tunerq, the bears from Star Island. "It'll look like I'm coming home weaker than when I left."

Kissimi bounced on his paws. "I want to take part!"

"You're too young to be good at anything!" Salik scoffed.

"I'm good at hiding!" Kissimi told him.

Iqaluk swiped playfully at the young bear. "Then go hide now, and let the grown bears talk."

Kallik turned to Illa. "Is this such a good idea?" she whispered. "What if everyone gets too competitive?"

"That shouldn't happen," Illa answered. "It's just like playing games. And it will keep us busy until the Longest Day."

"Is there enough time left?" Kallik wasn't sure how close the Longest Day was.

Illa nodded. "I was watching the evening shadows," she told Kallik. "Judging by their length, there are three more sunrises before the Longest Day. That gives us plenty of time to find a new leader."

Kallik hoped the gentle she-bear was right.

Anarteq got to his paws. "It's decided then. The first trial will be swimming underwater."

Qanniq's eyes lit up. Kotori stared across the lake, his eyes narrowing.

"We will meet at the water's edge at dawn." Anarteq looked around at the bears, his gaze solemn. "Good luck, everyone. See you at sunrise!"

CHAPTER TWELVE

Lusa

The sun was sinking when Lusa woke. Rosy light filled the forest. A cool breeze rolled in from the lake and streamed over her nest among the pine roots. Yawning, she climbed to her paws and stretched.

Her first thought was of the injured bears. Had Pokkoli brought them food? Had Issa changed their bedding? Lusa padded into the trees, toward the black bear camp. She smelled herbs as she neared, and freshly dug earth and root sap. When she reached the clearing, she admired the thick layers of fern that lined the nest of the wounded bears.

"Lusa!" Rudi spotted her first. The old bear looked bright-eyed. "Tell me I don't have to stay here anymore! The scent of fresh berries is driving me mad. I have to forage before everyone takes them!"

"Pokkoli brought you food, right?" Lusa checked.

"Loads." Rudi nodded to a pile of discarded branches. "But it's not the same as picking your own."

Lusa sniffed the old bear's wounds. The cuts on his shoulders smelled sharply of herbs, but no heat rose from them. They were healing well. And the swelling around his bruised back had eased. "You can go where you like," Lusa conceded. Foraging in the fresh air would probably help him heal more quickly.

Rudi dipped his head. "I don't know how to thank you for all you've done."

Lusa glanced away. *It's Ujurak you should thank.*

"And those white bears," Rudi went on. "Make sure you thank them from me. I owe them my life."

Lusa nodded, surprised. Was this the same bear who'd refused to let Kallik carry him? "I'll tell them."

Rudi turned to go, then hesitated. "I don't know how you ended up being friends with white bears," he grunted. "But I hope it's a friendship that lasts."

As the old bear shambled away, Lusa's heart lurched. *So do I.* She couldn't imagine not being friends with Kallik and Yakone, but they would be leaving for the Endless Ice soon. Was friendship still friendship if you never saw your friends again?

"Lusa!" Issa's call shook her from her thoughts. "Did you get some sleep?"

"Yes, thanks." Lusa studied the rest of the injured bears.

Tibik was fidgeting as if he had fleas in his pelt. Chula was dozing, her injured leg wrapped in thick leaves. "Has she been in much pain?" Lusa asked.

"She complained earlier, but I dripped water onto the leaves to make them damp and the sap seems to have eased it," Issa answered.

Lusa was impressed. "That's great!"

"The hardest part has been keeping Tibik in his nest."

"I'm bored," Tibik complained. "Can I go foraging with Rudi?"

"Not yet," Lusa told him gently. It would be better for Sheena if he stayed close.

"But I'm so bored!" Tibik wailed.

Lusa spotted a lump of moss at the bottom of the dip. Issa must have used it to drip water onto Chula's dressing. She grabbed it and found it was still damp. Squeezing it between her paws, she rolled it into a ball. "Where I come from, a bear could balance that on his nose." She gave it to Tibik.

He took it from her, his eyes lighting up. "Really?" He placed it on his snout. It rolled off and dropped to the ground. "That's impossible!"

"I've seen it," Lusa encouraged. "Keep practicing."

Paws scuffed through the leaves behind her.

Lusa turned and saw Miki approaching. "Where have you been? You should be resting."

"I needed a drink." Miki slid into his nest. "Did you rest?"

"Yes, thanks." Lusa checked the leaves swathing his ear. "How's your head?"

"Not as sore as it was." Miki watched Tibik as the cub placed the ball on his snout again. This time it stayed there for a moment before slipping off. "Did you really know a bear who could balance things on his nose?" Miki murmured.

"He could balance a stick, too," Lusa told Miki.

"A stick?" Tibik had overheard. "*I* want to balance a stick."

Miki plucked up the moss and pressed it onto Tibik's snout. "Learn to balance this, and I'll find you a stick." He glanced at Lusa. "You smell of white bears," he told her. "Did you visit them?"

"Kallik came to see me." Lusa searched his gaze for signs of accusation.

"She's one of the bears who helped save us, isn't she?" Miki checked. "The one who came back to the camp this morning."

Lusa nodded.

Miki frowned. "Why does she seem so familiar? She didn't rescue me."

"Not this time," Lusa mumbled.

"What do you mean?"

"Don't you remember last suncircle when Taqqiq and his friends took you?"

Miki's eyes narrowed. "Was she the white bear who rescued me?"

Lusa enjoyed the look of surprise on his face. "She's the one. And Toklo."

"The brown bear who carried me here?"

Lusa sat back on her haunches. "It seems like you've spent most of your gatherings being rescued by brown and white bears."

Miki sniffed. "I guess they have to be good for something!"

Lusa nudged him playfully. "They've saved my life a few times, too."

Ossi stepped up to them. "I'm going to look for grubs." He looked at Lusa. "Do you want to come with me?"

Lusa paused, waiting for Ossi to ask Miki as well, but as the pause grew longer, Miki spoke. "You go, Lusa. You must be hungry. I'll stay here and help Tibik practice balancing."

Tibik was sitting as still as a tree trunk with the moss ball resting on his snout. It dropped as Miki turned toward him.

"I've nearly learned it!" Tibik barked.

"I'd better start looking for a stick."

Lusa looked up at Ossi. "I shouldn't be gone long," she warned. "Chula might need me."

"I can take care of Chula." Issa leaned closer and lowered her voice. "I'm sure she wouldn't want to stop you spending time with Ossi." There was a knowing gleam in the she-bear's eyes.

Lusa blinked in alarm. "It's not like that," she hissed. "We're just friends."

Issa glanced at Ossi. "I'm not sure he feels the same way."

Pelt ruffled, Lusa climbed out of the nest. Ossi was kind and funny, but she could never be more than friends with him. "Come on." She marched past him briskly, hoping that he didn't think she was agreeing to anything more than a friendly forage.

He galloped after her as she headed between the trees. "Slow down!" he puffed. "Let me show you where the grubs are. I've found a patch that looks like perfect grub soil."

He looked so happy that Lusa couldn't feel anything but fond of him. She stepped to one side. "Lead the way."

She followed as he wove between trees and crashed through ferns until they reached a clearing where a tree stump sat in a patch of bare earth. The soil around the tree stump was dark and crumbly. Lusa sniffed, breathing in the sweetness of the earth and the grubs she guessed would be hidden beneath.

Ossi moved around the trunk and stopped with a gasp. "Oh no!"

Lusa trotted over to his side. Ossi was staring at a patch of freshly churned soil. Grubs were scattered across the untidy heap of earth.

Lusa frowned. "Who would do this?" No smart black bear would forage so messily, or wastefully.

"Perhaps some of the cubs did it." Ossi hooked a stray grub with his claw and popped it into his mouth. "It's hardly the feast that I promised you. Sorry."

Lusa hardly heard him. A pawprint at the base of the stump had caught her eye. She leaned close, her pelt prickling along her spine as she smelled an unfamiliar scent. "I don't think it was black bears at all. Look."

The pawprint was large and splayed out, edged by claw marks. But the indent was fuzzy, not sharp like a real bear print.

Lusa glanced nervously over her shoulder, scanning the undergrowth. "Perhaps we should go back."

Ossi shrugged. "We could try digging on the other side of the stump. There may be more grubs."

Leaves rustled a few bearlengths away. "I'd rather go," Lusa urged.

Ossi glanced at her. "Okay." He popped another grub into his mouth and headed down the slope.

Lusa followed him, listening for any unusual sounds. "Did you see anything strange when you came here earlier?"

"No," Ossi replied. "Are you worried other bears have been raiding our territory for food?"

"Perhaps." Lusa didn't want to encourage negative ideas about brown or white bears. Besides, the pawprint didn't look like it belonged to either. "It was probably just some cubs, like you said. Perhaps they scraped out the pawprint as a joke."

"Yeah." Ossi fell in beside her as the slope steepened toward the lake. "Cubs like to play tricks. Me and Miki used to climb trees and drop berries on the older bears. Rudi thought it was raining bilberries. Another time, we laid a trail of nuts through a bramble patch and lured Sheena right through it. Her fur was so full of thorns by the time she came out the other side, she looked more like a porcupine than a bear."

Lusa huffed with laughter.

Ossi stopped. "Look."

Ahead of them, Hashi's pine loomed among the alders and spruce. Dena and Leotie were piling berries on the grave. Sadness stabbed at Lusa's heart. The two she-bears were moving very carefully, placing their gifts as though trying not to disturb the spirits of Hala and Hashi.

As Ossi and Lusa joined them, Dena paused and gazed up at the branches. "Hashi was a good leader. So strong when he was young, and so wise as he grew old."

"The brown bears have lost their leader, too," Lusa commented. "I heard there have been arguments over who should take his place." She didn't dare mention Toklo.

"Brown bears like to fight." Dena patted the pile of berries and stems tighter together. "That's why they need a leader. We're different."

Lusa frowned. "Who will lead the Longest Day celebrations?"

"We know how it's done," Ossi pointed out. "We don't need someone to show us." He bent over a patch of ferns and pulled up a fat frond. Earth sprinkled from the thick root as he shook it. Then he laid it on the grave.

"I must go check on Chula and the others," Lusa told him.

Ossi nodded. "Is it okay if I stay here? I want to find more roots for Hashi. I know he liked them best."

"Of course." Lusa blinked at him fondly. "I'll see you later."

She headed back to the camp along the well-worn path. Issa had gone.

Tibik was sprawled on the leaves, fast asleep, a short, stout stick clutched to his belly. Miki sat beside him while Sheena held a wad of dripping moss over Chula's dressing. She let the moisture drizzle over the leaves.

As Lusa approached, Chula looked up, her eyes sharp with pain.

Lusa stiffened. "Is it worse?"

"Not worse," Chula grunted. "But I wish it would stop hurting for a while."

"I'll try to find something to help." Lusa went into the trees and plunged through a patch of bilberries, long picked clean. Nose twitching, she searched for an herb Ujurak had once shown her. *It's strong,* he had warned her. *It will make a bear sleepy. Too sleepy to feel anything.* Lusa headed downslope toward a stream that marked the edge of the camp. The herb grew close to water, and as she reached the stream, she was relieved to see dark-green leaves clustered at the edge. She picked two and, holding them softly between her jaws, careful not to swallow any of their sap, carried them back to Chula.

"Eat these." She held out the leaves. "They'll make you sleep. You won't feel the pain for a while." *And hopefully you will wake in the morning feeling much better.* Perhaps all she needed was a good night's sleep.

Chula lapped the leaves from Lusa's paws.

Sheena stood up and stretched. "I'll fetch some more water," she announced, gathering the moss under her paw. "Tibik might wake up thirsty."

Lusa watched her pad away, relieved that Sheena was focused on her surviving cub once more.

Miki shifted on his bed of ferns. "How was your walk with Ossi?" he asked softly.

Lusa avoided his gaze. "We didn't find many grubs. Some bear had already dug them up."

"Ossi likes you." Miki's growl was husky.

Heat seared through Lusa's pelt. "We're just friends, okay?" Why did everyone need to comment on her relationship with Ossi?

Miki grunted. "It's okay, you know."

"What's okay?"

"If you want to be more than friends with him," Miki told her.

"What's it got to do with you?" Lusa snapped.

Miki flinched. "I'm sorry. I just thought you might be worried that—"

Lusa cut him off. "I'm not worried about anything. Ossi and I are just friends. And it has nothing to do with you."

Tibik stirred beside her. "Lusa? I'm thirsty."

Lusa turned to the drowsy cub, relieved by the distraction. "Sheena's gone to fetch water."

Miki hopped out of his nest, his pelt ruffled. "I'll go help her."

Lusa watched him go with a strange feeling in her chest. Why did Miki care about her friendship with Ossi? Why did *anyone* care about her friendship with Ossi? It was as though suddenly everyone was trying to pair her off. She grunted to herself with annoyance. Who knew having friends could be so confusing?

CHAPTER THIRTEEN

Toklo

Toklo took a deep breath of dusky air. His belly rumbling with hunger, he scanned the bushes ahead. Pale evening light seeped like water between the trees. He was too close to the heart of the brown bears' territory for deer to be roaming, but a hare might have strayed into this part of the forest.

He wanted to take something good back to Aiyanna and the other bears from his home. *Home!* The word rang in his head. That was how he thought of the Forest of Wolves now. It was where he'd return to once he left the lake. It was where he belonged.

His heart leaped when he spotted a plump grouse, its dull plumage camouflaging it against the leafy forest floor. Softening his pawsteps, Toklo crept toward it. The grouse, pecking for insects among the leaves, had been too busy to see him.

The brambles behind him rattled. Paws hit the ground as something exploded from the bushes. The grouse squawked in fright and fluttered clumsily into the air. Toklo spun around, ready to snarl at whatever had ruined his catch.

Akocha skidded to a halt in front of him. The cub's pelt was ruffled and his eyes were wide with fright. "Is there anyone behind me?" he panted.

Toklo glanced past the cub. "No." Why in all the stars was this young bear crashing through the woods by himself? "Shouldn't you be on the shore with your mother?"

Akocha's flanks were heaving. "I saw a bear!"

Toklo looked around for the grouse, wondering if it had landed somewhere near.

"It was a scary bear!" Akocha puffed. "I think it was a spirit! It wanted to eat me."

Toklo met the frightened cub's gaze and tried to hide his frustration. "Spirit bears don't walk through the forest. They live in rivers. Are you sure you didn't just bump into some bear who was hunting?"

Akocha shook his head. "He wasn't hunting. He was just walking. I was looking for the waterfall again and I got lost. I heard the bear, so I went to find him to ask him how to get back to the shore. But when he saw me, he looked angry. I tried to tell him I was lost, but he said the forest was no place for a cub." Akocha was shaking now. "Then he *growled* at me like he wanted to hurt me."

Anger surged through Toklo. What sort of bear would frighten a lost cub? "Did this bear look familiar? Was he one of the bears from the shore?"

"I don't know." Akocha's eyes brimmed with fear. "He didn't look like them. He looked like a ghost."

Toklo frowned. Whichever bear it had been, he'd given

Akocha a serious fright. "Perhaps you'll recognize him when you get back to the shore. If you do, tell your mother or me which bear it was. No one should have scared you like that."

"I'm not going back to the shore by myself. The scary bear might have followed me." Akocha dug his claws into the earth. "Can I stay with you?"

"Okay," Toklo agreed reluctantly. "But you have to be quiet. I want to catch something to take back to my friends."

Akocha's eyes brightened. "Are they the bears from your old territory?"

My new territory, actually, Toklo thought with a surge of unexpected pride. "Yes. They're tired and hungry after their journey. I promised to bring them food."

"I can help you," Akocha offered. "My mother always sends me ahead to find prey."

Or to get you out of the way. Toklo headed toward a stretch of ferns.

Akocha followed. "I'm best at spotting birds because I like looking up. Look!" He stopped and raised his snout. "There's a pigeon up there."

Toklo saw a fat bird sitting in a high branch. "That'd be great if I could fly," he grunted.

"Perhaps I can climb the tree." Akocha was still staring at the pigeon.

"Leave tree climbing to black bears," Toklo muttered. Leaves rustled beyond the ferns. Was that the grouse? He padded forward, pushing through them so slowly that they hardly rustled.

A brown shape moved. It wasn't a grouse but a squirrel. Toklo tensed, ready to leap. *If I can move fast, I might—*

His thought was cut off by a *whump* and an indignant huff. The squirrel bobbed away and scooted up a pine. Toklo turned toward the noise that had disturbed it. Akocha was sitting at the bottom of a tree, bark scattered around him. Above him, the pigeon looked down from its branch, then flapped away through the trees.

Akocha heaved himself to his paws and shook out his pelt. "It's really hard to get a grip."

Toklo scowled. "Stay there," he ordered. "Don't climb any trees or call out if you see a pigeon. I need you to be quiet or I'll never catch any prey."

Akocha's eyes darkened. "Will I have to be quiet for long? I hate being quiet. There's always so much to say. If you knew half the things I *wanted* to say and didn't—"

"Hush!"

Akocha sat down. Shoulders slumped, he gazed at the ground.

Toklo felt a flash of guilt. "I won't be long," he promised. "And once I've caught something, you can talk all you like."

Akocha glanced at him hopefully but didn't speak.

Turning, Toklo pushed through the ferns. "I won't be far away."

Tiny pawsteps pattered over the ground, and a rabbit raced across his path. Quick as lightning, Toklo plunged after it, pounding through a patch of dogwood as the rabbit streaked ahead. Swiftly, Toklo leaped, slamming his paws onto the rabbit's spine.

It died as soon as he hit it, its neck cracking as he pinned it to the earth. It was a big rabbit—a buck. Not as good as a grouse, but it would be something to take back to Aiyanna. Snatching it up between his teeth, he turned and headed back to Akocha.

"That was fast!" Akocha leaped to his paws as soon as he saw Toklo. "You must be a great hunter."

Toklo couldn't speak with the rabbit dangling from his jaws. He headed toward the shore, Akocha padding beside him.

"Could I catch a rabbit?" he wondered. "I told you how fast I can run. Would that be fast enough to catch a rabbit? I won-der if I'm faster than you." He stood in front of Toklo, looking him up and down. "You're big, but that might slow you down. We should have a race on the shore. Then we'd know."

The scent of warm blood filled Toklo's nose. His empty belly twisted as he longed to gulp down the rabbit. He tried to concentrate on Akocha's chatter to distract himself from the smell, but Akocha was talking so fast, his words seemed to dissolve into a single growl.

At last they reached the shore. Toklo spotted Aiyanna straight away. He headed toward her, then realized that Ako-cha had stopped. He turned and saw the cub gazing along the shore. Tayanita was pacing the tree line, her face worried.

"I bet she's looking for me," Akocha murmured guiltily. "She's going to be angry that I went into the forest on my own."

Toklo laid down the rabbit. "You weren't on your own. You were with me."

Akocha gratefully blinked at him.

Toklo felt a twinge of sympathy for the young bear. "Here." He pawed the rabbit toward him. "You can carry this."

Eagerly, Akocha snatched it up and headed toward his mother, almost tripping over the rabbit's dangling hind legs.

Tayanita's eyes lit up when she saw her cub. "There you are!" She trotted toward him. "Where have you been? I've been worried half to death."

Akocha dropped the rabbit at her paws. "I was hunting with Toklo."

Tayanita flashed a knowing look at Toklo. She sniffed the rabbit, then snuffled Akocha's ear with her snout. "Is this for me?"

Akocha glanced uncertainly at Toklo.

"Of course," Toklo told her. He'd have to catch something else for Aiyanna and her friends. But it would be easy, now that he could leave Akocha safely with his mother. He turned, surprised to see Aiyanna staring across the beach at him. Feeling hot despite the cool breeze from the lake, he went over to her.

"I haven't found you any food yet, but I'll go hunting again."

Aiyanna nodded toward Akocha. "You've been too busy helping a mischievous cub, by the look of it. Poor Tayanita's been searching the whole shoreline for him. I thought she'd shred his ears when he got back." Her eyes sparkled at Toklo. "But it's hard to be annoyed with a cub who's brought you a special treat."

Toklo shrugged. "I found him in the forest. Some old bear had given him a fright."

Aiyanna's gaze didn't waver. "You're going to make a better father than Chogan ever was."

"I hope so." Toklo shuddered. He would always be ashamed to be the son of such a jealous, selfish, hostile bear.

Aiyanna moved closer. "You will never be like him, Toklo." She glanced at Akocha. The cub was holding up the rabbit while Tayanita admired it again. "It was kind of you to give them your catch."

"The rabbit was supposed to be for you."

"Don't worry. I've eaten. Hattack caught a deer for us. Wasn't that kind?"

"Very," Toklo grunted. "You should get some rest," he went on. "You've had a long journey."

"I napped all afternoon," Aiyanna told him. She glanced at the darkening sky. Stars were just beginning to appear. "I could do with a walk to stretch my legs." She beckoned Toklo with a jerk of her muzzle and headed along the beach.

Toklo fell in beside her, hoping his empty belly wouldn't rumble. He could catch a fish later. Right now, all he wanted was to walk beneath the stars with Aiyanna.

"It's so beautiful here," Aiyanna murmured.

"I know." Toklo groped for something interesting to say. "It looks even better from over there." He nodded toward Paw-print Island, no more than a shadow in the distance.

"Have you been to that island?" Aiyanna swung her head toward him, surprised. "It's a long way out."

"I swam there at the last Longest Day." Toklo tried to sound like it was no big deal.

Aiyanna brushed her flank against his. "I'd like to see you swim there again. It would make my journey worthwhile."

Toklo halted. "Isn't it worthwhile already?"

Aiyanna faced him. There was a gleam in her eyes. "Of course. I'm glad I came." She reached her muzzle forward, stopping a nose-length from his. "Can't you tell?"

Toklo shifted his paws. "I wasn't sure."

Aiyanna sighed. "I traveled for a moon to see you, and you're not sure!"

"I guess I'm sure now," Toklo murmured. Her sweet breath was washing his muzzle. He'd forgotten how much he loved the scent of her. They stood motionless for a moment, then Aiyanna turned and splashed into the shallows.

"Look at the white bears!" she called.

Toklo waded in beside her and gazed across the water. The white bears were sprawled on the shore as though the day's heat had exhausted them.

"I think they had a meeting earlier," Aiyanna told him. "We could hear their barks across the lake, but I don't know what they were discussing."

Toklo was only half listening. He'd spotted Kallik heading toward them along the beach. Yakone was close behind her.

Toklo broke into a run. "Come on!" He heard stones crunch as Aiyanna followed him.

Kallik reached them first, panting a little. "Aiyanna! How are you? Did you come here alone?"

"No, I came with Izusa, Makya, and their cubs," Aiyanna replied. Toklo thought she seemed a little shy around the white bears.

Kallik's gaze flitted toward the brown bears farther along the shore. "Izusa and Makya are here, too? Great!"

"Hi, Toklo!" Yakone greeted him with a nod. "How are you? I hear your friends have been fighting over who should be leader."

"Kind of," Toklo mumbled. He didn't want to be disloyal to the brown bears.

"It's good to see you again, Yakone," Aiyanna told him.

Yakone dipped his head. "Kallik said she thought it was you."

"We had to come and say hello," Kallik told her. "And we have news!"

Toklo tensed. "What?"

"We've decided how to choose a new leader," Kallik announced. "We'll have lots of trials to test different skills, and the bear who wins the most will lead the Longest Day ceremony."

"That's a great idea," Toklo barked.

"I know!" Kallik's eyes were shining. "The first trial, for swimming, is at dawn. After that, there'll be contests for stalking and fishing. I don't think I'll win. I'm so out of practice. I've spent too long away from the ice, living like a brown bear."

"You'll do fine," Aiyanna promised.

Toklo glanced at Yakone. The white bear's gaze had

darkened. *Why isn't he saying anything?* Was he going to take part? Something in Yakone's gaze warned him not to ask.

"I wonder if I can persuade the brown bears to do something like that," Toklo commented. "Our trials wouldn't be the same, I guess, but it might stop some of the arguments. At the moment it feels as if the leader of the Longest Day ceremony will be the one who has made the most noise!"

"You should tell Shesh about the trials," Aiyanna told him. "If it works for the white bears, why not us?"

"Have you seen Lusa?" Kallik asked Aiyanna.

"Not yet." The she-bear looked at Toklo. "Can we visit her now? I'd love to see her, and we could let her know about the trials."

"I'm not sure the black bears will welcome us barging into their camp in the middle of the night," Toklo warned.

"But it's barely dark!" Aiyanna pointed out.

Yakone grunted. "They weren't happy when we visited them this morning. They asked us to leave."

"I'm not frightened of black bears!" Aiyanna huffed.

"But they'll be frightened of you," Yakone murmured.

Aiyanna was already heading for the trees. "We'll be as gentle as rabbits," she promised. "Come on, Toklo."

Toklo nodded to Yakone and Kallik. "Good luck with the dawn trial!" he barked, before turning and trotting after Aiyanna.

"Look." Aiyanna had stopped.

Toklo caught up to her. A half-eaten rabbit lay on the moon-dappled earth.

"Spare prey." She looked at him, her eyes shining. "You must be hungry. Eat this."

Toklo sniffed the remains. There was a strange scent on them—something close to a bear scent but not one that he recognized from any of the territories by the lake. He backed away. "I'll catch my own prey," he told Aiyanna.

She snorted. "I forgot how proud you were." There was affection in her voice.

Toklo felt pleased, but he wanted to move her away from this place. The strange scent on the rabbit also lingered on the bushes around them. "I'll show you where Lusa's camp is."

He led her through the woods. Soon, he could smell the warm, fruity smell of the black bears, and he looked up, scanning the trees. He knew many of these bears preferred to spend the night above the forest floor. Perhaps Lusa was among them.

Paws scuffed the earth behind them. He heard a growl and turned to find a sturdy black bear with a patch of white fur on his chest. "Miki? It's me, Toklo. How's your head?"

Miki squinted into the darkness. "Hey, Toklo! It's good to see you. My head's still a bit sore, but I'm fine. Have you come to see Lusa?" His gaze flicked uncertainly to the bear standing beside Toklo.

"This is my friend Aiyanna," Toklo introduced her. "She knows Lusa, too."

"She's gathering herbs," Miki told him. He headed away from the camp, beckoning Toklo and Aiyanna to follow with a flick of his snout.

They found Lusa sifting through a pile of dewy leaves. She looked up as they approached. "Aiyanna?"

"Lusa!" Aiyanna trotted over to greet her, rubbing her muzzle along Lusa's.

"I didn't know you were coming to the Longest Day!"

"Izusa and Makya wanted to know what it was all about." Aiyanna glanced shyly at Toklo. "And I wanted to see Toklo again."

Toklo returned Aiyanna's gaze, feeling warm with happiness.

Aiyanna sniffed the pile of herbs. "Are these what you eat?" She wrinkled her nose.

Lusa snorted. "No! They're for treating the injured bears."

"Injured bears?" Aiyanna's eyes widened with concern.

"Yes," Toklo butted in proudly. "Lusa's been looking after bears wounded by a firebeast."

"I'm just doing what Ujurak taught me." Lusa shuffled her paws.

"We saw Kallik and Yakone just now," Toklo told her. "The white bears have decided to choose a new leader by holding trials."

Lusa looked alarmed. "Do you mean fighting?"

Aiyanna shook her head. "No, not fighting. Things like swimming, stalking prey, and fishing. The bear who wins the most will lead the Longest Day ceremony."

Lusa sat down beside her herbs, resting a paw on the pile. "That sounds like a good idea. Are the brown bears going to do that, too?"

"If I can persuade them," Toklo told her.

"We thought the black bears might want to do the same," Aiyanna put in.

Miki spoke from behind them. "I'm not sure we need a leader like you do," he growled softly. "There's been no fighting since Hashi died. We're happy just to be together."

Lusa looked at Miki. "The trials sound like fun, though."

Miki blinked at her. "So you think we should have them, as well?"

"In our own way." Lusa gazed into the trees. "No one can replace Hashi, but why shouldn't we find someone who can lead the ceremony? We don't have to compete like white bears or brown bears. But we can test our own skills like foraging and climbing trees."

"See?" Aiyanna whispered to Toklo, moving her muzzle close enough to brush his ear fur. "I told you she'd want to know."

Toklo rested his cheek against hers, relishing her warmth. "I'm glad you came to the lake," he murmured.

"Me too," Aiyanna chuffed softly.

CHAPTER FOURTEEN

Kallik

Kallik stood at the water's edge, relishing the cool before dawn. Pale-pink light spilled across the lake and made the bears' fur glow.

Tartok stared across the lake. "How far do we have to swim?"

Salik pushed past him and waded paw-deep into the shallows. "*I* could swim to the other side of the water if I wanted."

Kotori snorted. "If you could do everything you said you could do, you'd have been declared leader the moment you arrived."

Manik glared at Kotori. "Salik can outswim a seal."

Kallik narrowed her eyes to look farther along the shore. A few brown bears were gazing back at her. Beyond them, several black bears had ventured from the forest and seemed to be staring this way. Was Lusa among them? Kallik couldn't tell from here. She called over her shoulder to Yakone, "Do you think Toklo and Aiyanna managed to tell Lusa about the trials?"

He didn't answer.

Kallik turned, expecting to find him behind her, but he was hanging back, a few bearlengths up the shore.

She headed toward him. "Are you really not going to take part?"

Yakone's pelt ruffled. "What's the point? My paw is ruined. I will never be able to swim fast again. Do you want everyone to see me fail?"

Anger prickled beneath Kallik's pelt. *Why is he giving up so easily?* "You lost two toes, that's all. You've still got your paw! Stop acting like a scared cub."

Yakone glared at her. "You don't understand what it's like! I'm supposed to be strong."

"You *are* strong!" Kallik countered. But Yakone had already turned away. He stalked up the beach and clambered over the ridge.

Kunik's gruff call kept her from following him. "Bears, ready! Line up at the water's edge!"

Sliding between Shila and Taqqiq, Kallik scanned the other bears. Manik and Salik puffed out their chests, while Iqaluk stood beside them, his brow furrowed in concentration. Tonraq and Nukka looked nervously across the water, while Kotori swung his head confidently one way, then the other, as though sizing up the competition. Illa was lined up next to Tunerq and Imala. Beside Illa, Kissimi shifted from one paw to another, his eyes shining with excitement.

Kunik climbed onto a rock a few pawlengths from the shore. "Only bears older than one suncircle may take part."

Kissimi groaned. "That's not fair!"

Manik shouldered the cub away. "You'd never win anyway."

Qanniq guided Kissimi toward Kunik's rock. "Watch from here," she told him gently, nudging him up beside Kunik.

"I don't want to watch, I want to join in!" Kissimi growled.

Kunik raised his voice. "You will swim to Gull Island." He nodded to the rocky crags sticking up from the deep water. "You must climb out of the water, making sure your paws are clear before swimming back. The first bear to return will be the winner."

Kallik felt Shila tense beside her.

Taqqiq dropped his head, ready to charge forward. "I'm going to beat Salik," he muttered under his breath.

Kallik glanced at him in surprise.

Taqqiq growled. "He's always boasting. I'm going to prove he's not as great as he thinks he is."

Kunik lifted his muzzle to the sky. "Ancestors, we know you are with us, even without ice or the darkness that lets us see you. We race in honor of you. These trials will let us decide who will lead the Longest Day ceremony. Give your help to the most deserving."

Kallik glanced at the stars, each one fading as dawn pushed the night away. Her heart swelled as she imagined the spirits watching her. *I'll do my best,* she promised.

"Let's get on with it," Salik growled.

Kunik shifted on the rock, staring down at the bears lined up at the water's edge. "Get ready . . . go!"

At his bark, Kallik charged through the shallows, Shila bumping against her flank. Taqqiq was already belly-deep and, with a leap, dove for deeper water. Kallik chased after him, her paws slithering on the pebbles. She plunged forward, splashing Shila.

Shila spluttered behind her.

"Sorry!" Water filled Kallik's mouth. She closed it and swam.

Taqqiq was a bearlength ahead. Kotori and Salik were pushing ahead of him, crashing against each other as they fought for the lead. Shila had found her stride now and was neck and neck with Illa. Tunerq dove underwater, bobbing up a bearlength ahead of them. Manik lagged behind Iqaluk, and Kallik felt a surge of pride as she pulled past them. Ahead, the lake frothed. Bear heads bobbed and paws slapped clumsily at the surface as, in the struggle to break from the pack, the bears mistimed strokes.

Concentrate! Kallik focused on her paws. *Find your rhythm and just swim.* When she was a cub, swimming had been as simple as running across the ice. But after many moons of trekking through forests and over mountains, her muscles weren't used to being underwater. Frowning, Kallik forced her limbs to remember what they'd learned at Nisa's side.

The craggy island loomed ahead. She could see a small beach below the jutting rocks. No bear had reached it yet, but Salik was close. Kotori was right behind him. Kallik scanned the water for Taqqiq, her heart sinking when she didn't spot him beside the leaders. Glancing over her shoulder, she saw Iqaluk and Manik pulling closer. Her chest was burning. She gulped for breath, trying not to swallow water. Perhaps she should have paced herself better. Tunerq was falling behind Shila and Illa. Imala trailed at the back.

Where's Taqqiq? As Kallik faced forward, white shoulders broke the surface beyond Salik and Kotori. She recognized them at once. *Taqqiq!* Her brother surged ahead, reaching the island first. Scrambling out of the water, he raced clear of the waves and turned. Salik heaved himself out with Kotori on his tail. As Kotori headed up the beach, Salik turned, his paws still in the water, and followed Taqqiq as he plunged back into the lake.

"Cheater!" Kallik barked as she felt pebbles beneath her paws. Hauling herself out, she blocked Salik's way. Iqaluk and Manik scrambled after her.

Iqaluk stood beside Kallik. "You have to leave the water completely," he told Salik.

Manik nodded, panting. "If you want to win, then win fairly."

Frustration flickered in Salik's gaze. He cast a look at Taqqiq, already forging toward the shore, then bounded up the beach until his paws were clear.

Kotori was already splashing back into the lake. Salik chased after him, leaping with outstretched paws so that his belly hit the water first, sending up great splashes.

Illa chuckled as she pulled herself onto the shore. "He might be strong, but he's not elegant."

Shila shook the water from her eyes as she stumbled out after Illa. "Who's winning?" she puffed.

"Taqqiq!" Kallik told her proudly. Then she plunged back

into the water. Shila, Illa, Iqaluk, and Manik were on her heels.

The short break on land had let Kallik catch her breath. She pushed forward, cutting through the water as smoothly as an orca. Only Kotori, Salik, and Taqqiq were ahead of her. Kotori and Salik struck out at each other with massive forepaws as they fought over second place. As they splashed and rocked in the water, Kallik slid past them, diving beneath the surface and hoping they hadn't seen her.

Holding her breath, she swam until she thought her lungs would burst. Then she felt pebbles scrape her belly. She was nearly at the shore. She pushed up, exploding from the water, and gulped in deep drafts of air. Kunik's rock was only a few bearlengths away. Taqqiq was just ahead of her, and by the sound of the angry barks behind, Kotori and Salik were close on her tail.

Kallik's heart soared as Taqqiq reached the shore first. Kunik leaped down from his rock to greet him. Kallik's paws hit stones and she fought to find her balance, scrambling out after her brother.

"How did you pass us?" Kotori's surprised growl sounded behind her.

She turned, panting, as the large bear stumbled from the lake with Salik beside him. "I swam under you," she puffed.

Kotori dipped his head. 'Well done."

Salik snorted. "If I'd seen you, I'd have swum harder."

"Does that mean you weren't really trying?" Kallik asked innocently. Salik curled his lip at her and stomped up the beach. Kallik trotted to her brother's side and gazed at him proudly. "Taqqiq! Well done!"

He glanced at his paws. "Thanks."

Shila was climbing from the lake. She raced toward them, her eyes shining. "Did you win? I couldn't see! Illa was making more spray than a spouting whale."

Behind her, Illa emerged coughing and spluttering from the water.

"Did everyone finish?" Kallik scanned the bears. They were all back on shore. The first trial was over. She shook out her pelt, excited about the next one; then she remembered Yakone.

Her heart sank. She scanned the shore, hoping to see him ambling toward her. Didn't he care how she'd done? But he was nowhere to be seen. Anxiety tightened Kallik's belly. What was with wrong with him?

Leaving the others, she climbed up the shore and over the ridge. Beyond, the forest stretched steeply uphill and she slipped into its shadow, sniffing for a trace of Yakone. She picked up his scent at once and followed it along the winding trail he'd left through snapped brambles and flattened ferns. He must have been in a foul temper as he'd come this way.

Kallik caught sight of his white pelt among the lichen-covered trunks. He was pulling at the moss on a tree stump, peeling away great flaps and flinging them onto a heap beside him.

"What are you doing?" Kallik kept her growl soft as she approached him.

He glanced at her, then returned to moss gathering. "I thought if I gathered moss now, it could dry in the sun and be ready to line our nest by tonight."

"That's kind of you." Kallik searched his face, but he was intent on his task and she saw nothing but concentration. "Taqqiq won the race," she told him. He didn't reply.

"I came in second."

"You did?" He looked at her, surprise and happiness in his eyes, before looking back at the moss sternly, as though he'd remembered he was being annoyed. "I knew you'd do well. You're a strong bear."

"So are you." Kallik caught sight of his injured paw. He was using it to loosen another patch of moss. It looked swollen. "Stop." She pressed her paw gently over it. "You're hurting yourself."

Yakone grunted and snatched his paw away. "I told you. I'm useless. This paw is no good, even for picking moss."

"You'll adjust," Kallik soothed. "It will feel normal one day, and you'll be able to do everything the other bears can do."

"And until then?" He faced her, anger in his eyes again. "Why don't you go back to the others? They'll be planning their next trial. You wouldn't want to miss it."

Heat spread through Kallik's fur. "Perhaps I will. That's more fun than listening to you feeling sorry for yourself."

He met her fury with his own. "Does that mean you don't want to come to Star Island with me anymore?"

She felt as though he'd raked his claws across her cheek. "*What?*"

"You heard." His gaze bored into her. "Perhaps it's best if you don't. I'm no use to you now. I'm just a lame bear. You'd be better off among bears who can protect you and provide for you."

Kallik stared at him in disbelief. Was that what he thought? That she wanted him to *protect* her? Before she could speak, Yakone pushed past her and marched away through the forest. Kallik sat down, panic spiraling though her thoughts. She had thought Yakone wanted to be with her. Didn't he know how much she loved him? Had she been wrong about their relationship all along?

CHAPTER FIFTEEN

Lusa

Lusa dug her paws into the pebbly shore. Miki and Ossi shifted beside her. She could see the white bears splashing through the water as they raced back from the pile of rocks.

"Come on, Kallik!" Lusa knew her friend couldn't hear her, but she barked anyway, willing Kallik to beat the others. Water frothed as the white bears stormed toward the shore. Then, like a distant whale surfacing, Taqqiq emerged from the lake. Lusa's heart leaped as Kallik followed her brother out. "Look! Kallik came in second!"

Miki squinted. "How can you tell from here?"

"Can't you see?" She jerked her muzzle toward him. "Is your vision blurred again?" The swelling on his head was smaller, and his headaches fewer, but he was still having dizzy spells.

"No," he chuffed. "It's just such a long way away!"

Ossi was squinting, too. "Are you sure it's Kallik?"

The white bears' shore was far away, but Lusa would

recognize Kallik's outline anywhere. And Taqqiq was easy to spot—his great white flank as broad as Yakone's, his shoulders narrower.

Lusa frowned. Where was Yakone? Perhaps he was lagging behind because of his injured paw.

Ossi's voice broke through her thoughts. "I wonder if Dustu and the others have decided what trials we'll have? I'm so pleased you suggested this, Lusa."

Lusa thought back to the moment before dawn when she'd woken up. She'd quickly checked on Chula, Sheena, and Tibik, then headed for Dustu's nest.

"It's too soon!" Dustu had objected when she'd woken him and told him what Toklo and Aiyanna had said. "Hashi's only just died."

Leaves had swished around them as the other bears stirred, their faces still bleary with sleep.

"What's going on?" Ossi had ambled toward them, yawning, with Dena and Leotie behind him.

"The brown bears and white bears are holding trials to find new leaders," Dustu grunted. "Lusa thinks we should do the same."

"What sort of trials?" asked Dena.

"Races," Lusa explained. "Like who can pick the most berries or climb a tree fastest. It could help us decide who will lead the Longest Day ceremony."

Dena's eyes brightened. "It sounds like fun."

"What about a race to see who can build a den quickest?" suggested a bear behind her.

"Or a race to the top of the ridge and back?" another called.

A cub popped its head up. "Can I join in?"

"How can a cub lead the Longest Day ceremony?" growled Dustu.

Dena tipped her head on one side. "They can still take part, surely?"

Rudi put down the piece of bark he'd been chewing. "It seems disrespectful after all that's happened."

Lusa saw grief in his sharp black eyes. "The accident was terrible," she agreed. "We have lost bears we love, but—"

"Some of them are still injured," Sheena interrupted her. "Do you think Chula is fit to take part in these trials?"

"Of course not." Lusa shifted her paws. "But the Longest Day is about honoring the spirits. Is it right that we should only share sadness while we're together? Surely we should share joy, too? We don't even have to use the trials to choose a new leader. They will remind us what we're good at."

An old bear grunted stubbornly, "Do you want us to forget what happened?"

Miki pushed his way to the front. "Lusa would never want that! She was there when Hashi died."

Lusa watched Dustu's gaze narrow. "What would Hashi have wanted?"

Rudi rolled his bark beneath his paw. "He would want us to celebrate the Longest Day, not to mourn it."

"Does that mean we can do it?" Leotie chuffed.

Lusa glanced around the gathered bears, her heart lifting as she saw heads begin to nod.

"Very well." Dustu lifted his head. "We will hold trials like the other bears."

"What will they be?" Leotie demanded.

It was then that Lusa had noticed the dawn light breaking through the trees and remembered that the white bears would be starting their first trial. Slipping away, she hurried to the shore. Miki and Ossi had followed her.

Now that the white bears' race was over, Lusa wanted to know what trials the black bears would face. She turned to Ossi and Miki. "Come on! Let's go back to the others."

Ossi twitched his ears. "I hope we won't have swimming races!"

Lusa snorted with amusement as she headed up the beach. "Can't you swim, Ossi?"

"Like a stone," Miki teased.

Ossi sniffed. "I could swim if I wanted. I just don't want to."

Lusa's heart quickened as she thought about the trials. It would be fun to compete against bears who were just like her. Traveling with Kallik and Toklo had sometimes made her feel so small that she'd had to remind herself there were things they couldn't do, like steal honey from bees' nests or squeeze into hollow trees and search for tasty insects.

She felt a pang as she realized that Miki wouldn't be able to take part because of his injury. As they neared the black bear camp, she slowed until she was walking beside him. "I need someone to keep an eye on Chula and Tibik while we hold the trials."

"You mean you want to keep me busy while you're taking

part." He shot her a teasing look.

Guilt pricked in her belly. "You know you're not well enough to compete yet, don't you?"

"Of course." Miki shrugged. "But I don't want to spend the whole time watching Chula and the others. I want to watch the trials." He twitched his ears. "I want to see how you do."

"And me!" Ossi barged between them. "I'm going to win!"

Lusa nudged him. "If I don't beat you."

Dena's voice echoed through the trees. "Lusa! Miki! Ossi!"

"We're here!" Lusa trotted toward her.

"Quick!" Dena urged. "We're about to start the first trial."

Already? "What is it?" Lusa asked.

"Tree climbing." Dena led them to a patch of cedars. Bears circled each one, looking up into the branches. "Choose a tree."

"Hurry!" Dustu barked as he caught sight of Lusa and Ossi.

Lusa scanned the trees, looking for one with widely spaced branches that she'd be able to climb easily. She spotted one and headed for it. Ossi stopped at the tree beside hers.

Miki studied Lusa's tree. "I think you've picked a good one."

Dustu looked around the bears. "Ready? Go!"

Lusa stretched up and hooked her claws into the cedar wood. The sweet scent of its sap filled her nose as she hauled herself up to the first branch. Swinging her hind legs onto it, she reached up the trunk again. The next branch was some way above, but the bark was soft and easy to grip. Squeezing the trunk between her hind legs, she half pulled, half pushed her way upward.

She could see Ossi in the next tree. His stoutness hid impressive climbing skills; he raced up the tree, dodging between the branches, hardly stopping to plan his route.

Lusa pushed harder, pleased that the long moons of traveling had strengthened her paws. Tipping her head back, she saw a route clear to the top and zigzagged easily between the branches.

"Hurry, Lusa!" Miki called from below.

A branch cracked a few trees away, and Lusa caught sight of black fur tumbling. She paused, tensing as she heard a thump.

"Be careful!" Leotie's anxious cry rang through the trees.

"I'm okay!" Dena called. "I just slipped down a few branches."

Lusa pushed up again, suddenly remembering the tree in the Bear Bowl that she had climbed with Yogi. The memory swamped her, as powerful as a wave. How frightened she'd been. How high she'd climbed. For a moment the trees surrounding her seemed to fade, replaced by rows of watching flat-faces murmuring like the wind.

"Quick, Lusa! Ossi's nearly at the top." Miki's bark broke through her thoughts. Snapping back to the present, she scrambled past the next branch.

A moment later, her head popped through the spiky canopy and she found herself clinging to the top of the trunk and staring across the forest. Beyond the treetops, the lake sparkled in the sun. The narrow trunk swayed, and Lusa's belly tightened as it bent under her weight.

Quickly, she slid down, relieved as she felt the trunk thicken against her belly. Scooting between branches, she scrabbled backward down the tree. Halfway down she saw Ossi. Tangled branches surrounded him, and he was twisting around with a frown of determination as he tried to find a route down.

Lusa slithered down a few more branches. A black bear paced below. It must be Miki, waiting for her. She dropped down more quickly, feeling confident as the ground neared. "I'm almost there!" she called as she reached the bottom branch. Preparing to lower herself onto the leafy forest floor, she glanced down.

The black bear wasn't Miki. Her heart lurched as she recognized the broad shoulders and square brow. This was a bear who she hadn't seen in a long time—not since they had started their journey along the river from the Melting Sea. And it was not a bear she had hoped to see again. Lusa froze, clinging to the trunk. *Hakan!*

"I've won!" Ossi's voice rang out as he thumped onto the ground.

Lusa tried to find him, but the trunk blocked her view. She couldn't see Miki, either. Where had he gone?

Hakan scowled up at her. "Where's my sister?"

Lusa stared at him, her belly churning. Hakan had shared his territory on the Big River with his sister Chenoa, who had chosen to travel with Lusa and the other bears to escape her brother's bullying. Lusa felt sadness well inside her as she remembered Chenoa's death at a vast waterfall, not long after her journey began.

"Are you scared to come down?" There was menace in Hakan's growl.

Lusa clung harder to the trunk. How was she going to tell this angry bear that Chenoa had died?

"Where's my sister?" Hakan snarled again.

Miki's voice sounded from the other side of the trunk. "Sorry, Lusa. Ossi was faster than you." He blinked up at her. "Are you stuck?"

Lusa watched him notice Hakan. "Hello!" Miki greeted the black bear amiably. "Have you just arrived? I'm Miki." He followed Hakan's stare. "And that's Lusa."

"I know." Hakan's growl was cold. "Where's Chenoa?" he demanded.

"Chenoa?" Miki looked confused. "I haven't met a bear called Chenoa. Is she a friend of yours?"

Lusa clung tighter to the trunk, its sweet scent so strong now that she felt queasy. "Don't worry, Miki. I know where she is." Her voice was hoarse. She wanted Miki to stay, but she didn't want him to hear the awful news she had to break to Hakan. Such a young bear might be horrified, especially to learn exactly how Chenoa died. "Miki, go tell Ossi I'm pleased for him." Miki padded away, and Lusa lowered herself down the trunk.

Hakan thrust his face close as she touched the ground. "Where is she?"

Lusa backed away, her throat tightening. "She's dead, Hakan."

Hakan stared at her in horror. "What?"

"On the journey." Lusa could hardly make herself say the words. "She was washed over a waterfall. There was nothing we could do to save her."

Rage flared in Hakan's eyes. "She died on the river? She'd hardly left our home! You persuaded her to go with you and then you let her *die*?"

Lusa screwed her eyes shut as Hakan reared over her. Bracing herself for a blow, she backed against the tree.

Pawsteps thumped the ground and fur brushed in front of her. "Leave Lusa alone!"

Opening her eyes, Lusa saw Ossi shoving Hakan away.

"Don't hurt him!" she cried. She ran forward and pushed Ossi aside. "I can handle this."

"It doesn't look like it!" Ossi growled.

"Really," Lusa pleaded. "It's fine."

"You can't let some strange bear walk up to you and attack you! What's going on?"

Hakan curled his lip. "She killed my sister."

"What?" Ossi jerked his muzzle toward Hakan. "How?"

"It was an accident!" Lusa wailed. "A terrible accident."

Miki moved out from the trees. Dustu and Dena followed with Issa and Leotie, all of them looking worried. Lusa shifted uncomfortably as she saw even more bears heading toward her.

"Who is this?" Dustu asked.

"I'm Hakan. I came here to meet my sister." Hakan scored a line in the dirt with his claw. "But Lusa killed her."

"Don't be silly!" Issa scoffed. "Lusa wouldn't hurt anyone."

"She killed Chenoa," Hakan insisted.

"It was an accident," Lusa blurted out. "She fell into the river, and the current swept her over the falls. We couldn't have saved her."

"Murderer!" Hakan hissed.

"Hush!" Rudi pushed his way to the front and faced Hakan. "Lusa has done nothing but save lives here. She wouldn't harm another bear."

Dustu nodded. "Lusa is a healer, not a murderer."

"Try telling that to my dead sister," Hakan snarled.

Dustu met the angry bear's gaze. "We come here in peace, to celebrate the Longest Day and honor the spirits."

"Peace!" Hakan spat. "I will never know peace now I know that *she*"—he shot Lusa a poisonous glance—"took my sister from her home and killed her."

Paws shifted uncomfortably around Lusa. Did these bears believe Hakan? Most of them had known her only a few days. "I'm sorry." Her voice cracked.

Rudi straightened up. "You have nothing to apologize for, Lusa." He narrowed his eyes at Hakan. "Lusa has never shown anything but courage, kindness, and loyalty. If you cannot accept that your sister's death was an accident, then you cannot stay here."

Lusa saw heads nodding around her. She felt limp with relief. Yet guilt swirled through her belly. Were these bears going to drive Hakan away? Was that fair? Surely every bear was welcome at the Longest Day? And Hakan was grieving. He needed the spirits more than she did.

Should I leave? Lusa's paws started to shake. A shoulder pressed against hers. *Ossi.* Gratefully, she leaned against him.

Hakan curled his lip. "I wouldn't breathe the same air as that murderer anyway! But don't think I'll ever forgive this, or forget it." His gaze burned into Lusa's. "You'll be looking over your shoulder for the rest of your life—you and your friends!" Growling, he barged his way through the crowd and stalked into the forest.

Miki stepped forward, his eyes dark. "Let's go foraging." He tried to sound bright. "Come on, everyone. There will still be dew on the berries if we hurry." He began to shoo them away, pacing one way, then the other until they began to leave. Encouraging the last stragglers, he guided them between the trees. "You must be hungry after the trial."

Lusa was left alone with Ossi. "It was an accident," she whispered.

Ossi didn't seem concerned about Chenoa's death. He was peering suspiciously into the forest. "Do you think it was Hakan who destroyed that grubs' nest?"

Lusa stared at him. She remembered the chilling sensation of being watched during Hashi and Hala's burial. Had Hakan been stalking her? But why had he waited until now to ask about Chenoa? Surely he'd have wanted to know where his sister was as soon as he arrived?

Once more, Lusa pictured Chenoa's eyes, wild with fear as the river swept her toward the falls. "I need to be alone." Dizzy with grief, she pushed past Ossi and stumbled between the trees. Her paws led her to a shady patch, and she slumped against a trunk. She remembered seeing Chenoa's face in the swirl in the bark of a tree near the river. Was she at peace there?

If only Hakan could find peace. It must have been a

devastating shock to travel all this way expecting to see his sister, only to learn that she was dead.

"Lusa?" Miki's soft growl made her lift her head. "Are you okay?"

"Yes," Lusa huffed wearily.

"You shouldn't be hanging around on your own while that bear is around."

Lusa let her haunches slide down the trunk until she was sitting. "I can look after myself."

"Obviously." Miki sat down next to her. "Did you really travel along the Big River?"

"Yes." Lusa stared between the trees without focusing.

"I've never met a bear who's traveled as far as you." Miki sounded impressed. "You must have seen and done so many things."

"Not all of them good." A lump rose in Lusa's throat.

"You don't have to tell me now. But—" Miki hesitated. "But maybe one day?"

Lusa looked at him, searching his gaze. *I'd like that.* Was it okay for her to think about her future when Chenoa had none? "Maybe," she whispered. "One day."

CHAPTER SIXTEEN

Toklo

Toklo stood on the shore, watching the white bears climb from the water. He couldn't tell from here who had won. His pelt pricked, and he glanced toward the trees behind him. There it was again—the feeling that someone was watching him. Last night, as he and Aiyanna had trekked back from Lusa's camp, he'd been sure eyes were watching from the darkness.

He snorted. *Don't be silly.* It was probably an owl. And yet he scanned the tree line, looking for a shape among the undergrowth.

When he saw nothing, he glanced along the beach to where Aiyanna was entertaining Yas, Wapi, Flo, and Fala by hiding white stones for them to find among the driftwood. Yas, Wapi, and Flo had each collected a small pile. Fala was frowning. "It's not fair," she complained. "I haven't found a single stone yet."

Close by, Hattack and Holata were watching the white bears, too. Their gazes flicked from the far shore to each other, as though each bear was thinking about the upcoming fishing trial. With the sun rising, the fish would be swimming near the surface, their shimmering backs easy to spot.

Toklo called to Shesh. "Have you decided which river we'll fish in?" Brown bears didn't hunt for prey in deep water, but in shallow tumbling rivers. Shesh would choose which of the rapids close to the lake would be best for the trial.

"Not yet."

Akocha scampered up to Toklo and whispered in his ear. "You won't tell them about our secret river, will you?"

"No." Toklo thought of the falls and the hidden cave behind them. He wouldn't admit it to Akocha, but he was happy to keep the river secret. He wanted to share it with Aiyanna, perhaps on the Longest Day itself; it would be a surprise that would make the day even more special for both of them. Besides, that river was too deep and ran too slowly for a fishing trial.

"I know a river that might be suitable," Wenona called from beside the driftwood. She'd just slid a large white pebble beneath a branch while Fala and the other cubs were hunting farther along the shore. "There's a river behind the white bears' territory that was full of salmon when I passed it on the way here."

Shesh narrowed his eyes. "Can you show us where this river is, Wenona?"

She nodded. "It means crossing the white bears' shore."

"They'll understand," Toklo grunted. "They're holding trials, too."

Hattack snorted. "And if they don't, we'll cross their dumb shore anyway."

Toklo felt a rush of irritation. Did Hattack have to fight about everything? He glanced at Aiyanna, hoping she'd noticed Hattack's bad-tempered comment. But Aiyanna was busy congratulating Fala, who had just discovered Wenona's stone and was fluffing her pelt out with pride.

Growling under his breath, Toklo headed along the shore toward the white bears' part of the lake as Shesh and the others followed behind him.

Aiyanna caught up to him, the cubs chasing after her. "I'm glad they decided to hold the trials in a river and not the lake," she admitted. "You still haven't shown me how to catch lake fish."

"It's not hard, so long as you don't mind diving."

"Underwater?" Wapi bounced in front of them. "I thought only white bears dove for fish."

"We have paws and snouts just like them," Toklo answered. "There's no reason we can't dive, too."

Yas splashed into the shallows. "Will you show us how to dive?"

Izusa called to the cubs, "Leave Toklo and Aiyanna in peace."

"We're only talking!" Wapi objected.

Aiyanna glanced back at Izusa. "They're not bothering us."

Toklo didn't comment as Yas swerved in front of him. He'd rather walk with Aiyanna instead of tripping over a crowd of tiny bears. Was he going to have to fish with them bouncing around his paws, too?

Akocha raced over to them. "Do you think cubs will be allowed to fish?" he panted.

"I don't see why not," Aiyanna answered. "It'll be good practice."

"Flo and Fala caught their own fish on the journey here," Makya barked proudly.

"Mine was the biggest," Flo announced.

"No, it wasn't!" Fala glared at her sister. "Mine was."

Toklo was relieved to see that they were nearing the white bears' stretch of shore. The white bears were lying in the sunshine, letting their pelts dry after their race, but one by one they clambered to their paws as they saw the brown bears heading toward them.

Manik padded forward to meet them, damp fur rippling along his spine. "What are you doing here?"

Shesh, at the head of the group, halted. Holata passed him and stopped in front of the white bear. "We're holding a fishing trial in the river behind your shoreline," he explained.

Salik lowered his head aggressively. "They've come to take over our part of the lake."

Toklo snorted. "Would we bring cubs if we were planning an invasion?"

Kunik stepped in front of Salik. "There is a good salmon river up there." He nodded toward the ridge at the head of the shore. "You are welcome to pass."

Shesh dipped his head. "Thank you."

Salik growled under his breath as the brown bears filed past. Some white bears ignored them; others watched angrily, muttering to one another as they stepped aside to let the brown bears pass.

As the beach turned from pebbles to larger stones, Toklo spotted Kallik. She was sitting beside Taqqiq, her pelt damp. She nodded quickly, hardly catching his eye, and Toklo did the same.

Aiyanna nudged Toklo. "Aren't you going to say hello?"

"No." Neither white bear nor brown would be pleased to see them greet each other like old friends.

Aiyanna shook her head. "It's fish-brained, having to keep your friendship secret."

"It's not secret, believe me," Toklo muttered.

"Hey, Toklo!" Holata called. "Why don't you stay here with your white bear friends? You've probably forgotten how to catch river fish anyway."

Toklo glared at him, refusing to rise to the bait. His pelt felt hot as he sensed the gaze of white bears and brown bears on him.

"Holata is a dung-breath," Aiyanna hissed.

Hattack stopped at the ridge and waited for Toklo. "Don't listen to Holata," he growled. "He's just showing off." Hattack's gaze was on Aiyanna as he spoke.

Toklo winced as Aiyanna blinked gratefully at Hattack. He longed to tell her that Hattack was just pretending to be kind. But would she believe him? Clenching his jaws, he scrabbled up the rocky ridge and down into the forest. The ground turned to earth, and Toklo relished the musty scents of prey, bark, and leaves.

"It's this way." Wenona led the way through the trees.

The river was wide and shallow, the water splashing and

foaming as it tumbled over boulders.

Wenona frowned. "It's shallower than it was when I fished here."

"We've had no rain," Shesh pointed out.

Yas and Wapi leaped in and began wading upstream.

Holata blocked their way. "Young bears fish downstream," he told them, shooing them away.

"They can fish where they like!" Izusa protested.

Shesh called from the shore. "Holata is right, Izusa. I'm sorry, but this is a serious trial to see who will lead the Longest Day ceremony."

Muna splashed past Izusa, heading upstream. "The cubs can catch what we don't," she murmured, finding a good spot where the river began to widen. Hattack took the place next to her.

Toklo jumped down from the bank, relishing the cool water streaming around his paws. As Aiyanna followed, he nodded to a spot behind Muna, where a rise in the riverbed made the water run faster. "You could try there," he suggested.

Aiyanna touched his cheek with her nose. "Thanks."

Toklo pushed his way through the swift-flowing water, enjoying the surge of it against his legs. Stopping beside a wide, flat rock hidden just below the surface, he lowered his muzzle in and drank. The water tasted of the mountains. This was a perfect fishing spot. The fish would be easy to see against the rock.

Toklo glanced around. Wenona was staring intently at the surface, her ears pricked. Toklo was looking forward to fishing, but he wasn't going to take the trial as seriously as the others. Were they really so desperate to lead the Longest Day ceremony?

Shesh stood on the shore, waiting while each bear found a place in the river.

Flo and Fala stood close to Makya. Akocha had chosen a spot a little way downstream from Tayanita. The older bears were dotted like gigantic rocks across the wide stretch of river. Toklo had never seen so many bears fish a single river before. He remembered the river his mother had fished when he was a cub. The bears who fished there had guarded their places ferociously, lashing out at any bear who waded too far into their area. He hoped the trial wouldn't be so competitive. After all, they weren't fishing for survival.

"Begin!" Shesh's bark took Toklo by surprise. He scanned the water, alert for a flash of silver against the yellow riverbed. A soft wind ruffled his fur, and the sun felt warm on his back. *Where are the salmon?* He looked up, wondering if the others had caught anything yet. But all the bears were staring, motionless, at the water.

There must be *one* fish in the river!

Hattack lifted his head, looking puzzled. "Where are the fish?"

Wenona shook her damp fur. "There were loads last time I fished here."

Grumbles rose from the other bears.

"I haven't seen a single fish."

"This river must be poisoned."

Toklo shook his head. "I drank some," he argued. "The water tasted fresh."

Muna grunted. "Then what's happened to the fish?"

Hattack began to push farther upstream, the water lapping against his chest where it deepened. Toklo headed for the bank and hopped out. He passed Hattack and followed the river around a bend. He stopped as he saw the river narrow to a little waterfall between two great boulders. In the gap between, a leafy branch blocked the flow. Water flooded between the twigs and leaves, but nothing else could get through.

Hattack rounded the bend and clambered out. Stopping beside Toklo, he stared at the branch. Shesh and the others caught up to them a moment later.

"That's what's blocking the fish," Hattack announced, climbing onto one of the boulders and peering into the water behind. "Look!"

Toklo heaved himself onto the boulder and looked down. Salmon teemed in the river, buffeted by the current.

Muna squeezed up beside them and sniffed the branch. "It must have fallen in and blocked the fish."

Hattack growled. "Really?" He looked pointedly toward the trees, set back several bearlengths from the riverbanks on either side.

Shesh frowned. "How did it get there?"

Hattack turned and addressed the others from the boulder. "Isn't it obvious?"

Toklo blinked at him. *Obvious?*

"The white bears put it there to ruin our trial." Hattack's pelt spiked with rage.

"But why would they want to spoil—"

Toklo's words were drowned by the angry barks of the other bears.

Holata bared his teeth. "We'll make them sorry."

"What a dumb trick!" Wenona snarled.

"It's just the sort of thing a white bear would do." Muna turned and headed toward the trees.

"Where are you going?" Toklo called in dismay.

"Those white bears need to be taught a lesson!" Muna called over her shoulder.

Toklo's heart sank as more bears streamed after her, the undergrowth swishing as they crashed through the forest toward the white bears' shore.

Shesh and Aiyanna stayed on the bank. Izusa and Makya beckoned their cubs close.

Akocha was staring after Hattack. "Let's go! I want to make those white bears sorry!"

"No." Aiyanna blinked at the cub. "We have no proof it was the white bears."

Shesh shook his head slowly. "Why would the white bears want to spoil our trial?"

"There's no time to talk!" Toklo leaped down from the boulder and chased after the others. "We have to stop them from fighting!"

CHAPTER SEVENTEEN

Kallik

Kallik's heart lurched as brown bears streamed from the forest and leaped onto the shore.

She backed toward the lake, alarmed by the anger burning in their eyes. Around her, the white bears bristled. Yakone, who had been lying in the shade of the pines, scrambled to his paws.

"Kissimi!" Illa waded, dripping, from the water. "Come here!"

The young bear was chasing beetles farther along the shore. He hurried to Illa's side. "What's happening?"

"I don't know," Illa whispered.

The largest brown bear reared onto his hind legs and bellowed at the white bears. "You ruined our fishing trial!"

Grunts of surprise rose from the white bears.

Kunik stepped forward. "What are you talking about?"

Another brown bear swung his muzzle accusingly toward Kunik "You blocked the river!"

Just then, Toklo burst from the trees. "Stop!" He bounded

SEEKERS: RETURN TO THE WILD: THE LONGEST DAY   197

down the stones and pushed his way to the front. "There's been a misunderstanding."

Pride swelled in Kallik's chest. Toklo was so brave! She looked at Yakone, hoping to catch his eye. But Yakone was glaring at the brown bears. Kallik felt a stab of disappointment.

The huge brown bear glared at Toklo. "There's been no misunderstanding."

"Shut up, Hattack!" Toklo snapped.

Aiyanna joined Toklo. "Listen to him, Hattack," she pleaded. "Why would the white bears want to spoil our trials? It doesn't make sense."

"Who asked you?" Hattack hissed at her. "You've never been to a gathering before. You don't know anything!"

Kallik saw shock glitter in Aiyanna's eyes.

Kunik blinked at the brown bears. "We haven't tried to spoil your trials. This young bear is right." He nodded to Aiyanna. "Why would we bother? We are busy with our own."

Hattack curled his lip, revealing sharp yellow teeth. "Then who blocked the river and stopped the fish running?"

"No one!" Kotori squared his shoulders. "How dare you invade our territory with your fish-brained accusations? Get away from here!"

Salik swaggered forward. "Unless you want to fight!"

"Go stand beside Tonraq," Illa told Kissimi. Then she crawled forward and faced Hattack. "You say the river is blocked," she announced calmly. "Then why not just unblock it?"

Hattack stared at her. "Because—"

Another brown bear growled. "Why should *we* unblock it when *you* blocked it?"

"Nonsense." Illa pushed past them and climbed up the ridge. "Show me this blockage. Perhaps we can figure out how it got there."

Fur ruffling, the brown bears followed.

"Someone put it there," growled one.

"A *white* bear," grumbled another.

Kotori leaped up the ridge after Illa. Kallik followed.

"Stay here," Kunik told the other white bears. "We'll sort this out." He hauled himself up the stones behind Kallik.

As she followed the bears through the forest, warm fur brushed her flank. She jerked her muzzle around, hoping it was Yakone. But it was Toklo.

"Hi." He glanced sheepishly at the brown bears marching through the forest ahead of them. "Sorry about this."

"Why do they think it was us who blocked the river?" she asked.

Toklo shrugged. "I guess they don't think it could be anyone else."

"Couldn't the river have blocked itself?"

"There's a branch stuck in a gap," Toklo explained. "It looks too well wedged in to have been washed there by the river."

"So you think someone put it there?"

Toklo's pelt rippled. "I've had a feeling that there's someone else in the forest."

"What do you mean?" The lake was the gathering place for the Longest Day. Surely every bear had a right to be here?

"I keep thinking I'm being watched." Toklo sounded embarrassed. "I know it sounds dumb, but I get this creepy feeling when I'm alone. Like someone is following me."

Kallik bumped her shoulder against him. "There are so many bears around the lake, you're probably being watched all the time by someone."

Toklo grunted. "I guess." He glanced at her. "Where's Yakone? I thought he'd come with you."

Kallik looked away. "So did I."

"Have you had an argument?"

"Yes." Side by side, they crunched over the last stones and plunged into the trees.

"What about?" Toklo sounded concerned.

Kallik shrugged. How could she explain their argument? She hardly understood it herself. "He's worried that he won't be able to take care of me when we reach Star Island because of his injured paw."

"You don't need taking care of," Toklo huffed.

"I know that!" Anger surged beneath Kallik's pelt. "It's ridiculous." But if it was ridiculous, why hadn't they made up yet? Yakone had walked away from her earlier without even trying to make peace. Was he only worried about his own feelings? *Am I only worried about mine?* Perhaps they were both being selfish.

The river sparkled ahead. The other bears were already following the bank upstream. Kallik broke into a trot to catch up. Talking about Yakone was making her miserable.

"Is this it?" Illa had reached the boulders first and stared at the branch as the brown bears clustered around her.

"It's enough, isn't it?" Hattack growled.

Kotori pushed past him and grabbed the end of the branch between his teeth. With a grunt, he hauled it from between the stones. The water flooded free, salmon plopping into the shallows below.

"You can fish to your heart's content now," Illa declared. She let her gaze travel around the brown bears. "Do you really want to fight? Why don't you just get on with your trial?"

Kallik watched several brown cubs break away and leap into the river. Chasing the fish, they slapped the water excitedly.

"I'm going to catch the first one!" barked the smallest.

"No! I will!" yapped another.

One by one, the brown bears began to scramble down the bank. Before long, they were all wading downriver, pushing past the cubs in their race to catch the fish. Only Hattack, Toklo, Aiyanna, Kotori, and Kunik remained beside the boulders.

Hattack swayed from paw to paw, glancing hungrily downstream.

Aiyanna jerked her muzzle toward him. "Go fish," she growled. "I know how much winning means to you."

Hattack snorted, and Kallik noticed a flash of satisfaction in Toklo's eyes.

Kotori was examining the branch. "There are teeth marks here." He poked the thick end with his paw. Deep scratches in the bark betrayed the teeth and claws of a large bear, though it was impossible to tell whether they were made by a white bear or a brown.

Toklo leaned over and sniffed it. "They don't smell like brown bear," he decided.

Kotori sniffed it, too. "Nor white."

Kunik shrugged. "Perhaps a black bear put it here."

"It must have been a huge black bear," Toklo commented.

Hattack let out a snarl. "I've had enough of this." He glared at Kunik. "Just keep your bears away from our trials in the future."

As he waded into the river, Kotori growled. "He's lucky it's the Longest Day gathering or I'd claw his pelt off."

"It's not worth fighting over," Kallik muttered. The whole incident had been a big fuss over nothing. Perhaps Manik and Salik had put the branch there. It would be like them to stir up trouble.

As she followed the bank toward the lake, she saw a young brown bear splashing in the shallows. He was struggling to keep his balance, a huge salmon thrashing in his jaws. Scrabbling onto the bank, the young bear dropped it and gave a killing bite.

"Nice catch, Akocha!" exclaimed Aiyanna.

The young bear lifted his muzzle proudly. "I won! I won!"

Hattack was the first to look up, his eyes darkening when he saw the young bear's salmon lying on the shore. "You started fishing before us!" he objected. "It doesn't count."

"Of course it does!" Aiyanna insisted. "We agreed that the first brown bear to catch a salmon wins. Akocha was the first."

Hattack frowned. "Well, it makes no difference. Akocha isn't going to lead the Longest Day ceremony, no matter what happens!"

Kallik headed into the forest, leaving the brown bears to quarrel.

Illa caught up to her. "What a strange way to fish," she commented. "All that splashing about, chasing every sparkle and shimmer. I prefer hunting seals in deep water. It's far more dignified."

Kallik glanced at Illa. Unlike Illa, she'd caught fish like a brown bear. She'd learned to be quite good at it. Should she mention that it was actually fun, chasing salmon through the rapids? But Illa went on.

"I remember my first catch. It took me ages to haul the seal out through the ice hole. I nearly lost it, and once it pulled me back into the water. But I got it." She chuffed with amusement. "I remember Yakone's first catch, too. He waited beside an ice hole for half a day. Then he jumped on a white bear surfacing for air."

Kallik's heart twisted. Yakone had never told her that story. Perhaps they hadn't been as close as Kallik thought. Had their whole relationship simply happened because they'd been traveling together? Now they were with other white bears, Yakone could see he had other choices. Perhaps worrying about his injured paw was just an excuse to get rid of her.

When Kallik didn't speak, Illa slowed her pace. "Have you and Yakone argued?"

Kallik stared ahead. She'd already spoken to Toklo about

it. That hadn't helped. She didn't want to talk about it any-more.

"It will pass," Illa murmured. "Yakone knows where his heart lies."

Kallik quickened her pace and tried to ignore the thoughts spinning in her head. *Yakone knows where his heart lies. But what if it doesn't lie with me?*

By the time they reached the shore, the rest of the white bears had begun the next challenge. Each bear had to stalk a wading bird at the water's edge and get as close as possible without being spotted by the bird.

Kallik watched Manik creeping along the beach, his gaze fixed on a curlew as it picked its way through the water.

Beside her, Iqaluk gave a grunt. "It's a cloud-brained challenge. We should be testing our courage and strength, not how good we are at creeping up on birds."

Taqqiq twitched his ears. "When prey is short, stealth can be more important than strength."

Yakone was standing beside Anarteq. Kallik tried to catch his eye, but he was staring at the lake. She lifted her muzzle. If he didn't want her to go to Star Island with him, he was going to have to tell her why. She marched across the beach, slowing as she grew near to him. She felt sick.

"Yakone," she began. "We need to talk—"

"It's not fair." Kissimi popped up in front of her. "Why shouldn't cubs be allowed to take part? The brown bears took cubs to their fishing trial."

"And what if you won?" Tunerq pointed out. "Do you really think the spirits want a cub to lead the celebration?"

"Why not?" Kissimi stopped, blocking Kallik's way. "The spirits watch over cubs, too, you know!" He turned to Kallik. "You think I should be allowed to take part, don't you? Stalking's not dangerous like swimming to the island."

Kallik dragged her attention from Yakone. "I know it's not fair, Kissimi. But Tunerq has a point. The ceremony should be led by an older bear." She looked at the bears along the beach. Manik's bird had flown away and Iqaluk was tiptoeing through the shallows, stalking a sandpiper a few bearlengths ahead.

"Okay," Kissimi growled. "So I can't lead the ceremony. But I can take part in the trials, can't I?" He looked pleadingly at Kallik.

"I'm sorry, Kissimi. You can't." She rubbed the top of his head with her chin. "But I'll take you stalking later," she promised.

Kissimi snorted and padded away. "I never get to have any fun."

Kallik looked up at Yakone.

He had gone! Her heart ached as she saw him pad into the shade of the pine trees and flop down. He really didn't want to talk to her. Sadness flooded through her, so sharp it stole her breath.

"Kallik!" Taqqiq called. "It's your turn."

Iqaluk was stomping from the lake, his eyes dark with anger as his sandpiper flapped away.

Flustered, Kallik hurried to the water's edge, aware of the other bears' eyes on her as she waded into the shallows. If Yakone didn't want her to go to Star Island, what would she do? She fought back panic and forced herself to concentrate on the trial.

A snipe was wading a few bearlengths away. It stopped and ducked its curved bill into the water before moving on. Kallik crept toward it. As she neared, she realized that her shadow was moving ahead of her. No wonder Manik and Iqaluk had frightened their birds away. Their shadows had betrayed them. Backing quietly away from the water, Kallik moved down-shore and waited, like a rock, for the snipe to move. She heard the other bears whispering behind her and guessed that they were wondering what she was doing. As soon as the snipe turned its back, she crept into the shallows.

Her shadow was behind her now. All she had to do was move quietly. Placing each paw carefully, she felt for loose stones that might roll and send ripples through the water. Half a bearlength away, she felt a stone slide beneath her paw. She froze, as still as ice, then withdrew her paw and placed it to one side where the pebbles gave her a firm footing.

She was good at this. She knew it. The moons of trekking over strange terrain, learning new ways to hunt and to fish, had made her as sensitive to the landscape as any bear. Pride warmed her pelt as, with another pawstep, she leaned forward and reached for the snipe's tail feathers. As her nose touched them, the snipe squawked and fluttered into the air. The wind from its wings swept her face as it escaped.

She heard the approving grunts of the watching bears. As she turned to face them, Taqqiq dipped his head to her.

Kallik gazed at the pine trees. Had Yakone been watching?

He was lying in the shade, his back toward the lake. *He doesn't even want to look at me.* She felt cold, as though the blood had drained from her.

"Kallik!" Kissimi was calling her from the shore. "Kallik!" He was running toward her. "Take me stalking like you promised. Please!"

She stared at him blindly, her throat tightening. "Okay." As the cub charged down the shore, Kallik stumbled after him.

Oh, Yakone. What did I do wrong?

CHAPTER EIGHTEEN

Lusa

"They're gone!" Pokkoli skidded to a halt at the edge of the injured bears' nest.

Lusa looked up at him in surprise.

"The white bears led them back into the forest," he went on.

"I wonder what they're up to?" Lusa mused.

Pokkoli, Dena, and Leotie had been watching the brown bears, taking it in turns to rush back into the forest to report what was happening. First the brown bears had crossed the white bears' territory and climbed over the ridge into the forest beyond. Then they'd returned, barking angrily at the white bears.

Pokkoli's eyes were bright with excitement. "I thought they were going to fight. But a brown bear stopped them. And now they've gone back into the woods."

Miki sat back on his haunches. "Do you suppose it's one of their trials?"

Chula grunted. "Picking fights with other bears is probably an important brown bear skill."

"Not for *all* brown bears," Lusa put in. She wondered if Toklo had been the bear who had stopped the fight. She turned her attention back to Chula's leg.

The she-bear stood on three legs, her sprained paw unbandaged. Lusa felt the swelling with her paws. It was still warm, but the inflammation had eased. "Can you put any weight on it?" she asked.

Gingerly, Chula pressed her injured paw to the ground. "It hurts, but it feels strong."

"Good." Lusa felt a twinge of satisfaction. "Take it easy for another few sunrises," she warned.

"Does that mean I can leave the clearing?"

"Yes," Lusa told her. "But make sure you rest."

The brambles rustled nearby and Rudi appeared, leaves caught in his fur. "The others are ready to start."

Lusa blinked. "Is it the honey gathering trial already?"

Rudi nodded. "Ossi's found a patch of forest with three bees' nests."

"Good old Ossi," Miki chuffed.

"Is it far?" Chula asked.

"Deep in the woods, where the spruce turns to pine," Rudi told her.

Lusa met Chula's gaze. "Too far for you to walk."

"I'll stay with you," Miki offered. "I can't take part anyway." He patted his head gently. His ear wasn't swathed in leaves any longer, but the bump was still easy to see.

"No, you should go with Lusa," Chula insisted. "I'll walk down to the shore and cool my paw in the lake."

"You'll be careful, won't you?" Lusa reminded her. Perhaps she should stay after all.

"I'll walk with her," Rudi grunted. "I never liked climbing pine trees. They make my paws ache."

"We'll bring you back some honey," Miki promised.

"I'll fetch Dena and Leotie." Pokkoli was heading back through the trees. "They're still watching the white bears."

Miki trotted across the clearing. "Come on, Lusa!"

Lusa ran to catch up. Ahead of them, Sheena was racing after Tibik. The cub was zigzagging through the forest. "Do you remember that bees' nest we found on the way here?" he barked happily.

"Yes," Sheena panted. "It took me a whole day to wash the honey out of your fur."

Issa and Dustu were waiting among the pines when Lusa and Miki reached them. The other black bears were sifting through the thick layer of pine needles that covered the forest floor, picking out bugs and digging for grubs. Above them, the dark-green canopy blocked the sunshine. Lusa glanced up and saw bees hovering busily among the trees.

Ossi pushed his way from behind a clump of brambles and stopped beside a broad, deeply scarred trunk. "This is one of the bee trees. The others are over there." He pointed with his muzzle over his shoulder.

"Which bears should go first?" Sheena asked.

"Pokkoli, Lusa, and Ossi," Dustu decided. He nodded to the tree beside Ossi. "You take that one, Lusa. Ossi and Pokkoli can take the other two."

"Good luck, Lusa!" Miki barked.

Dustu looked at the bears. "The bear who gathers the most honey is the winner. Ready?"

Lusa rested her paws against the bark.

"Go!"

Lusa heaved herself upward, weaving between the jutting branches. The bark scraped her belly, and the sound of buzzing grew louder. Looking up, she could see bees swarming around a dark hole in the tree trunk. She licked her lips, smelling the honey. She was going to have to be quiet and move as slowly as a shadow. She edged closer to the hole. Bees buzzed around her ears. More flitted beneath her haunches. Holding her breath, Lusa pulled herself level with the hole and reached inside. *Ouch!* A sting sent pain stabbing through her paw. She ignored it and stretched until her claws reached soft, wet honey. She dug her paw deep into the comb, scooping out a thick pawful.

Gripping the trunk with three paws, she eased herself down. Honey dripped onto her fur as she reached the ground and landed with a thump on the needle-strewn earth.

Miki admired her piece of honeycomb. "Well done!"

"Let's see how the others did." Lusa went over to Pokkoli's tree. The young bear was sitting at the bottom, a huge chunk of honeycomb—far bigger than Lusa's—in his paws. Lusa felt a twinge of disappointment, but she was happy for Pokkoli. More bears gathered around him.

"I've never seen a better piece," chuffed an old male.

"The nest must be huge," grunted another.

A she-bear peered up through the branches. "I'm going to get an even bigger piece."

Tibik pushed his way through the crowd and stopped beside Lusa. "Can I have a taste?"

Sheena appeared behind him. "Will you share it, Lusa?"

"Of course!" Lusa snapped the honeycomb and gave half to Tibik. "Promise to take some back to Rudi and Chula."

Tibik nodded as he scooped a pawful into his mouth.

Lusa licked the comb. "Do you want some?" She broke off a piece for Miki.

"Yes, please!" His eyes lit up as he took it. "Thanks," he told her, stickily.

Issa and Dena were lining up at the bottom of the bee trees. They looked to Dustu, who raised his muzzle.

"Go!" The bears began to climb.

Ossi crossed the forest floor toward them. His fur was clumped where it was smeared with honey.

"Did you get much?" Lusa asked, licking the final smudges from her paw.

"Not as much as Pokkoli." Ossi shrugged. "But I think I got the most stings."

A breeze whisked between the trees and the brambles rustled. Lusa glanced around, her heart pounding. "What was that?"

"Just the wind," Ossi told her.

Lusa scanned the shadows, forgetting the sweetness on her tongue as she thought of Hakan. Was he still here, watching? "I need to warn Toklo, Kallik, and Yakone about Hakan."

Miki twitched his ears. "Hakan can't hurt them. They're bigger than he is."

"They should know he's here," Lusa insisted. Suddenly she needed Toklo to tell her not to worry, and Kallik to reassure her that there was nothing they could have done to save Chenoa.

"I'm coming with you," Miki told her.

"No, it's too far. You should rest."

"I'll go with her," Ossi offered.

Miki narrowed his eyes. "Of course you will," he grunted.

Lusa peered at him, surprised. It wasn't like Miki to be grumpy. "You'll soon be well enough to travel as far as you like," she reassured him.

Tibik distracted her with a loud burp. He was leaning against Sheena's flank, wiping his tongue around his sticky muzzle.

When she turned back, Miki was padding away. Worry churned in Lusa's belly. "Do you think he's annoyed because I didn't share enough of my honey?" she asked Ossi.

Ossi didn't meet her gaze. "Maybe his head is hurting."

"Do you think? Perhaps I should go check on him."

"He'll be fine," Ossi told her. "Look. He's surrounded by friends. They'll take care of him."

Miki had joined the bears at the base of Issa's tree. Settling among them, he looked up and watched Issa climb.

"You're right. He'll be fine." Relieved, Lusa headed through the trees, following the slope down toward the lake.

"Follow me." Ossi slipped past her and disappeared over a mossy rise.

"Where are you going?" Lusa raced after him, the ground soft beneath her paws. As she reached the top, she saw Ossi standing in a stream. His snout was deep in the bubbling water.

The sweetness of the honey had left Lusa's mouth dry, and she bounded down the slope and splashed into the stream beside Ossi. Closing her eyes, she drank. Then she ducked down and let the water sweep over her shoulders. It was refreshingly cold. As she stood up, she saw Ossi staring at her. Was there still honey on her face? Lusa swiped a paw across her muzzle, but it was dripping with water, no stickiness left. She stared back, wondering why he was watching her with such warmth in his eyes.

She jumped onto the bank and shook out her pelt. "What's wrong?" He was still blinking at her like a drowsy rabbit. "*What?*" she demanded.

"Where are you going when the gathering's ended?"

Lusa looked down at her paws. "I don't know." She sensed Ossi was working up to something, but she couldn't imagine what.

"Are you going to keep traveling with those brown and white bears?"

Sadness tugged at her heart. "No," she answered softly. "This is the end of our journey together."

"What did you plan to do next?"

"I hadn't planned anything really." Thinking about the future sent worry worming beneath Lusa's pelt. "I guess I thought I'd make some friends here and travel on with them.

They might know a good place to live."

"You could come home with me," Ossi murmured.

Lusa lifted her head.

"My home is a moon's journey from here," he went on. "It's full of rowan trees and cedar and beech. You can climb from tree to tree forever. There are other black bears, and more berry bushes than you can imagine. And no flat-faces to bother us."

Lusa gazed at Ossi. He was so kind. And yet sadness tugged at her heart. *Why?* This was a future she'd dreamed of, and yet she couldn't picture it with Ossi.

When she didn't answer, Ossi shook his fur. "Oh, I see." He dragged himself out of the stream. "I guess you don't want to come with me."

Lusa's mouth felt dry. *I've hurt him.* "Can I think about it?"

"Of course." Ossi brushed past her. "It's not important." But he didn't meet her eyes, and she knew he was lying.

"I can feel the wind from the lake." She changed the subject. "It feels warm. Do you think the weather's going to get hotter?"

"Probably," he grunted, pushing past a patch of ferns. He headed through the forest, making for the white bears' stretch of shore.

Lusa tried to keep up, but Ossi managed to stay a few paw-steps ahead. As they neared the beach, he quickened his step and disappeared around a bramble. She heard his paws crunch over the pebbled shore and hurried to catch up. Was he going to be angry at her forever? Couldn't they be friends now?

The rustle of leaves sounded at the edge of her thoughts. Still half thinking about Ossi, Lusa turned. Her heart lurched.

Hakan was striding toward her, his gaze fiery with rage. "You killed my sister."

"No!" Lusa scrambled backward as Hakan lunged at her, teeth bared. She shoved him away, but he rose to his hindpaws and towered over her.

"Hakan! No!" Fear spiked through Lusa's pelt.

She leaped sideways as his forepaws slammed down. He missed her, thumping earth instead and sending leaves fluttering around them.

Lusa backed through the brambles, her thoughts whirling. "We would have saved Chenoa if we could!" she barked desperately.

"But you didn't!" Hakan pushed after her through the spiky branches, his pelt bristling with rage.

Lusa felt pebbles beneath her paws and hot sunshine wash her flanks as she stumbled backward onto the beach. Stones clattered behind her, and a moment later, Ossi was barging past her toward Hakan.

"Leave her alone!" Ossi roared, shoving Hakan against the bramble.

Hakan staggered, and then found his balance. Ducking past Ossi, he hurled himself at Lusa, knocking her onto her back. Pressing his claws against her throat, he hissed into her face, "Chenoa's dead because of you!"

Ossi grabbed Hakan's scruff between his teeth and grunted as he tried to pull the black bear away. But Hakan was bigger than Ossi, and he was gripping tight to Lusa's throat.

She gasped, blood roaring in her ears as his claws pressed her throat. Was Hakan going to kill her?

As terror swamped her, white fur flashed at the edge of her vision. Stones crunched under huge paws, and Lusa smelled the familiar scent of Kallik.

Kallik swung a blow at Hakan. Lusa felt fur rip at her throat as Hakan staggered sideways, releasing his vicious grip. She heaved herself up onto her paws, panting.

Kallik had pinned Hakan to the ground, her ears flat with rage, her muzzle a hairbreadth from the black bear's face.

Ossi hurried to Lusa's side and watched wide-eyed. "He's gone crazy!" he growled.

Lusa frowned. Perhaps he had. Her chest ached with pity.

"Leave Lusa alone!" Kallik hissed. "Chenoa's death was an accident. There was nothing we could have done to prevent it."

Hakan snarled at her. "You should have let her stay with me. She'd still be alive."

Kallik snorted. "What kind of life would it have been? With a bully like you for a brother!" She swiped a paw across Hakan's muzzle.

"No!" Lusa darted forward. "Don't hurt him!"

Kallik swung her head around. "Why not? He tried to hurt you!"

Lusa twitched her ears. "He's grieving, Kallik."

Kallik hesitated, anger melting from her round black eyes. She let go of Hakan and backed away.

Hakan heaved himself to his paws and stared at Lusa, his gaze suddenly bleak. "Why did you take her with you?" Sadness choked his growl. He wasn't crazy; he was heartbroken.

Lusa faced him. "She *wanted* to come with us. We couldn't have stopped her, even if we'd tried. Nor could you. She would have followed us anyway."

Her heart twisted as she saw Hakan's shoulders slump. "If I had been kinder to her, she wouldn't have wanted to go."

Kallik shifted her paws. "Every bear needs to choose the path they follow. Chenoa chose hers."

"She was happy with us," Lusa offered. "And her death was quick. She didn't suffer."

Ossi padded forward and stopped beside Lusa. "It hurts to lose someone you love. But she'll be at peace now."

Lusa nodded. "I saw her spirit in a tree."

Hakan jerked his gaze to meet hers. "You did? Where?"

"Near the Big River," Lusa told him. She hoped, with a pang, that the flat-faces hadn't started cutting down the trees where Chenoa's stood.

Ossi was still staring at Hakan. "Come and make a nest in our camp," he growled softly. "No bear should grieve alone. You can find comfort among your own kind."

Lusa tensed, watching Hakan's face. Would he agree to make a nest in the same camp as her? She hoped so. Ossi was right. He need friendship more than anything.

"Okay." Hakan dipped his head. He flashed a look at Lusa, more reproachful than angry, and she guessed that, although he hadn't forgiven them for what had happened to his sister, he was starting to accept that it was a tragedy no bear could have foreseen.

Ossi blinked at her. "Let's take him back to join the others."

"You take him, Ossi," Lusa told him. "I want to speak with Kallik." She wanted to thank Kallik for saving her, and she guessed that Hakan would rather travel without her.

Ossi seemed to understand. He met her gaze for a moment, then turned to Hakan. "You can make a nest near mine," he told the black bear gently. "There's a thick clump of ferns. It'll be comfortable. And there are berry bushes just up the hill." Talking encouragingly, he nudged Hakan into the forest.

As they disappeared past the bramble, Lusa turned to face Kallik. "Thank the spirits you saw us!" She glanced past Kallik, wondering where Yakone was. She couldn't see him and only recognized Nukka close to the edge of the group. Lusa remembered the she-bear from the Melting Sea.

Kallik touched her muzzle to Lusa's head. "I'm glad I did! Where did Hakan come from? Did you know he was here?"

"He came to our part of the woods earlier," Lusa told her. "He was looking for Chenoa. He was angry when I told him Chenoa was dead. The other bears sent him away, but he must have been following me."

Kallik frowned. "Do you think you'll be safe, sharing a camp with him?"

Lusa nodded. She felt sure that with the friendship of his own kind, his anger would ease. "He can mourn properly now. And I won't be alone with him."

Kallik's gaze darkened. "I wonder if it was Hakan who blocked the river."

"What?" Lusa didn't understand.

"Someone used a branch to block the salmons' path to the shallows where the brown bears were holding their trial," Kallik explained.

"Why would Hakan do that?" Lusa asked.

"I can't see who else would want to spoil the trials." Kallik shrugged and glanced toward the trees where the black bears had disappeared. "Ossi seems nice."

"He is."

"Is he a special friend?" Kallik's question was edged with meaning.

Lusa stepped back. "No!"

"Oh." Kallik looked crestfallen. "He just seems to be very loyal."

"We're not like you and Yakone," Lusa snapped. Kallik's eyes clouded, and guilt washed over Lusa. "I'm sorry!" she gasped. "It's just that everyone seems to be trying to push me and Ossi together." *Even Ossi.*

Kallik touched her nose to Lusa's cheek. "It's okay. You must make your own decisions now. After all, it's your future, no one else's."

Lusa's heart ached as she rested her cheek against Kallik's muzzle. The white bear's fishy breath smelled comforting and familiar. *My future. After all these moons, I still have no idea where my journey will end.*

CHAPTER NINETEEN

Toklo

"I want to carry it!" Akocha picked his way down the rocky ridge after his mother.

Toklo grunted, amused, as Tayanita headed back to camp with Akocha's salmon clamped proudly between her jaws. The fish was too big for Akocha to hold. Even the white bears glanced at it admiringly as they crossed the stone beach.

Hattack was still complaining. "We should have kept fishing until we found a real winner."

Toklo scanned the white bears, looking for Yakone and Kallik. They had sometimes bickered on their journey, but they'd never fallen out like this. He caught sight of Kallik beyond the edge of the white bears' stretch of shore. He blinked in surprise. Lusa was with her.

"Hi!" Toklo stopped beside them as the other bears streamed past, heading for their own beach.

"Turned into a white bear, have you?" Muna hissed in his ear.

Toklo ignored her. Lusa was looking troubled. "What's wrong?"

"Hakan's here," Kallik told him. "He attacked Lusa. He said if it wasn't for us, Chenoa would still be alive."

Anger made Toklo's fur spike. "The coward! Why didn't he come looking for me? I'm the one who persuaded Chenoa to leave with us."

"It's okay," Lusa reassured him. "We managed to reason with him. Ossi's taken him to join the others. He's grieving, that's all. Perhaps the Longest Day ceremony might help him to accept Chenoa's death."

Toklo snorted. "Hakan couldn't accept his mother's death. He blamed Chenoa for it, remember? Why would he accept Chenoa's?"

"He'll be okay now," Lusa promised. "He's with his own kind."

Kallik was still frowning. "We think it was Hakan who spoiled your fishing trial."

Toklo blinked. Hakan couldn't have known that Wenona would suggest the fishing trial, unless . . . he had been lurking in the forest, following the brown bears.

Would he really go that far?

"Toklo!" Aiyanna called. "Hurry up. It's the fighting trial next." The brown bears had reached the edge of their shoreline and were pacing restlessly.

Toklo looked at Kallik and Lusa. He didn't like the idea of Lusa sharing a camp with a bully like Hakan. But he had to trust that she knew what she was doing. "Be careful," he warned.

"And you!" Kallik replied, watching the brown bears. Some of them were already facing each other, fur rippling as though they couldn't wait to start fighting.

"Are Lusa and Kallik okay?" Aiyanna asked as Toklo reached her.

"They're fine." There wasn't time to tell Aiyanna about Hakan.

Shesh was nodding the bears into groups. "Toklo, you're in this group," he directed. "Aiyanna, are you taking part?"

Aiyanna shook her head. "This is my first gathering," she told him. "I wouldn't know how to lead the ceremony."

Shesh raised his voice. "We fight in pairs, without tooth or claw. This is a test of cunning and skill, not a real fight. The winner is the bear to hold his opponent down for three heartbeats. The winners will fight until one pair is left. Their fight will decide the winner of the trial."

Toklo went over to the group Shesh had pointed to. Wenona, Tuari, and Muna moved aside to let him join. "I'll fight Tuari," he offered.

Wenona bristled. "Let Muna fight Tuari. I'm fighting *you*."

Toklo frowned. Was that fair? "I'm bigger than you—"

She silenced him with a snort. "This is about skill, not brute strength."

Shesh shooed the bears away from each other so that each group had space to fight.

Farther up the beach, Akocha was wrestling with his catch

on the stones. "I won again!" he barked, planting his paws on the smooth silver fish. The other cubs were watching.

"Can we eat some?" Elki asked, eyeing the fish hungrily.

"Only if you fight me for it." Akocha squared up to the cub and showed his teeth. Tayanita and Izusa hurried over.

"No teeth or claws," Tayanita reminded them.

Izusa pulled the fish out of harm's way. "This is play-fighting, remember?"

Toklo pulled his attention away from the cubs. There was a real trial to focus on. He glanced around the other groups, seeing the same hardness in the gaze of every bear. *They all want to win.* Something stirred in Toklo, a feeling he hadn't had since he faced his father on his home territory. He'd wanted to show his father he was stronger. He'd wanted to prove he could take Chogan's territory for himself. The same competitiveness throbbed in his belly now. He didn't want to be leader of the brown bears, but he *was* going to win this fight.

He faced Wenona and waited for Shesh to give the signal. Nearby Tuari and Muna stood snout to snout. Silence fell around him as the bears prepared to fight.

"Begin!"

Shesh's bark rang across the shore. Wenona was on her hindpaws before Toklo could move. He tried to stand up with her, but her forepaws crashed onto his shoulders. Stiffening, he pushed back against her weight, then sank back, letting Wenona fall to one side. One fast move now and he could pin her shoulders to the pebbles. He lunged, but she was faster.

She rolled out of the way. Toklo's paws smashed onto the stones, sending them flying.

Wenona leaped to her paws, narrowing her eyes. She rammed her shoulder into his. He was surprised by her power and staggered. With a growl, she tried to heave him over, but he pushed back, driving her toward the water's edge. She ducked away suddenly, and he stumbled forward. As Toklo regained his footing, Wenona darted behind him. Confused for a moment, he froze. *Where are you?*

Paws slapped heavily onto his spine. He jerked around, shaking her off. As her paws thumped onto the ground, Toklo saw his chance. Wenona's gaze dropped for an instant as she stumbled. He reached out with a forepaw and hooked her hind legs from beneath her. With a bark of surprise, she toppled over. This time, Toklo was faster. In a flash, he slammed his paws into her shoulders and held her firmly down for a count of three.

Rage flared in Wenona's gaze. Grunting, she shook him off and clambered to her paws. "You were lucky," she hissed. Barging past him, she lumbered away.

Tuari was sitting on his haunches beside a pile of driftwood, looking beaten. Wenona sat next to him and glowered.

Muna nodded to Toklo. "It looks like we're the winners of this round."

Toklo dipped his head to her. "Congratulations."

Around them, the other fights were ending. Toklo glanced toward Hattack. He was watching a young bear limp away. Hattack was the largest bear here, and Toklo knew that if he was going to win the trial, he would have to beat him.

Toklo won fight after fight until finally he stood head to head with Hattack. His paws stung from the pebbles, and his flanks were bruised from the blows of the other bears. Holata had been the hardest to beat. Toklo had admired his speed and quick thinking. He'd almost toppled Toklo twice, turning as fast as a deer. But Toklo was light on his paws, and the moons of traveling had given him enough stamina that when Holata had finally begun to tire, Toklo still had the strength to knock his opponent to the ground.

Hattack glared at Toklo. He had made easy work of a young she-bear before a long, fierce fight with an older male that had led him to the final round. Hattack's ear was bleeding. Perhaps he had torn it on a jagged pebble. But Toklo suspected both bears had used their teeth and claws in the previous fight.

Toklo squared his shoulders and met Hattack's burning stare. *I can win,* Toklo told himself, trying to ignore the doubt tugging in his belly.

Shesh stepped from the crowd of bears encircling them. "Ready?"

"Ready," Hattack growled without looking away.

Toklo nodded.

With a jerk of his muzzle, Shesh shooed the others backward. Toklo shifted his paws as the space widened around them. The air seemed to crackle, as though a storm were coming.

"Begin."

At Shesh's growl, Toklo braced himself for the attack. But

Hattack didn't move. He watched Toklo, a mocking glint in his eyes. Uncertain what to do, Toklo studied his opponent, checking for weakness in a paw or a patch of ruffled fur that might betray a tender spot. Hattack was larger, but only just. Muscles showed beneath his pelt. *I have muscles, too.* Toklo lowered his head, his heart pounding. *I guess it's up to me to make the first move.* Taking a step backward, he fixed his gaze on Hattack's left shoulder. Satisfaction pricked as Hattack's gaze momentarily followed his. *He thinks he's guessed what I'm going to do.*

Still staring at Hattack's shoulder, Toklo lunged around the other side and slammed his paws into Hattack's flank. He felt Hattack stumble. But Hattack was quick. He jerked around, rearing onto his hind legs. Toklo lifted his forepaws to meet him, and they clashed heavily.

Toklo staggered, gripping Hattack's sides with his paws. Pebbles clattered beneath them as they wrestled. Hattack's hot breath washed his muzzle, then pain seared his cheek as teeth ripped his fur. *No claws or teeth!* Yanking his head away, Toklo glanced at the watching bears. Had anyone seen that? Outrage surged through him as the other bears leaned forward, eyes bright, growling as they cheered the fighting bears on. Either no one had noticed, or none of them cared now that the trial was about to be decided.

As his thoughts wandered, Hattack jerked him to one side. Toklo's weight shifted to a single hindpaw, which twisted painfully beneath him. With a roar, he shoved Hattack away. Hattack reeled backward, surprise showing in his eyes. *You didn't think I was so strong, did you?* Toklo dropped onto all fours and shook out his hindpaw, relieved as the pain eased. Then he rushed at Hattack, his cheek still stinging. He met Hattack chest to chest. The heavy thump made them both stagger until Toklo gripped Hattack's shoulders once more. He felt Hattack's claws dig hard into his pelt, tearing his flesh. *You want to fight dirty?* Anger burned in Toklo's chest, and he prepared to dig his claws in.

No, Toklo. A whisper sounded in his ear. The scent of Ujurak wreathed around him, taking him by surprise. *You are better than that.*

Toklo uncurled his claws. The air shifted around him as though some unseen bear was giving him space.

His hindpaws are sore and tired. Ujurak's whisper sounded again. *Push him over the sharp stones.*

Toklo glanced at the patch of jagged pebbles behind Hattack and, with a bellow, heaved the brown male toward them. He winced as the rough edges jabbed into his own pads, but he felt Hattack flinch, too. Satisfaction surged through Toklo, giving him fresh energy. Hattack was struggling.

Be careful. A desperate bear is more dangerous. Ujurak's voice brushed his ear fur. Toklo broke free of Hattack's grip, feeling claws scratch his skin as he pulled away. Scowling, Toklo ducked behind him, leading him farther over the jagged pebbles. Around them, the bears shifted to make room as Toklo led the fight closer to the water's edge. Cold water would make Hattack's scratched pads sting.

Hattack spun around. "Are you running away?"

Toklo backed into the shallows. "Why would I?"

"You want to fight like a fish?" Hattack splashed into the water with a snarl.

Get him onto his hindpaws again, Ujurak urged. *He's trying to disguise a limp.*

Hattack reared first. Toklo rose to meet him. They clashed, the lake swirling around their legs. Hattack's paw slipped on the wet stones. His stumble unbalanced Toklo. Alarm flashed though Toklo as he felt himself topple. Letting go of Hattack, he slammed his paws into the water.

Hattack thumped onto Toklo's back and dug sharp claws into his flanks. Toklo staggered under his weight, his paws buckling beneath him. Teeth sank into the back of his neck. Panic flared beneath his fur. *Don't fall!* Toklo felt himself start to crumple, pain deafening his thoughts.

His hindpaw! Ujurak called. *It's weak.*

In a last, desperate move, Toklo swung out a back leg. His paw found Hattack's. With a vicious kick, he knocked Hattack's hind leg from beneath him.

Fur tore from his neck as Hattack fell. Roaring with pain, Toklo turned as Hattack splashed into the water. The great male thrashed like an overturned beetle, waves washing his belly. Fast as lightning, Toklo thrust his paws against Hattack's shoulder and shoved him down.

Rage showed in Hattack's eyes as his face disappeared underwater. Toklo felt him struggle, his snout barely breaking the surface. He held him for a moment. Then he let Hattack go.

Hattack burst from the water, fury glittering in his gaze.

"You fight like a white bear," he hissed.

Toklo stared coldly at him. "What a shame you don't."

The others rushed toward them.

"The winner is Toklo!" Shesh barked.

"Great fight!"

"Nice move at the end, Toklo."

Toklo felt dizzy as the bears swarmed around him. Hattack shouldered his way through the crowd and lumbered down the beach. Pride swelled in Toklo's chest. He lifted his muzzle, scanning the faces for Aiyanna's. He saw her at the edge of the throng, her eyes glowing. Toklo pushed his way toward her.

"Well done." Aiyanna pressed her muzzle to his as he reached her.

He leaned against her, suddenly exhausted. "I won." He could hardly believe it.

"You were great." She nuzzled him again, then pulled away. "You're bleeding!"

"Just a bite."

Aiyanna's eyes lit up with outrage. "But Shesh said no teeth or—"

Toklo blinked at her. "Did you really think Hattack would fight fair?"

Before she could answer, Shesh's bark silenced the crowd. "The final trial will take place tomorrow, when the sun is at its height, one day before the Longest Day. It will be a hunting challenge. Get some rest and eat well. Tomorrow we'll know which bear will lead the Longest Day ceremony!"

As grunts of excitement rippled through the crowd, Aiyanna

guided Toklo away. Exhausted, he let her steer him up the beach and into the shelter of the forest. She led him to a fern-lined scoop between the arching roots of a pine. "Rest here."

The scents of Izusa, Wapi, and Yas filled Toklo's nose. "This is Izusa's nest," he objected.

"And mine," Aiyanna told him. "But you can stay here while I hunt. You must be hungry."

Toklo nodded. Without arguing, he stumbled into the nest and lay down, wincing as his cuts and scratches stung. Closing his eyes, he felt sleep tug at him. "Thank you, Ujurak," he whispered.

A few moments later, he felt a tongue lapping a throbbing scratch. He smelled the sharp scent of herbs. "Lusa?" Had she come to heal his wounds? Blearily, he opened his eyes and saw Izusa beside him.

"Go back to sleep," she murmured. "I'm just licking herb juice into your cuts."

Wapi and Yas leaned over the edge of the nest.

"I knew he'd win!" Wapi whispered.

Yas sniffed. "You said Hattack would win, but I told you it would be Toklo. Toklo's the best."

Toklo closed his eyes and let himself drift into sleep.

A chorus of frightened barks awoke him. He scrambled to his paws, alarm shrilling through his pelt. Izusa was gone. Wapi and Yas, too. A knot of bears was clustered farther up the slope. Toklo ran toward them, fear pushing tiredness away. He could see their fur standing on end.

"How badly is she hurt?"

"Was it wolves?"

Fear sparked in Toklo's belly. Had Aiyanna been attacked while she was hunting? He pushed his way through the crowd and gazed at the crumpled figure lying at the center.

Elki. He recognized the cub at once. Muna was crouched beside her, lapping desperately at the bloody wounds that marked her flank. Holata stood over them, his eyes bright with rage. "I'll kill whoever did this!"

"Are there wolves here?" Toklo asked. What wolf would be dumb enough to roam a forest full of bears?

"The white bears must have attacked her!" Wenona snarled.

"She was nowhere near their shore," Muna sobbed.

"Where was she?" Toklo demanded.

Muna lifted her clouded gaze. "I'm not sure. She said she was going to catch a rabbit. I told her not to wander far."

"Where's Elsu?" Alarm jabbed Toklo's chest. Elki and Elsu were never far apart. "Is he safe?"

"I'm here." Elsu squeezed past his father, trembling as he pressed against Holata's flank.

"Were you with her? Did you see what did this?" Toklo prompted.

Elsu shied away. "I was fishing in the lake."

Holata curled his forepaw around his cub. "Leave him alone. He's had enough of a shock," he told Toklo. He looked at Elki. "The most important thing now is to make sure Elki is okay."

Izusa was picking her way through the crowd, a wad of

leaves clamped in her jaws. She ducked down beside Elki and began working sap into the cub's wounds.

"This gash is deep." Muna sniffed at a cut on Elki's throat, where blood seeped into the fur around her neck.

Izusa dropped green pulp onto it. "This will help," she reassured Muna before working it into the cut with gentle laps.

Elki stirred, moaning.

"Elki?" Muna leaned closer as the cub half opened her eyes. "What happened? What did this to you?"

Elki's eyes flickered and closed again.

Muna stiffened. "Is she okay?"

Izusa glanced at the cub's flank. "Her breathing is steady and strong. She'll be fine."

Toklo turned away. Makya was watching from a distance, Flo and Fala huddled beside her. Suddenly Aiyanna crashed out of a clump of ferns, dragging a young deer. She dropped it when she saw the crowd. "What's happened?"

"Something attacked Elki," Toklo told her.

He blocked her way as she began to hurry toward the injured cub. "Izusa's with her. She's going to be okay."

Aiyanna stared at him in horror. "Who would do something like that?"

Toklo shrugged. "Wolves?" His belly rumbled.

"You're hungry."

"I haven't eaten all day." He grabbed the deer in his jaws and helped Aiyanna haul it toward the nest. They dropped it on the needle-strewn earth and ate.

Aiyanna's eyes were wide as she chewed. "I didn't see any

signs of wolves while I was hunting." She looked puzzled. "Is everyone sure it was a wolf?"

"We won't know for sure until Elki wakes up." Toklo glanced toward the knot of bears. The warm meat in his belly was making him sleepy again. He tried to fight the heaviness in his eyes and pushed himself to his paws.

Aiyanna must have seen him sway. "Sleep." She nudged him into the nest. "I'll check on Elki and see if Izusa needs help."

Gratefully, Toklo lay down. He closed his eyes and sleep enfolded him again.

He dreamed he was on the lakeshore. Darkness hid the forest and mist curled on the water. He looked up, trying to make out the stars, but the sky was dull. Only the moon shone, cold and alone.

"Toklo." Ujurak's voice echoed along the shore. His pelt pricking, Toklo searched the shadows for his friend.

A shape moved, and Ujurak padded from the darkness. His sleek pelt shone in the moonlight.

Toklo met his gaze warmly. "Thanks for helping me in the fight."

"I didn't want you to become like Hattack. He is a bear who will always cheat to get what he wants. But nothing is worth having if you have to cheat to get it." Ujurak's growl was soft. "Everything you have—friendship, love, respect— you have earned honorably."

Happiness flickered in Toklo's belly for a moment . . . until he saw Ujurak's eyes darken.

"You must try to hold on to what you have," Ujurak warned.

A cold wind lifted from the lake and billowed through Toklo's fur. He tried to move closer to Ujurak, but his paws were rooted to the pebbles. His heart quickened. "What's going to happen?"

"Never underestimate the power of hatred, Toklo," Ujurak told him.

Toklo struggled to hear over the rising wind. "Whose hatred?"

"You have made enemies, Toklo." Sadness filled Ujurak's gaze. "You, Lusa, Kallik, and Yakone have traveled far and ruffled more than one pelt. And now you will have to fight to save what you love."

"Fight what?" The wind whipped Toklo's ears, buffeting his flank. He strained to see Ujurak, but the young bear was fading into the shadows. "Help me, Ujurak!"

"You must save yourselves. I cannot—" The wind snatched the last of Ujurak's words away.

Toklo was left alone on the shore in darkness. *Save ourselves.* Blood roared in his ears, louder than the wind. *From what?*

CHAPTER TWENTY

Kallik

A hot wind tugged at Kallik's pelt. The fierceness of it stirred her from sleep. As she opened her eyes, sand whisked into them, whipped up from the stony shore. The other bears were stirring around her. She climbed stiffly to her paws. The dip in the stone where she'd curled for the night had been hard. She hadn't bothered to line it with moss.

She'd gone to her nest last night—the nest she and Yakone had built in the shelter of the ridge—but it had been empty and smelled stale. She'd turned away and found a place on the shore near Illa and Kissimi. Curling up tight, she'd tried to ignore the pain in her heart. How strange it was to breathe air that didn't smell of Yakone. The warm night was all that had enfolded her. She kept hoping that Yakone would come find her, and when he didn't, she'd felt the same white-hot grief she'd felt when Nisa had been killed.

Did Yakone miss her, too? Kallik blinked the sand from her eyes and scanned the shore. There he was, lying in the shallows, letting the cool water wash over his back. He stared out across the lake. *He's not even looking for me.*

"Kallik!" Taqqiq was weaving his way through the others toward her. "Kunik and Anarteq are hiding a fish over there." He nodded toward the rocky outcrop that marked the end of the lake. Beyond, the beach cut into a wooded cove.

Kallik knew that the last trial was to test the scent skills of the bears. The ability to detect food at a distance was crucial to survival on the ice. She followed her brother's gaze, wishing that she could feel as excited about the trial as he did. Around her, bears shifted restlessly, murmuring to one another.

"Aren't you looking forward to it?" Taqqiq asked.

"I don't care about the trial," Kallik murmured.

Taqqiq's gaze darkened. "Haven't you and Yakone made up yet?"

"He won't speak to me."

"Have you tried?" Taqqiq looked worried.

"Every time I approach him, he walks away."

"Did you do something wrong?"

Kallik stared at her brother bleakly. "If I did, I don't know what it was. I just wanted him to take part in the trials, and he said that he couldn't because of his injured paw." She tried to remember exactly what had happened, but the only words that rang in her mind were the words she would never forget. *I'm no use to you now.* "Then he said it was best if I didn't go to Star Island with him."

Taqqiq's eyes widened. "He didn't mean it, surely?"

"That's what I thought, but he's been avoiding me ever since." A lump rose in her throat.

Taqqiq leaned closer. "You have to speak with him, Kallik. You can't let him go without finding out why he's behaving like this. He's too important to you."

Kallik stared at her brother, surprised by his concern. And his wisdom. He was right. Whatever happened, she must speak to Yakone, even if it meant hearing that he didn't want her anymore.

Taqqiq touched his nose to her cheek. "You can come back to the Melting Sea with me and Shila."

Kallik rested her head against his. "Thank you, Taqqiq."

"I've changed, Kallik." Taqqiq pulled away and met her gaze. "I know I've done bad stuff in the past, but I've learned how important it is to be with the bears you love, and who love you." He dropped his gaze shyly. "Shila has taught me that."

Kallik's heart swelled with affection. "She's a great bear, Taqqiq. I'm glad you have her."

As she spoke, Shila trotted toward them. "Glad he has who?" Her eyes flashed teasingly.

"You," Kallik huffed.

"Of course." Shila brushed against Taqqiq as she halted. "Are you ready for the last trial, Kallik? Taqqiq says you have a good sense of smell."

"She'll probably win," Taqqiq chuffed.

"If she does, she'll lead the Longest Day ceremony." Shila met her gaze happily.

"If Taqqiq wins, he'll lead it," Kallik pointed out.

Taqqiq shrugged. "I don't mind who wins. I'm just looking

forward to going home." He glanced at Shila. "Perhaps next time we come to the gathering, we'll bring our cubs." Shila nuzzled his cheek with her nose.

Along the shore, Kunik and Anarteq were climbing back across the jagged rocks.

"The fish is hidden!" Kunik called.

Anarteq jumped heavily onto the beach. "The first bear to find it wins the trial."

Shila started trotting toward the cove.

Taqqiq lingered beside Kallik. "Are you coming?"

Kallik glanced at Yakone. He'd gotten to his paws and was shaking the water from his pelt. "I should talk to Yakone instead."

"You can do that afterward," Taqqiq urged. "Let's find the fish first. You can think about what you're going to say to him while you're looking."

Kallik hesitated.

"Come on!" Shila called. The other bears were already streaming over the rocks. Manik, Salik, and Iqaluk jostled against one another, fighting to be the first into the cove.

Kallik let her brother steer her after the others. The rocks were sharp beneath her paws, and she was relieved to jump down the other side onto a patch of soft sand. Ahead, the narrow strip of shore was covered with boulders. Pines reached to the edge, their branches sticking out over the water. White pelts glowed in the shadow of the trees as bears picked their way through the undergrowth, heads down as they sniffed for the fish.

Shila broke into a run toward the top of the beach. Taqqiq followed.

Kallik clambered over the boulders instead, following the edge of the lake. The large stones rocked beneath her paws as clear blue water lapped against them. Kallik sniffed halfheartedly. Pine scent filled her nose. She could hear Illa calling to Kissimi in the trees.

"Don't stray far!"

"What if I smell the fish?" Kissimi called back.

"Tell me!" Illa answered.

"But the others might hear and find it first!"

As their barks faded away, Kallik picked her way along the shore until it widened. She stopped, a heavy stone tipping beneath her paws, and looked back.

Yakone was standing on the outcrop. His muzzle high, he seemed to be scanning the shoreline. *Is he taking part in this trial?* Kallik frowned as Yakone hurried down the rocks and began to head along the shore.

The other bears were all in the forest now. This time she could speak to him without any interruptions. Kallik walked toward him. Let Iqaluk, Salik, or Kotori find the fish. If Yakone didn't want her to go to Star Island, he had to tell her why. She could go back to the Melting Sea with Shila and Taqqiq. She could be happy eventually. Perhaps they'd let her take care of their cubs.

"Kallik." Yakone greeted her with a grunt.

"Be careful on the rocks," Kallik warned, not knowing what else to say. "They move when you step on them." As she spoke, one shifted beneath her and she stumbled.

Yakone didn't seem to notice. "Is that why you came?" he growled. "Were you worried I couldn't take care of myself?"

Rage sparked beneath Kallik's pelt. "I came to talk to you! Is that okay or are you going to walk away again?" When he didn't speak, she went on. "I hardly know who you are anymore."

Yakone held up his paw. "I'm a lame bear! If you don't like that, leave me alone."

"You lost two dumb toes!" Kallik exploded.

"I lost more than that," Yakone snarled.

"It's always about you, isn't it?" Kallik accused. "*Your* paw. *Your* home. *Your* feelings! What about me?"

"I'm doing this for you!"

"Doing what?"

"I'm saving you from a life with a crippled bear in a place among bears you hardly know."

Kallik shook with rage. "Thanks for deciding what's best for me!"

"Would you rather I didn't care?" Yakone barked.

"Is this you *caring*?" Kallik couldn't believe her ears. He'd let her spend two days breaking her heart over him. "I remember you when you really cared. When you lay down as bait for coyotes to save your friends. When you trekked for a moon to find Lusa. You were missing your toes then, remember? You haven't starved since you got caught in that trap. You can still do everything! This is just an excuse."

Yakone's eyes glistened with pain.

Guilt stabbed Kallik's heart. She'd hurt him. "If you don't want me to come to Star Island, that's fine." Her growl thickened. "I loved traveling with you, but our journey is over now, and I understand if you don't want to start a new life with me. It's okay to change your mind."

Yakone stared at her. "Is that what you think?" He sounded amazed. "That I don't want to start a new life with you?"

"That's what this is about, isn't it?"

"I told you why I don't want you to come." Yakone lifted his paw once more. "I might be able to hunt now, but not like I used to. When we get to Star Island, I'll be weaker than I was before. I won't be able to take care of you."

"I've been taking care of myself since I was a cub," Kallik told him. "I don't need you to take care of me. I want to take care of you. And I don't understand why you won't give me the chance. Don't you love me anymore?"

Yakone lowered his head. "Of course I love you. I could never stop loving you."

"Then how could you try to drive me away?"

"What if you don't like Star Island? What if you miss your home on the Melting Sea? What if you get bored staying in one place? What if it's not the same without Lusa and Toklo?" The questions tumbled out, his growl growing hoarser with each one.

Love flooded Kallik's heart. It had never been about Yakone's injured paw. He was frightened she wouldn't be happy on the Endless Ice. "I only ever want to be with you," she breathed. "You gave up everything to come with me.

Everything we have, we have made together. I won't ever miss my home, because my home is with you."

Yakone stumbled forward and buried his muzzle in her neck fur. Kallik breathed in the scent of him, dizzy with emotion.

As he pressed harder against her, a stone rocked beneath his paw. The fresh smell of fish wafted around them. Stepping back, Kallik looked down. A fish gleamed beneath the boulder. "You've found it! You've found the fish!"

Her loud bark made several white heads pop out from the tree line.

Yakone grabbed the fish in his jaws and headed back toward the outcrop. Kallik hurried after him, pride warming her pelt. She clambered over the rocks after him as he crossed the shore and dropped the fish at Kunik's paws.

Behind them, the other bears were hurrying from the cove. "Yakone won the trial!"

"I didn't think he was taking part," Salik muttered.

"He must have been. He found the fish!" Shila barked.

Illa raced along the beach, scrambling to a halt beside Kallik. "Where was it?" she whispered.

"Under a rock."

Kunik stepped forward, looking troubled. "This means we have no winner for the trials."

Illa sniffed. "We have three winners: Taqqiq, Kallik, and Yakone."

Malik shouldered his way to the front. "They can't all lead the ceremony."

"They should fight to find out who the real winner is," barked Salik.

Taqqiq turned on him. "We come here to honor the spirits in peace!"

Murmurs of agreement rippled among the others.

"Perhaps the spirits will decide who should lead the ceremony," Anarteq rasped.

"How will they tell us?" Salik scoffed.

Anarteq looked up at the sky. "They will find a way."

Kallik followed the old bear's gaze. Perhaps they'd send a message through Ujurak? As she stared into the vast blueness, she saw clouds bubbling on the horizon. The hot wind was bringing a change in the weather. Would there be a storm on the Longest Day?

She shivered. Then she remembered she'd never told Yakone about Hakan. She lowered her voice. "Hakan's here," she murmured. "He attacked Lusa."

Yakone's eyes widened. "Is she okay?"

"He didn't manage to hurt her. I pulled him off. But he's grieving for Chenoa. I think it was Hakan who sabotaged the brown bears' fishing trial."

"Will Lusa be safe with him around?"

"Lusa's friend persuaded him to join the black bear camp," Kallik explained. "They think that with the help of his own kind, Hakan can come to terms with Chenoa's death. I can't imagine him attacking her again, not with so many bears around. She'll be okay."

"We don't know that for sure. We should go and check on

her." Yakone headed toward the far shore. "We've helped Lusa get this far. We can't abandon her now."

Kallik hurried after him, her heart swelling with pride. This was the brave, decisive Yakone she'd traveled beside for all those moons. She noticed with a rush of joy that he wasn't limping anymore. *You're as strong as you ever were,* she thought as she fell into step beside him.

CHAPTER TWENTY-ONE

Lusa

Lusa felt a paw nudge her, and sleepily, she opened her eyes.

Ossi was standing beside her nest. "Wake up! It's not cold-earth yet."

Bright sunshine sliced through the branches above her. She must have slept late. The breeze from the lake had picked up, but Lusa was hot. The forest was stifling. Still drowsy, Lusa heaved herself to her paws. "Has the last trial begun?" she yawned.

"It's about to," Ossi told her. "That's why I woke you. I hope you don't always sleep this late."

Lusa's pelt prickled. Ossi's easy familiarity irritated her. She felt that there was something more than friendship in his tone, as though he'd decided after their talk yesterday that she was going to travel home with him after all. She stretched, feeling guilty. Perhaps she was imagining it.

"Come on." Ossi was nudging her from her nest. "Dustu's about to announce the start of the foraging."

Lusa shook him off. "I want to check Chula's leg. And

Tibik. He seemed sleepy yesterday."

"Hot weather makes everyone drowsy." Ossi was shifting impatiently from paw to paw.

"I'll catch up." Lusa shooed him away with a jerk of her snout. She headed for the nest of wounded bears.

Chula was pacing around the edge, putting gentle weight on her sprained paw. "It's much better!" she called as she saw Lusa.

Lusa chuffed with delight. "Does it hurt?"

"Just a bit."

"Don't walk too much," Lusa warned.

The bushes at the edge of the clearing rustled, and Miki emerged. His pelt was wet.

"Have you been for a swim?" Lusa asked, surprised.

"I just went to cool off in the lake." Miki sounded distant. Perhaps the hot weather was making him cranky.

"I guess it feels good to get your fur wet on a day like this," Lusa ventured.

"Yes." Miki nodded to her politely, then turned to Chula. "Come and soak your leg, Chula! The water's cold enough to freeze the fish."

Lusa bristled. *Why is he being friendly with Chula and not me?*

Chula glanced at her. "Do you want to come?"

Miki answered before she could. "Lusa will want to take part in the final trial." He looked at her, his eyes betraying nothing. "Won't you?"

"Oh, yes!" Chula exclaimed. "I'd forgotten. We'll come see how you did later!"

Lusa watched Miki and Chula head away between the trees, feeling something sharp and heavy in her chest. Then she remembered Tibik. She hurried to his nest.

Sheena was leaning over her son. "He's so sleepy and hot," the she-bear fretted.

Lusa touched the sleeping cub. He did feel hot, but the weather was suffocating. All the bears probably felt hot.

"He keeps waking up and falling asleep again." Sheena's eyes glittered with worry.

"It's probably all that honey he ate yesterday," Lusa guessed. "Let him sleep it off." She sniffed Tibik's pelt. She smelled sourness there. The heat? She saw a dead bee caught in his pelt. Plucking it out with a paw, she tossed it away. "If only honey came without stings," she murmured.

She pictured Chula and Miki at the lakeside. Chula would be limping though the shallows by now. Miki would be bouncing around her, splashing water over her fur.

Swallowing back irritation, Lusa headed for a shady patch in the forest where she could see the other bears gathering for the trial. "Keep an eye on him," she called back to Sheena.

Ossi was pacing when she arrived. "I thought you were going to miss the start!"

Pokkoli was studying the slope above them, as though already picking out the best plants to forage from.

With his paw, Dustu drew two lines in the leaf litter where sunshine striped the forest floor. "When the shadow hits this line, you can begin foraging. When the shadow reaches the next line, you must stop. Collect as many leaves, grubs, berries, and insects as you can. The winner will be the bear who has collected the most variety and best quality."

Rudi stepped forward. "Each bear should forage alone and bring what they've found back here."

Lusa felt Ossi's flank brush hers. "We might have to forage alone, but there's no reason we can't forage in the same part of the forest," he whispered.

"I guess." Lusa forced herself to sound enthusiastic. *Isn't he going to give me any space?*

The bears leaned forward as the shadow slowly moved across the forest floor.

"Good luck," Ossi whispered.

"Have fun," Lusa reminded him. These trials weren't about winning, they were about enjoying themselves.

"Begin!" Dustu called out as the shadow hit the first line.

Paws swished over leaves as the bears scampered into the forest.

"Which way should we go?" Ossi asked.

Lusa wanted space to think. She couldn't get Miki out of her head. She was sure she could hear him and Chula barking happily beside the lake. Ossi gazed at her, round-eyed. She couldn't disappoint him. They were friends, after all. "Let's find somewhere cool."

"This way." Ossi led her up the slope to a cluster of mossy rocks. "There'll be a few grubs' nests here," he told her.

Lusa peered past a half-rotted fallen log. She could see the glossy leaves of a cloudberry bush on the other side. "I'll go this way," she told Ossi.

"Okay," he grunted. He was already digging in the soil.

Lusa clambered over the log and began to pick cloudberries from the bush. She popped one in her mouth, grunting as the juice burst on her tongue. When she'd gathered a small pile, she left them and padded toward the roots of a spruce. The earth here was soft and damp, and she didn't have to dig far to unearth a fat worm. Working her paws deeper, she uncovered a clump of grubs. They were fat and white, as big as any she'd seen. Happily, she picked a few to take back with her and popped the rest into her mouth. She sat back on her haunches and enjoyed the musky flavor.

A foul scent touched her nose. It made her wince. Curious, Lusa got to her paws. Circling the spruce, she saw an opening in the other side. The trunk was hollow and she looked up, realizing that the needles on the branches were long dead. The stench was worse here, and, screwing up her nose, Lusa leaned in to see what was making such a smell. It was too early in the season for fungi. Her nose wrinkled when she saw a half-eaten squirrel rotting inside the hollow. Maggots wriggled over its carcass.

Lusa pulled away, feeling sick. Who'd eaten this and left the rest to rot?

Her pelt rippling with unease, she backed away from the spruce and scanned the forest. Had brown bears been hunting in the black bears' forest? Not all of them were as friendly as Toklo. Lusa scooped up the grubs and decided to find Ossi. She could look after herself, but it would be easier if she had a friend.

She halted as she reached her pile of cloudberries. A thought sparked in her mind. The stench of the rotting squirrel had reminded her of something. Pausing, she frowned. She'd smelled sourness earlier.

Tibik!

Lusa's heart lurched. It wasn't the heat that made him smell sour. It was infection! How had she missed it?

"Ossi!" Panicked, she called through the trees.

She heard paws thump the ground. "Lusa? Are you okay?" Ossi skidded around a tree and stopped in front of her. Berry juice smeared his jaws.

"Tibik's sick!"

"How do you know?"

"I remembered the smell." Lusa's pelt bristled with fear. "He's got an infected wound." She pelted down the slope.

Ossi raced after her. "But he didn't have any wounds."

"He must have one I didn't see!" Lusa scrambled over the mossy rocks, scattering her grubs and berries behind her. Her thoughts whirled. She knew what herbs would stop infections from taking root, but what could she use to cure an infection that was already sour?

She stumbled to a halt beside Tibik's nest. Sheena jerked around. "What's wrong?"

"Infection!" Lusa puffed. She leaned over Tibik. Heat pulsed from his pelt. He was damp, and when she touched him, he felt as limp as dead prey. There must be a cut somewhere. She ran her paws over his fur, searching for an injury. "Has he trodden on a thorn?" she asked Sheena.

"No." The she-bear was leaning close, stiff with fear.

Lusa checked Tibik's pads for grazes. They were fine.

The bee sting! Didn't Ujurak once tell her they could get infected? Lusa ran her paws over the patch of fur where she'd knocked the bee away earlier. It felt swollen and even hotter than the rest of Tibik. She pressed the fur aside and saw yellow pus straining beneath the surface. She wrinkled her nose at the foul stench. She turned to Sheena. "The bee sting is infected. Squeeze as much of this pus out as you can. I need to fetch herbs."

Anger flashed through the fear in Sheena's eyes. "You said he was sick from eating too much honey!" she growled. "You left him and went to the trial."

Lusa's belly tightened. "I know. I was wrong. I'm sorry."

Ossi peered into the nest. "How is he?"

"Sick," Lusa told him. "Stay with Sheena while I fetch herbs."

She raced into the trees. The usual herbs she needed to prevent infection wouldn't be enough. They might help clean out the wound once the pus was gone, but what would help Tibik fight the infection that had found its way inside? She swerved around a clump of brambles, running half-blind as she tried to think.

Black fur loomed ahead of her. Pulling up, Lusa skidded and thumped into the flank of a male bear.

"Lusa?" It was Miki. "What's wrong?"

"Tibik's really sick!" Lusa blurted out. "I have to find herbs, but I don't know which ones!"

Miki brushed his flank against hers. "Calm down," he growled. "Take a deep breath and think."

Lusa stared at him, her thoughts slowing as she drew in a deep breath.

"What herbs did you use for Rudi's cuts?" Miki prompted.

Lusa tried to hold on to her moment of calm. "Those leaves only help the infection of the wound. I need herbs to help the infection inside."

"Okay." Miki glanced around. "Let's gather some leaves to help the outer infection. While we do, you can think about what else we need." He nodded toward the bottom of the slope where the forest opened onto the shore. "Didn't we gather leaves for Rudi there?"

Before Lusa could answer, he walked down the slope. She followed, concentrating on breathing steadily. She could already see the bright-green leaves that would cure the sourness in the pus-filled bee sting. They were growing in thick swathes around the base of a rowan. She stopped as Miki began to tear up pawfuls.

"This is the right stuff, isn't it?"

Lusa nodded. She sat on her haunches beside him and began to rip leaves from their stems. Methodically, she stripped a patch and moved on to the next. She knew they were collecting far more than she needed, but she could feel her mind turning over everything she had learned and kept picking.

She'd had to find flat-face medicine to treat Yakone when his paw went sour. There was no flat-face medicine here, but there must be an herb that would help. Lusa reached back through all Ujurak had taught her. She pictured gathering leaves beside him from rocky outcrops, in lush meadows, alongside streams.

She paused. There was one herb that grew beside water. Ujurak had told her that if a bear ate enough, it could slow a pounding heart and ease a burning fever. Wasn't that the same as curing an infection?

"That's it!" she barked.

"You've remembered an herb?" Miki's eyes shone.

"It grows near water." Lusa jumped up and made her way down onto the shore. She raced to the edge of the lake, but there were no plants there, only water and stone.

"Over here!" Miki was heading toward a patch of green where a stream emerged from the forest.

Lusa bounded toward him. Plants grew thickly along the narrow rivulet. Jumping into the water, Lusa followed it back under the trees. Long, thin leaves covered small, round ones. Furry leaves poked out among straggly, paw-shaped ones. In her mind Lusa saw Ujurak plucking a long, limp leaf that trailed in the water. She smelled its musky odor. Opening her mouth to taste the air, she scanned the edge of the water. There must be some here! Tibik's life depended on it.

"Have you found it?" Miki's bark interrupted her thoughts.

"Hush!" A faint scent touched her nose. She plunged her paws into the leaves. Drawing them back, she saw the precious herb floating on the surface of the stream. She leaned in and grabbed the main stem between her jaws, ripping the whole plant away. The leaves trailed through the water as she looked up triumphantly at Miki.

"I'll fetch the other leaves and meet you at Tibik's nest," he told her.

She nodded and climbed out of the stream. Pounding across the forest floor, she raced for the camp. Was this really the right herb? *Ujurak, help me!*

Tibik was moaning when she reached his nest. Sheena met her with wide, frightened eyes. "He's in pain!"

Ossi was crouched beside Tibik. "We got the pus out. The wound's running clear now."

There was no time to explain what she was going to do. Lusa chewed a mouthful of leaves into a pulp and leaned over Tibik. He wriggled, whimpering as she opened his jaws with her paw. Letting the pulp drop into his mouth, she shut his mouth quickly, then pressed his cheek to make him hold still. "Swallow, Tibik, swallow!"

Behind her, Sheena growled. "What are you doing to him?"

Tibik was twisting beneath Lusa's paws, struggling to open his jaws. She could feel his heart pounding beneath her flank. "I know it tastes bad, but it will make you better," she whispered. She felt him swallow and let go.

He lifted his head and stared at her, his glassy eyes wide with panic, then collapsed back into his nest and lay still.

Sheena lunged forward and knocked Lusa away. "You've killed him!"

Paws came to a halt beside her. *Miki!* Lusa stared at him desperately as he dropped the leaves on the ground. "I made him swallow the water herbs."

Miki looked at Tibik. "How long will they take to work?"

"I don't know." Lusa watched Sheena stroking Tibik's flank.

The cub was still breathing. She could see his flank rising and falling, fast and shallow. Sheena glared at her. "What did you give him?"

"Herbs that will help," Lusa murmured, hoping it was true. She grabbed a mouthful of Miki's leaves and chewed them into a poultice. Ignoring the foul flavors washing over her tongue, she lapped them into the bee sting. Ossi was right, the pus was gone, and she could taste only fresh blood beneath the herb tang. "You and Sheena did a good job clearing the wound, Ossi," she told him as she lifted her head.

She stepped back, her heart fluttering like a captured bird. She stood between Ossi and Miki to watch Tibik. The cub wriggled and moaned as Sheena tried to soothe him with gentle licking.

Please let him be okay. Lusa stiffened with grief. Why had she gone to the trial? She should have realized how sick he was. She began to tremble. Miki pressed softly against her.

Voices sounded from higher up the slope. Cheery and loud, the other bears were returning.

Leotie came bounding into camp. "Issa found the most!"

"I found the biggest berry!" Dena announced.

"It wasn't a trial to find the biggest berry," Rudi reminded her.

Issa halted beside the nest. "What's happened?"

"Tibik's sick," Lusa replied.

The returning bears fell silent. Dustu and Dena padded over while the others retreated quietly into the trees.

Dena crouched next to Sheena. "He's a strong cub," she told the other she-bear. "He'll pull through."

Sheena didn't take her eyes from Tibik. "I can't lose him, too." As she spoke, Tibik stopped whimpering and fell still.

Lusa's heart dropped like a stone. Was he dead?

"Tibik?" Sheena touched her muzzle to his. "Tibik!"

Lusa leaned forward and sniffed the cub's fur, bracing herself for the scent of death. She saw his flank rise, then fall. He was breathing again, gently and evenly. She reached a paw toward him, already feeling less heat pulsing from his pelt.

"He's going to be okay!" Ujurak's herbs had worked! Lusa looked up at Ossi. "Can you find moss and soak it in water for him to drink?"

Ossi nodded and headed away.

Miki stepped forward and touched his nose to Lusa's ear. "You did it, Lusa. You saved him."

Lusa turned her muzzle and rubbed it happily against his. "I did, didn't I?" She breathed in Miki's warm scent. Pressing against him, she closed her eyes.

"Lusa! Shall I use lake water or stream water—"

Lusa opened her eyes and saw Ossi staring at her in dismay. She pulled away from Miki, feeling suddenly hot. Ossi turned and blundered away through the undergrowth.

Lusa watched him go. *I'm so sorry.* But how could she change what she felt?

She turned back to Tibik. Sheena was curled around her son, licking his ears. *Tibik is safe.* Nothing else should matter. She glanced at Miki. He was staring after Ossi.

Nothing else should matter, Lusa repeated to herself.

CHAPTER TWENTY-TWO

Toklo

The sun beat down on Toklo's fur as he waited for Shesh to start the final trial. He stared into the forest where the bears would be hunting, a shiver running along his spine despite the heat. Elki's wounds hadn't seemed as bad once the blood had been washed away, but she still hadn't been able to explain what had happened. Fear had haunted her eyes, and Toklo suspected that she had been frightened into silence. Wolves hadn't done this. The bears had searched the forest and found no sign. *Who could have hurt her?* Toklo scanned the shadows. Was someone watching now? Suddenly he remembered Akocha. A strange bear had frightened the cub. Was a rogue bear roaming the woods? It couldn't be Hakan, could it, still out for revenge? Toklo flexed his claws.

Aiyanna brushed against him. "Are you nervous about the hunt?"

"No," Toklo grunted.

Aiyanna followed his gaze toward the trees. "The cubs are

safe," she reminded him. "They won't wander off by themselves."

"We need to find out who hurt Elki."

"We can't do that now," Aiyanna soothed. "Focus on the hunt. If you win, you'll be leading the ceremony."

"It's not fair," Holata huffed beside him. "Akocha spoiled the fishing trial."

"I did not." Akocha marched forward, looking sulky. "I won it. Now I'm not allowed to take part in the hunt in case I win again."

Tayanita cuffed him over the ear. "You're not allowed to take part because it's not safe in the forest for cubs."

Before Akocha could argue, Shesh climbed onto a rock. "Is everyone ready?"

The brown bears grew still. Only the trees moved, swishing as the scorching wind tugged at them. Toklo shifted his paws. The strange heat seemed to signal danger. *You have made enemies, Toklo.* Ujurak's words echoed in his mind.

Shesh lifted his muzzle. "The first bear to return with prey will be the bear who leads the ceremony. . . . *Go!*"

Holata plunged forward, barging through the crowd of bears who were swarming into the forest.

Toklo hesitated and looked at Aiyanna. She had agreed to take part in this trial so that she could bring back food for the cubs. He nodded toward an inlet farther along the shore. The stone tower loomed beyond. "Let's head that way," he suggested. "There'll be no prey left in this part of the forest."

He led the way down the shore, heading into the trees as they neared the inlet. Aiyanna slid past him and vanished into the shade of the branches. Toklo followed, hoping the forest would be cooler than the sun-baked shore, but the air beneath the trees was stifling.

Aiyanna was standing beside a bramble, her ears pricked. "I see a squirrel trail," she whispered over her shoulder. "I'm going to follow it."

"Good luck." Toklo veered the other way, scanning the undergrowth for signs of life. He clambered up a slope, dry leaves crunching beneath his paws, and crossed a patch of dappled sunlight. Following a deer track, he climbed higher. As he trampled a shriveled bilberry patch, he saw movement ahead. Pausing, he narrowed his eyes. A grouse was pecking through leaf litter beneath a gnarled pine. Toklo trod more softly, avoiding a patch of ferns that would rustle if he crossed it. Excitement flickered in his belly. The scent of the grouse touched his nose. Closing in, he broke into a run and leaped.

The grouse heaved itself up and Toklo flung his paws into the flurry of wings, feeling the plumpness of its body as he knocked it to the earth. Gripping it with one paw, he killed it quickly, snapping its neck between his jaws. He couldn't hold back a bellow of triumph. If he raced back to the shore now, he was sure he would win. *I'll lead the ceremony!*

As he began to head for the lake, Aiyanna's bark rang through the trees.

"Leave me alone!"

Toklo dropped the grouse. Was it a rogue bear, as he had

wondered earlier? The same rogue bear who might have frightened Akocha and hurt Elki? He charged toward Aiyanna, fur bristling.

"Stop talking to me!" he heard her growl.

Toklo burst into a clearing. A flat-face den stood in the middle. Dry ferns and brambles smothered the dusty log walls. Aiyanna stood at one end of the den. Toklo strained to see who she was talking to, but the corner of the den blocked his view.

"You must be wrong!" Aiyanna gasped. "Toklo would never do anything like that!"

Toklo's hackles rose. Who was she talking to? What was the other bear saying?

Hakan! His thoughts flashed to the grieving black bear. It *must* be him. He'd tried to spoil the trials, and now he was telling Aiyanna they'd killed Chenoa!

Toklo charged forward. "It was an accident!" he snarled.

Aiyanna swung her muzzle toward him. Shock gleamed in her eyes. "Then it's true? You did kill them?"

Kill them? Toklo halted, confused. What was she talking about?

A scent touched his nose that turned his blood cold, and he stared in horror as a half-brown, half-white bear stepped from behind the den. It was Nanulak from the Island of Shadows. The bear Toklo had once called a friend.

"What are you doing here?" Toklo hissed.

Nanulak stared at him with pure hatred in his eyes. His mottled brown-and-white fur was ragged and coarse with leaf scraps, and there was a deep scratch above one eye, as if he had been fighting.

Beside him, Aiyanna whimpered. Toklo turned to look at her. She was gazing at him as though she hardly knew him. "You killed his family!" she whispered. "Then you left him. He nearly died."

"Is that what he told you?"

"I know your journey has been hard. I know you had to fight to survive. But did you really—"

Toklo cut her off. "Of course not! Nanulak's always been a good liar. I don't think he's ever told the truth in his life." He tried to ignore the pain jabbing at his heart. *How could Aiyanna believe I'd kill a bear's family?* "We met him on the Island of Shadows. He pretended his family had abandoned him. So we looked after him and let him travel with us. But then he tried to trick me into killing his father, who had only ever loved him!" Toklo shuddered as he remembered. Nanulak's mother—a brown bear—had come looking for her son, too, but Nanulak had turned on her, driven crazy by his belief that he didn't belong to any group of bears.

Toklo turned back to Nanulak. "You attacked Elki, didn't you? You tried to spoil the trials, not Hakan! Is that why you came?" He didn't give Nanulak a chance to answer. "Did you want to ruin the gathering for everyone? The Longest Day should be peaceful. You don't belong here. You don't belong anywhere that decent bears meet." He flexed his claws. "You have only ever hated those who love you."

Nanulak growled. "You left me! You rejected me just like

everyone else. As soon as you found out I was half-brown, half-white, you turned your tail on me!"

"That's not why I left you—" Toklo began angrily.

Nanulak raged on. "You must have known I'd hunt you down. I'm going to make you sorry you abandoned me. I thought you were different. But you're just as cruel as the others. I'm going to make you suffer like every other bear who has ever hurt me." His gaze flicked toward Aiyanna. "And when I've finished with you, I'm going to make her suffer, too."

Blind fury blazed through Toklo. Rearing, he lunged for Nanulak. The bear ducked beneath his outstretched paws and rammed his head hard into Toklo's belly. Winded, Toklo staggered backward. Dropping onto all fours, he felt a violent blow to his shoulder. For a heartbeat, his leg went numb, and he lurched against the wall of the flat-face den.

Claws raked along his side. Then he felt the weight of Nanulak on his back. Teeth sank into his neck. Panic spiraling, Toklo tried to shake him off. Backing along the side of the den, he felt the wood yield behind him, and he crashed backward through the wall.

Surprise flashed beneath his pelt as he found himself inside. Nanulak must've been surprised, too, because his grip faltered. Toklo staggered clear and swung a hefty blow at Nanulak's muzzle. Wood splintered as Nanulak crashed sideways into a pile of flat-face clutter. Toklo hit him again, feeling flesh rip beneath his claws.

With a roar, Nanulak turned on him. He reared up and gripped Toklo's head with his front paws. Wrestling, they lurched across the den. Toklo grabbed Nanulak's throat between his jaws and heaved with his hind legs until Nanulak began to stumble. Toklo tasted the salt tang of blood and bit harder. Roaring with pain, Nanulak swung him around with strength Toklo had never felt in a bear before. Unbalanced, he let go and fell onto something hot and jagged with a bright light inside. Pain seared Toklo's flank, and he glanced around to see flames leaping beside him. The fire caught some pelts fluttering beside an opening in the wooden wall and bloomed like huge yellow flowers.

Toklo swung his gaze back to Nanulak. The brown-and-white bear was staring in horror as the fire licked the wood above his head. Turning, he fled toward the opening. Toklo raced after him, crunching over the shattered flat-face mess.

As he burst from the den, he saw Nanulak push past Aiyanna and flee into the forest. Behind Toklo, flames started to reach through the opening, lapping hungrily at the dry wooden walls.

"What happened?" Aiyanna stared past him toward the den.

"We spilled fire on the ground!" Toklo nosed Aiyanna toward the trees. Pain throbbed where Nanulak had torn his pelt. Toklo knew that in a moment the flames would touch the dried ferns and brambles and spread faster than they could run. Blood roared in his ears as he chased after Aiyanna.

"Keep going!" he roared as an explosion ripped through the air behind him.

CHAPTER TWENTY-THREE

Kallik

A loud blast echoed from the pine-covered hillside.

"What was that?" Kallik lifted her head from the fish she was sharing with Yakone.

Beside her, Yakone tensed. "It sounded like a huge firestick."

Kallik narrowed her eyes. Smoke was rising from the trees at the top of the slope. Then she glimpsed flames leaping through the branches.

The hot wind, whipping fiercely down to the lake, tugged at Kallik's fur. She saw the fire flare and brighten. Horror hollowed her belly as she watched flames spring from treetop to treetop, growing taller as the wind drove them toward the shore. The scent of smoke touched her nose. "We have to get out of here!"

Farther along the shore, the brown bears were watching the fire, too. Barking with alarm, they backed toward the water. Suddenly Kallik saw Toklo and Aiyanna burst from the trees near the edge of the white bears' territory. Terror shone in their eyes.

"Get the others into the water!" Kallik ordered Yakone. Smoke was starting to gust over the shore. It stung her eyes as she swung her muzzle toward the nearest island. "Tell everyone to head there!"

"Quick! Everyone! We have to swim!"

As Yakone began to bark at the others, Kallik raced toward Toklo.

"It was Nanulak!" Toklo snarled. "He's here! We fought in a flat-face den. It caught fire."

"Nanulak?" Kallik could hear the flames now. They were swallowing the forest, as hungry as wolves. She stared at Toklo in panic. "Have you seen Lusa?"

"No!"

Aiyanna was staring at the trees. The fire was roaring closer and closer to the shore.

"The black bears will be heading for the lake." Toklo blinked against the smoke billowing from the trees. "I'll go see if they need help."

"Wait!" Aiyanna jerked her muzzle toward the brown bears. Panicked, they were crashing into one another as they backed into the shallows. "Can you see Wapi and Yas? Where's Flo? I can't see Flo!"

"Kissimi!" Illa's terrified wail sounded from the white bears' shore.

Kallik turned and saw Illa darting back and forth at the edge of the lake. Clouds of smoke rolled over the rocks. Through the choking darkness, Kallik glimpsed a small white shape charging for the tower. *Kissimi!*

Flames raced down the hillside toward the great stone den. Kallik pelted toward it, barking at Kissimi. "Get away! Go back to Illa!" As a gust of wind cleared the smoke for a moment, she glimpsed his terrified face. He was bolting, panic-stricken, his gaze fixed on the tower.

Kallik ran harder as Kissimi scrambled up the rocks toward the opening at the bottom of the tower. As he disappeared inside, her heart lurched. "Kissimi! No!"

The roar of the flames drowned Kallik's cry. She leaped the rocks and climbed over the scrubby grass surrounding the tower. Her eyes streamed as smoke engulfed her, but she blundered her way to the opening. Stone walls scraped her sides as she heaved herself in. Steep steps curved upward in front of her. Kissimi was vanishing around the first bend.

"Come down!" Kallik's voice echoed up the tower. But the cub kept running. Kallik charged after him, her heart bursting with fear each time she passed a gap in the wall and saw the fire rolling down the hillside toward them. Her chest roared as she climbed. "Kissimi! Stop!" She stumbled on a step. Pain shot through her paw, but she ignored it and kept climbing.

Looking up, she saw Kissimi disappear through an opening at the very top of the tower. *He'll fall!* Terror pulsed in her paws as she followed him out through the square gap at the end of the steps. "Stop!"

Kissimi turned and stared at her, smoke billowing over him. Behind him a short wall stood between him and the long, long drop to the ground.

"We can't stay here!" Kallik barked. The flames were so

close she could feel their heat, driven by the wind. She glanced over her shoulder at the brown bears down on the shore. Toklo and Aiyanna were herding cubs toward their mothers. The others crowded in the shallows. Some were swimming toward a cluster of rocks a little way out.

In the white bears' part of the water, bears were plunging into the lake and striking out for deeper water. Near the shore, Yakone stood belly-deep, barking encouragement as the others streamed past him. Anarteq and Kunik hung back, circling anxiously. Taqqiq and Shila paced behind them, their pelts spiked in fear, while Illa was staring toward the tower. Kallik wondered if Illa could see her and Kissimi through the smoke.

Where are the black bears? She searched the forest where the pines gave way to birch and spruce. The flames were closing in on every side, but there was no sign of the black bears on the shore.

"We can't stay here!" Kallik repeated, leaning forward and snatching Kissimi's scruff between her jaws. Swinging him toward the opening, she began to carry him down the steps. He was heavy, no longer the tiny cub she'd carried on the Endless Ice, and Kallik's neck pulsed with the strain.

"Don't take me down! There's fire outside!" Kissimi whimpered.

It'll be inside before long. As Kallik's flanks scraped the walls, she could feel heat through the stone. Kissimi howled as she bumped him against a step. *I'm sorry! But we have to get away!*

Stumbling to the bottom, she saw flames licking the

entrance. Smoke billowed beyond, hiding the lake and the trees. Kallik took a deep breath around her mouthful of Kissimi's fur and closed her eyes. Then she put her head down and charged through the fire, stumbling over the rocks, feeling thorns scrape her pelt. Kissimi swung and jerked in her jaws. Kallik fought to keep her balance and kept going. The acrid stench of burnt fur touched her nose.

The rocks and bushes under her paws gave way to pebbles. Kallik opened her eyes. She had made it to the shore. Behind her, the tower filled with flame, bright-orange tongues leaping from the gaps in the wall. Kallik dropped Kissimi with a grunt. Blinking away tears from the smoke, she checked him for burns. Soot smeared his white fur, but she couldn't see any singed pelt. She glanced along her own flank and saw patches of her fur blackened at the tips. But it didn't hurt. She was okay.

"Where's Illa?" Kissimi wailed.

"Waiting by the water."

The cub jumped up and tore across the stones. "Illa!" he howled.

Kallik followed him, reaching the edge of the lake as Kissimi buried his snout in Illa's flank. Hardly hearing Illa's bark of gratitude, Kallik raced toward Yakone. She stopped beside him, her flanks heaving. Most of the bears were swimming now, heading for the island. Aside from her and Yakone, only Anarteq, Kunik, Taqqiq, Shila, Illa, and Kissimi remained on land.

"They're too old to swim that far." Yakone nodded toward

Anarteq and Kunik. "Not in this smoke." He coughed as another cloud billowed over them. Embers sparked in it, hissing as they hit the water.

Kallik looked at the bears. Kissimi trembled beside Illa. He was too shaken to risk the long swim, and she knew Illa wouldn't leave without him. "Let's take them to the brown bears' territory," Kallik suggested. "We might be able to get them to those rocks near the shore." Most of the brown bears were swimming for the rocks now, but a few lingered on the beach. Aiyanna was among them, huddling close to a group of cubs.

Kallik nodded to Shila and Taqqiq. "Head for the island!"

Taqqiq shook his head. "I'm not leaving without you."

Kallik blinked at him. "But you need to get away—"

Shila stepped forward. "We'll swim to the island when everyone is safe."

There was no time to tell Taqqiq and Shila how much this meant to her. "Come on, then." Kallik headed for the group of brown bears. Toklo was emerging from the trees.

"There's no sign of the black bears!" he called.

Yakone scowled. "Where are they?"

Kallik didn't want to imagine. She herded Anarteq, Kunik, Illa, and Kissimi toward the brown bears. Aiyanna and another female hurried to meet them.

"Some of the bears are too weak to swim," Aiyanna barked.

Like the white bears, it was the oldest and youngest brown bears who were trapped on the shore. But at least they were out of the forest. Kallik's heart lurched as she thought about

Lusa. "Get them as far into the water as you can." She nosed Anarteq, Kunik, Illa, and Kissimi toward Aiyanna. "Take these bears, too. Toklo and I have to find Lusa and the other black bears."

Aiyanna shook her head. "I'm coming with you." She turned to the female beside her. "Izusa, you heard what she said. Take them as deep as you can."

Izusa stared at her. "Where are you going?"

"We have to help the black bears." Without waiting for a response, Aiyanna started running up the shore toward Toklo.

Kallik turned to follow Aiyanna. She felt Yakone's flank brush hers and leaned against it for a moment. Ahead of them, smoke rolled in thick black waves from the trees. Kallik could see fire illuminating the shadows inside. Somewhere in there, Lusa was fighting for her life.

If she was still alive.

CHAPTER TWENTY-FOUR

Lusa

Lusa stared in terror at the flames licking at the edge of the clearing. The fire had come so fast. They hadn't known which way to run. And now it was too late. She spun around, searching for a way out, but the fire was on every side. "We're trapped!" she whispered to Miki. Another cloud of smoke drifted through the trees before the wind swirled down between the burning branches. The fire roared louder. The trees screeched, hissing steam. Lusa shuddered. Was that the shrieking of spirits as the fire clawed at them?

"We're going to die!" Dena pelted past her, racing toward a patch of brambles, then veering away as flames crackled behind it. On the far side of the clearing, Hakan grabbed a cub by its scruff and carried it to its mother, his eyes wild with panic. Leotie cowered in the middle of the camp, whimpering, while Dustu stared around, wide-eyed.

"This is how it ends," he murmured.

"No!" Miki nosed him backward, away from the wall of heat. "There has to be a way out."

"Hashi's tree!" Lusa gasped. "He'll protect us!" She raced to Tibik's nest, but Sheena had already hauled the weak cub onto her back.

"I've got him," Sheena grunted.

"Take him to Hashi's tree!" Lusa ordered. "Chula, you must come with us."

Chula stared up at her with terrified eyes. "I can't run!" She flinched as a burning tree creaked behind her.

Ossi raced past Lusa and leaped into Chula's nest. Shoving his shoulder beneath Chula's, he started to boost her to her paws. Behind them, the tree began to lurch.

"Look out!" Miki roared.

Ossi lunged forward, pushing Chula ahead of him. The tree snapped and crashed down into the nest where Chula had been lying one heartbeat earlier. A few flaming branches broke off and rolled across the clearing.

"All of you, head for Hashi's tree!" Lusa barked. She began to herd the frightened black bears downslope. There was a stretch of unburned forest ahead. The bears streamed through it.

Lusa felt Miki's pelt brush hers as she raced after the others. "We might be able to get to the lake from Hashi's tree." She looked hopefully at the strong pine, which towered into the smoke-gray sky. Her heart sank as orange flames leaped up behind it.

"We'll find a way out," Miki growled.

The bears clustered beneath Hashi's tree, hiding their faces from the heat. Lusa pushed between them and reared up, pressing her forepaws against the bark. "Protect us, Hashi!

Hala, save us!" Perhaps the two spirits could keep the flames at bay.

Lifting her snout, Lusa stared in horror as she saw the tips of the branches catch light. A moment later, fire flashed through the tree as the needles flared like dry grass. There was a deafening roar as though Hashi's spirit was raging against the destruction.

"Get away from here!" Lusa shrieked.

Dena stared at her. "We'll be safe here! It's Hashi's tree!"

Panic surged in Lusa's chest. "The tree is going to fall!" She began to shove the bears away, nosing at them fiercely and rearing up with her paws to push them clear. The bark whined and crackled above them.

"Hurry!" Miki began to push, too, steering the bears toward the small clearing beside the tree.

Dustu pressed against the trunk of the pine as flames roared above his head. "Hashi will protect us," he insisted.

"Not from this!" Pokkoli grabbed the old bear's scruff between his teeth and began to haul him away.

Surprise flashed in Dustu's gaze as his paws slithered over the earth. "But Hashi won't let us die."

The pine creaked ominously.

Pokkoli grunted with effort as he dragged Dustu toward the clearing and shoved him toward the bears already crowding into the small space. Then he stumbled. The tree cracked behind him. The top snapped and hurtled down.

Chula shrieked as it smashed, flaming, onto Pokkoli.

No! Lusa rushed forward. Teeth snagged her haunches.

Miki dragged her back. "You can't save him."

Lusa stared in horror at the burning pine. Pokkoli was hidden by the fiery branches. There was nothing she could do. Lusa turned her head away, burying her muzzle in Miki's neck. Were they all going to die?

Miki jerked away. "Look!"

Lusa followed his gaze. Shapes moved beyond the burning trees between the clearing and the lake, looming brown and sharp white through the smoke. "Toklo! Kallik!" Yakone was with them, and Aiyanna. They'd come to save the black bears.

"Lusa!" Kallik's roar sounded above the fire. "Are you there?"

"I'm here!" she called back. "We're all here!" She could see the white bear racing back and forth beyond the flames.

Toklo reared up, peering over the burning brambles. "There's no way through!"

As he spoke, a mighty bellow sounded through the trees. Lusa spun around. A massive creature was striding through the flames toward them, unflinching as burning branches tumbled around it. As it drew nearer, Lusa made out vast antlers trailing fronds of fire.

"What is an *elk* doing here?" Miki rasped.

Lusa felt a pool of calm spread through her. She looked into the eyes of the elk, past the flames reflected in the dark-brown depths. "Ujurak?" she whispered.

The elk turned away and strode toward a burning spruce. It lowered its head and braced its mighty antlers against the trunk. Lusa could see the elk's muscles straining beneath its skin. The spruce creaked, then slowly tipped over, its roots lifting as it toppled.

Flames licked around the elk, but it didn't seem to feel them. No fire caught its fur, no soot colored its pelt. Lifting its head, it moved to the next tree, then braced its antlers against the trunk and pushed until, groaning, the flaming birch crashed down.

"He's clearing a path!" Ossi gasped.

Lusa watched, her heart swelling with joy. *Thank you, Ujurak!*

A third tree fell. Toklo bounded into the space it created. Behind him, the lake gleamed.

"Quick!" Lusa turned to the bears around her. "Run through the gap!"

The fire bellowed as the wind rose. Lusa's throat burned as heat and smoke swirled around her. She felt a shoulder press against her and let herself be guided forward. "Are the others coming?" she coughed.

"Everyone's running for the shore." Miki's voice sounded close to her ear.

Her eyes streaming, Lusa stumbled forward until she felt the earth turn to pebbles beneath her paws. As the air cooled around her, she turned. Toklo, Kallik, and Yakone were guiding the black bears through the gap. Behind them, framed against the flaming forest, stood the mighty elk.

"Thank you!" Lusa called as Ujurak turned and galloped into the inferno.

"Lusa!" Kallik raced to her side, pressing close. "Are you hurt?"

Lusa was aware of her flanks stinging beneath scorched fur. "I'm fine." She met Kallik's gaze. "Did Chula escape? And Tibik?"

Kallik nodded toward the water. The black bears were plunging into the shallows. Only Pokkoli was missing.

At the top of the beach, the forest erupted in flame. Smoke billowed onto the shore. Lusa coughed, feeling a sharp pain in her chest. They couldn't stay here while the forest burned. The smoke would choke them. She looked at the islands dotted in the lake. White bears and brown bears stood on the island shores, staring back across the water. *Could we swim that far?*

Toklo lifted his head. "I think I know where we'll be safe," he growled. Turning, he began to trek along the shore. "Follow me."

CHAPTER TWENTY-FIVE

Toklo

Toklo headed for the white and brown bears still gathered in the shallows. Through the smoke billowing from the forest, he spotted Shesh, Izusa, and Makya with Flo, Fala, Wapi, and Yas. Tayanita was there, too, with Akocha. They watched him approach, their eyes round with fear.

Along the tree line, flame crackled through great swathes of dark smoke. Flecks of fire whirled in the wind, hissing as they touched the water. Toklo fought down the panic that swirled inside him. He had to get these bears to safety.

Aiyanna's voice broke into his thoughts. "I'll go help Izusa and Makya with their cubs. They'll be frightened."

As she ran ahead, she passed Tayanita, who bounded over to Toklo with Akocha at her heels. "What are we going to do?"

"Can we stand in the water until the fire stops?" Akocha asked.

Toklo shook his head. "The smoke will choke us." He leaned closer to the young bear. "Do you remember our secret place?"

Akocha's gaze flashed toward the far side of the lake. The

fire hadn't reached there yet but was roaring toward it. He nodded. "The waterfall?"

"That's right. I think we should go there. We'll have to walk through the forest, but if we hurry, we can beat the flames."

Tayanita stared at him. *Walk through the forest?* Disbelief glittered in her eyes.

"I know a place we'll be safe until the fire passes," Toklo told her.

The black bears were streaming past him now. The others shifted to make room for them in the shallows.

Tayanita watched them gather around her. "There are cubs and elders here. Do you really think we can outrun a fire?"

"If we start now, we can make it," Toklo urged. He hoped he was right. Padding past Tayanita, he stopped in front of the throng of frightened bears. "We can't ask you all to swim to safety," he called. "But I know somewhere we can hide!"

Hopeful murmurs rippled through the crowd.

Toklo went on. "But we must walk through the trees, ahead of the fire." He nodded to the far side of the lake.

"We can't go back into the forest!" Anarteq growled.

Kallik stood beside the old bear. "Toklo says we'll make it if we keep moving." She blinked at Toklo. "If he says it, it must be true."

Toklo stared back at her. Did he really deserve such trust?

Muna turned in an anxious circle. "Elki can't walk. She's still hurt."

"Holata can carry her." Toklo looked around. Where was Elki's father? Where was Elsu? Only Elki was with Muna, leaning against her flank, her wounds showing through her wet fur.

Muna nodded toward the cluster of rocks. "Holata took Elsu. I stayed with Elki."

Toklo dipped his head. Sometimes splitting up meant the best chance of survival. "Then you must carry her as far as you can," he told her. "If you get tired, others will help."

He didn't wait for a response. She had no choice. None of them did. He glanced around the bears. "Will you come with me?"

Taqqiq stepped forward. "If Kallik says we can trust you, then I'm coming."

"Me too." Shila nodded.

"Lusa?" Toklo looked at his friend. "Can the black bears do this?"

Lusa lifted her muzzle. "Black bears were born to walk through forests."

Grunts of agreement sounded from her camp-mates.

Toklo's fur prickled along his spine. "We should leave now." He turned, flinching against the blast of heat from the blazing forest. He forced himself to walk slowly. There were injured and elderly bears to think of. If he just kept them moving, they could beat the flames.

He heard Kallik's voice behind him. "Up you go, Tibik. You can ride on Yakone's back." He glanced over his shoulder and saw her boost a young black bear onto Yakone's shoulders. "Hold on tight," she urged.

Aiyanna was carrying Yas while Izusa and Makya walked

beside her, their cubs pressing close.

Pawsteps crunched on the stones as Shesh caught up to Toklo. "Oogrook was right about you," the old bear murmured. "You caught that salmon for a reason. You were destined for this."

Toklo grunted. "Let's decide that after I get us to safety."

They reached the trees. The fire was burning steadily around the curve of the lake, but the forest here was still green and unscorched. The wind was driving the smoke out across the water, leaving clear air. Toklo breathed the musty scent of the forest, his heart twisting. Even if the bears made it to the waterfall, he knew the fire would come. Was this the last time he'd smell the lush fragrance of leaves and moss?

He paused, looking back. A few black bears were straggling, but Kallik had stopped to hurry them on. He waited for them to catch up before heading into the trees. Fear was heavy in his belly. Would he remember the way to the waterfall in time to beat the fire?

"Lean against me."

Toklo heard Shesh's rasping growl behind him. He glanced back and saw the brown male press his shoulder against an old white bear's flank. Behind them, he saw Muna stumble. Elki was clinging to her back, but the she-bear looked exhausted. Toklo lifted his muzzle. "Will you carry Elki?" he called to Kallik.

Kallik was walking beside Illa, encouraging Kissimi to keep moving with small nudges of her muzzle. She looked up as he spoke, but it was Taqqiq who hurried forward.

"I'll carry her," the white male offered.

Muna's eyes shone with relief. "Thank you," she croaked as Taqqiq crouched beside her. Dropping her shoulder, Muna let her cub slither onto the white bear's back.

"I'll walk beside you," she promised Elki. "I'll make sure you don't fall."

"I won't fall," Elki barked. "There's lots of room here." She wriggled into the thick fur between Taqqiq's shoulder blades.

Toklo pushed on, following a deer track he thought he recognized. The ground sloped up, and as it grew steeper, he smelled smoke. He heard the roar of flames. He peered through the trees, his heart lurching as he glimpsed a bright-orange glow in the distance.

"We must hurry!" he called over his shoulder. He veered off the path, suddenly unsure where to go. The river was beyond a ridge, but which ridge? The forest seemed to slope in every direction here.

Small pawsteps pattered behind him. He turned to see Akocha hurrying toward him.

"It's this way!" the young bear barked. "I remember that tree stump." Akocha cut across the slope, clambering over a fallen tree, and raced to where a mossy lump of wood stood beside a deer track. "This track takes us straight to the top of the rise. The river's just beyond it."

Toklo stared at Akocha. "Well remembered!" As hope flickered in his heart, smoke rolled between the trees.

He heard wood crackle. Behind him, frightened growls rose from the bears. He turned and saw flame moving like a wave toward them.

"We're nearly there!" he urged. "Akocha, show them the way!"

Akocha bounced past him. "We're going to make it, aren't we?"

"Of course." Toklo tried to sound convincing, but smoke was stinging his eyes. The crackle had become a roar, and he could feel the first heat of the flames as they raced closer. He stood beside the mossy stump, shooing the bears past. "Climb to the top of the rise and head down to the river," he told them.

Following, Toklo reached the top as Shesh and the old white bear disappeared through the undergrowth beyond. Lusa, Kallik, and Yakone plunged down the slope after them, Akocha at their heels. Toklo felt relief wash over his pelt. They had reached the valley where the river cut through the woods. Trees grew thickly on the slope, and undergrowth spilled down to the river's edge.

Aiyanna was waiting for Toklo as he reached the bank. She touched her muzzle to his cheek.

Toklo noticed the empty space on her shoulders. "Where's Yas?"

"She wanted to walk the last part." Aiyanna glanced toward the trees. The roar of the fire was so close that she had to raise her voice. Smoke billowed over the ridge and rolled down to the river. "We *are* nearly there, aren't we?"

Toklo looked upstream, but trees and brambles blocked his view. "I think so." As he spoke, he heard a rumble. He recognized it at once. Not the roar of the flames, but the thundering of water. "The falls!" Breaking into a run, he pushed past the bushes and saw the waterfall tumbling into the pool where the river widened.

The other bears were standing on the edge of the pool, staring at the tumbling water.

Shesh looked confused. "Is this the place?" Ash fluttered down onto his patchy fur. The hiss and crackle of green wood sounded just beyond the ridge.

"There's a cave behind it!" Toklo barked. "Quick! Get into the water."

"I'll show them!" Akocha leaped into the pool.

The black bears teetered at the edge, half falling, half jumping as the others pushed from behind. Shesh jumped in clumsily. Ossi guided Chula farther along the bank, where it was less crowded, then helped her slither into the water and followed her.

"I can't swim!" Yas wailed.

"That's okay. I won't let you drown!" Miki scooped Yas up by his scruff and bounded in.

Muna hurried to Taqqiq's side. Elki was still clinging to the white bear's back. "Hold on tight, Elki!" Muna panted.

"Don't worry," Taqqiq told her. "I'll keep her safe." Carefully he eased his front paws down the steep bank and slid into the water. Muna plunged in after him, her gaze fixed on Elki.

On the far side of the pool, Akocha disappeared beneath the wall of water. The other bears ducked in after him.

Pain jabbed like claws into Toklo's back as embers scorched his pelt. He turned to Yakone, Lusa, Aiyanna, and Kallik. They were the only ones left on shore. "We'll be safe once we reach the cave." He had to bellow to be heard over the roar of the flames. Heat blasted over him. He glanced up the slope behind them.

A shape had appeared at the top.

Toklo narrowed his eyes. Had they left someone behind? Then he recognized the outline.

Nanulak!

Flames illuminated the brown-and-white bear.

Yakone growled beside Toklo.

"He's back!" Aiyanna gasped.

"Get into the water," Toklo ordered. "It's me Nanulak has come for."

A few bearlengths upstream, a tree toppled and bounced down the slope. It crashed into the water with a hiss. "Go!" Toklo barked.

As Lusa, Kallik, and Yakone scrambled down the steep bank, Aiyanna pressed against him. "Don't leave me now," she whispered.

"I won't." Toklo nudged her away and climbed toward Nanulak. The heat of the fire scorched his face. He stopped a muzzle-length away. "You attacked your own family, Nanulak," he growled. "You betrayed everyone who loved you. You can't blame me for what happened."

Nanulak curled his lip. "I thought you were my friend. But as soon as you learned that my father was a white bear, you hated me just like everyone else."

"That's not true," Toklo shouted over the hissing of the fire. "You lied to me from the start. You betrayed our friendship.

You've done terrible things, Nanulak. Stop blaming everyone else!"

With a roar, Nanulak shoved Toklo backward.

Toklo slid down the slope, brambles tearing his belly fur. As he found his paws, mottled fur flashed ahead of him. Pain seared his cheek as Nanulak ripped into him with a swiping blow. Toklo lashed out with a forepaw, swinging it hard against Nanulak's muzzle. Nanulak staggered but regained his footing and leaped at Toklo. Rearing, they clashed together, their chests thumping. Smoke swirled around them, stinging Toklo's eyes. Barely able to see, he grappled desperately with Nanulak, his hindpaws slipping on the muddy bank.

Teeth sank into his shoulder. He swung his head, knocking his skull against Nanulak's with such force that Nanulak let go. Flames flashed at the edge of his vision as a burning branch crashed down beside them. "Get into the water, Aiyanna!" Toklo roared. He could see her hanging back, her eyes streaming as smoke swirled around her. *"Now!"*

As she plunged in, Nanulak swiped at Toklo again. Toklo ducked, pain searing through his paw as he trod on the smoldering branch. Nanulak's claws dug into his back. He whipped around, shaking the brown-and-white bear off, and dove beneath his belly. Pushing up with all his might, he flung Nanulak backward. Nanulak staggered. His hindpaw slid off the bank. Flailing wildly, he fell into the water.

A crack rang through the hot air. Toklo raced to the edge and leaned over. Nanulak lay still, his body limp in the ash-speckled water, his head bleeding where he had hit a jagged rock.

Toklo froze.

"Watch out!" Aiyanna barked from the pool.

He glanced over his shoulder. Fire was swarming down the slope. Its heat seared his muzzle. Heart lurching, Toklo hurled himself into the water beside Nanulak.

"Leave him, Toklo!" Aiyanna's teeth sank into his scruff, and she tried to haul him away.

"But he'll burn!"

Aiyanna let go and stared at Toklo. "So what?"

"He was my friend once!"

"He's your enemy now!"

As Aiyanna stared at him in disbelief, another burning tree rolled down the bank. It hit the water with a crash. Fire spat from the trunk and stung Toklo's muzzle. Bristling with shock, Toklo pushed Aiyanna backward as flaming twigs showered around them. The tree had cut across the pool between him and Nanulak.

How could he reach the brown-and-white bear now?

Aiyanna splashed the water in terror. "If we stay here, we'll die!"

Toklo stared at the burning tree, grief scorching his heart as he pictured Nanulak behind it. *I can't save you.* Determination charged through his pelt. *But I can save Aiyanna.*

"Hurry!" He hurled himself toward the falls and dragged Aiyanna with him as he ducked beneath the crashing water. Hugging her tight, he let the current tumble them to safety as behind them the fire surrounded the river in a wall of flame.

CHAPTER TWENTY-SIX

Kallik

Kallik huddled closer to Yakone. "Will the rain stop the fire?"

Yakone gazed through the shimmering wall of water as thunder rumbled outside. "I think so," he murmured.

The storm had begun in the night, lightning outshining the flame beyond the hazy falls. The bears had huddled at the back of the cave when the rain started, and it wasn't until the sun had begun to sink that the hiss of embers finally died and the bears were able to emerge from behind the waterfall and swim back across the pool to the forest.

Now, Kallik walked among the others in silence. Like them, she had no words as she crunched over the charred debris of what had once been a forest. *Their* forest. This land had belonged to the bears. And fire had destroyed it.

A fine drizzle still darkened the far side of the lake, but here late sunshine was breaking through the clouds. Blackened tree stumps stretched along the hillsides. Ash covered the beach. The acrid smell of charred wood filled Kallik's nose. The only glimpse of green was in the distance.

As they neared the shore, Lusa brushed Kallik's flank. "We'll be leaving after the ceremony."

Of course! Today is the Longest Day! "Then these are our last moments together." Kallik scanned the mass of pelts for Toklo's. He had reached the spot where brown bears were wading from the shore. They'd begun swimming as soon as the others had emerged from the blackened remains of the forest. The white bears who'd found refuge on the islands were already out of the water and trekking toward the brown bears' shore.

Kallik walked closer to Lusa, wanting to feel her soft pelt for a little longer. She could hardly believe that in the coming moons, she would wake up every day without her friends. *At least I have Yakone.* Who would Lusa have? "Will you be okay?" she asked. "By yourself, I mean."

"I won't be by myself," Lusa promised. "I've made friends here."

Kallik touched her nose to Lusa's head, hoping that the little black bear would always be as loved as she had been on her journey.

Toklo and Shesh had climbed onto a wide, flat rock. They were talking quietly with Kunik and Anarteq as the others caught up.

"Come on." Izusa shooed Wapi and Yas toward the water. "Let's wash the soot from our fur." She waded in behind them.

Kallik saw tension ease from the brown bear's shoulders as water washed around her paws. Before long, she was splashing Yas and Wapi playfully. As the cubs barked with delight, the others began to join them. Illa waded in with Kissimi, and soon most of the bears from the cave were rolling in the water, rinsing the ash from their pelts.

Kallik leaned against Yakone. "We survived." The forest behind her had been destroyed, but the lake rippled toward the horizon, darkened by ash and dotted with burnt branches and splintered wood. The forest would grow back. In seasons to come, the fire would become no more than a story.

Yakone rubbed his muzzle along her cheek. "We survived *together*. We all did."

Kallik saw his gaze flit toward Toklo. Aiyanna had joined him on the rock. Warmth filled Kallik's heart as she watched the pair lean closer. "Do you think she's a good match for him, Yakone?"

"Yes." Yakone pressed against her. "Like you are for me."

Shesh lifted his head and barked to the crowd. "It is time for the Longest Day ceremony."

"Who will lead us?" Izusa called.

Hattack pushed his way to the front. "The trials didn't decide a winner."

"Do we need bears to lead us?" asked Illa, raising her damp white head.

Taqqiq stepped to the edge of the rock. "We survived because we joined together and helped each other. We should perform the ceremony together."

Several bears murmured in agreement.

"No!" Salik shouldered his way from the crowd. "It's never been done that way."

Hattack was nodding. "We should celebrate separately as we've always done."

"Black bears have never celebrated with white bears and brown bears," Rudi grunted.

Yakone's muzzle brushed Kallik's ear fur. "At least they agree on something," he murmured.

"No." Toklo was standing beside Shesh, his shoulders braced as if he was ready for battle. "We must celebrate together."

Hattack frowned and dropped his gaze. Salik stomped from the lake, scowling.

As Rudi looked away, Dena stepped forward. "This Longest Day is different from the others," she rasped.

"We should give thanks together," Illa called from the water.

Barks of agreement rose from the groups, and the bears shuffled into a wide arc around the stretch of rock where Shesh and Toklo stood beside Aiyanna, Anarteq, Kunik, and Dustu.

Toklo beckoned Hattack to join them. "Will you help say the words for our ceremony?"

Hattack narrowed his eyes for a moment, then padded forward. Taking his place beside Toklo, he began. "This lake has been here since the time before bears. It was a cold and barren place. The wind swept over it, snow and rain and sunlight fell onto the ground, but no creatures dared live here."

"Then the Great Bear Arcturus came this way." As Shesh took up the next part of the story, Kallik noticed Lusa leaning against a black bear. She recognized Miki, the young male who had dozed beside Lusa in the cave while they waited for the fire and the storm to leave. Miki was whispering into Lusa's ear. Lusa blinked at him, her eyes lighting up. Kallik's heart pricked with hope. Had Lusa found more than just friendship among the black bears?

Toklo was speaking now. "And ever since then, we bears have taken this lake for our own, and every suncircle, on the Longest Day, we return and give thanks to his spirit."

Kallik felt a nudge from Yakone. Anarteq was staring at her. "Join us, Kallik," he called.

She glanced at Yakone. Pride warmed his gaze. "Go," he urged.

Her pelt spiked self-consciously as she climbed onto the rock. Toklo caught her eye as she took her place beside him. "This is quite an ending to our journey," he whispered.

Anarteq began the white bears' ceremony. "Sun, we welcome you on this, the Longest Day. Hear my words. Your reign is ending. From now on, the dark will return at the end of each day, bringing with it snow and ice, and striking stillness into the melted ice."

Kunik went on. "White bears will be able to return to their feeding grounds once more. Bear spirits, bring back the dark, so that you may shine again in your tiny fragments of ice." He nodded to Kallik.

Raising her eyes to the darkening sky, she sought out the first glimmering star. "Drive the sun lower in the sky, so that we can honor you from our ancient home on the ice." She looked at Yakone. *Our home on the ice.* Was he thinking of Star

Island, too, their home for the rest of their moons together?

Dustu nodded to Lusa. "I think you should lead our ceremony." His gaze flicked around the others. "Without Lusa, many would have not survived the accident with the firebeast. She and her white and brown friends saved us from the fire. The power to heal, the power to trust, the power to make friends—all these are mightier than the greatest strength."

Surprise flickered in Lusa's eyes. She stared around, until Miki nosed her forward.

Lusa climbed onto the rock beside Dustu and looked across the lake. "Thank you, spirits of the trees, for the long days of sun that have brought us berries and leaves and warmed the earth so that grubs could grow." She kept her gaze on the water, avoiding the charred stumps encircling the lake.

Suddenly a fresh breeze whisked in from the lake, sweeping away the stench of the burnt forest, bringing instead the scent of distant pines.

Dustu lifted his muzzle, the wind rippling through his fur. "The spirits have heard us and replied."

Lusa peered at the old black bear. "Does that mean they are safe in new homes?"

"I think it does."

The black bears chuffed happily to one another.

"I wonder where Hashi is?" Ossi's voice rose above the others.

Sheena stared hopefully into the distance. "He's found a new place with Hala, where they can watch over the lake forever."

Anarteq stepped to the water's edge and faced the bears. "At the last Longest Day, we were all hungry, all fighting to survive. We survived the last suncircle, and now the fire. And we will keep on surviving, because we have no other choice. But perhaps survival is not enough on its own. Perhaps we should remember the power of friendship. We cannot live our lives separate from all the other living things—either prey or bears." Anarteq dipped his head. "Go in peace, friends."

Kallik watched the bears shift, drifting apart like clouds blown by the wind.

Lusa jumped down onto the pebbles. "I'll be back in a moment!" she promised Kallik.

Only Toklo and Aiyanna remained beside her.

"I guess we're all going home now," Toklo grunted.

Kallik jerked her gaze toward him. This couldn't be the end. Not now! She wasn't ready. Anger flared beneath her pelt. "How can you sound so calm about it?"

Toklo met her gaze, and she saw grief in his eyes, so sharp that she felt guilty at her outburst. He would feel their parting as sharply as she did.

"Toklo!" Akocha bounded toward the rock. "I want to come home with you!"

Aiyanna blinked at the cub. "What about your poor mother? What will she do without you?"

Akocha looked at her gravely. "She makes too many rules. I can never remember them all, and I'm always breaking them."

Toklo nuzzled the young bear's ear. "You need to listen to her rules and learn as much as you can. She's teaching you how to grow up into a strong, brave bear."

"Like you?"

"Just like Toklo," Aiyanna agreed.

"Akocha!" Tayanita was calling from farther up the shore, where the brown bears were gathering, ready to leave.

Akocha jumped down. "See you next suncircle!" he called over his shoulder. Aiyanna followed him, shooing him toward Tayanita.

Yakone joined them on the rock. He nodded toward Lusa, who was standing beside Miki. Kallik could hear their soft growls.

"You're really coming home with me?" Miki asked.

"Of course!" Lusa gazed at him happily. Then her gaze darkened as Ossi approached.

Miki turned to greet him, but Ossi spoke first. "You're a lucky bear, Miki."

Miki dipped his head. "I know."

"Good luck to you both." He turned toward Chula, Rudi, Sheena, and Tibik, who were waiting for him at the edge of the blackened forest. "See you next time," he called over his shoulder.

Kallik noticed that the Star Island bears were gathering at the water's edge. Kissimi was wading in the shallows, slapping his paws down as he tried to catch the tiny fish that flitted there.

"I think they're waiting for us," Kallik whispered to Yakone.

Lusa scrambled onto the rock, and the four bears stood in silence for a moment, muzzles close.

"Time to leave," Lusa whispered.

Toklo's eyes clouded. "We've seen more than any bears will ever see."

"We swam with orca," Kallik murmured, the memory so fresh in her mind it seemed like only yesterday.

"We learned to ride the currents in the Big River." Lusa's eyes shone.

"You saved my life." Yakone stared fondly at Lusa before lifting his gaze to the others. "You all did."

"We saved each other more times than I can count," Toklo growled.

A lump swelled in Kallik's throat. "And now it's over."

"Not over," Lusa corrected her. She glanced at Miki, waiting on the shore. "We all have new beginnings."

Every day is a new beginning, a voice breathed with the wind. Kallik blinked. Had the others heard it, too? Toklo lifted his head sharply. Lusa's fur tingled along her spine. As Kallik looked at Yakone, she glimpsed a shape moving among them. Hardly more than a shadow, it wreathed around them. A familiar scent touched her nose. *Ujurak.*

Wordlessly, the bears made space for him.

He shimmered, barely visible between them. "I'm very proud of you all." His voice stirred Kallik's ear fur like a warm breeze. "I'll be watching over you forever."

Kallik strained to see him better, longing for the rippling haze to become real. But a wind whipped in from the lake, and like smoke, he disappeared.

Kallik caught Toklo's eye. Sadness shone in his dark gaze.

"Toklo!" Aiyanna called to him softly across the shore. "We should go."

Toklo nodded to her, then turned to Lusa. "Thank you, Lusa, for never losing hope. And Yakone." His gaze settled on the white male. "Without your strength I'm not sure we would have survived." Finally he met Kallik's gaze.

Her breath caught in her throat.

"Kallik." Toklo's voice was husky with emotion. "You have taught me the importance of trust." He glanced at Aiyanna. "You all have given me so much. Now I know how to be happy."

As he turned away, Kallik's heart swelled.

"Good-bye." Lusa reached up. Her fruity breath bathed Kallik's muzzle as they touched noses. "I'll miss you." She turned to Yakone. "You too." Nuzzling him quickly, her eyes glistening with sadness, Lusa bounded from the rock and joined Miki on the shore.

Kallik gazed at Yakone. Sorrow choked her.

"It's time to go," Yakone murmured. "Star Island is waiting for us."

She followed him along the shore, to where Taqqiq and Shila were waiting to say good-bye, pausing to blink away grief. One more parting to go, and then they would begin the long journey home.

CHAPTER TWENTY-SEVEN

Lusa

Lusa's paws ached. The hot sun scorched her back. "We must be near now." Weary to the bone, she looked at Miki.

He was a little way ahead, following the winding deer track up the wooded slope. "I'm sure this is the last hill," he puffed.

"It is!" a male cub barked from the top. "I can see it!"

"I saw it first!" his sister huffed.

"You did not!"

"Now, now." Miki caught up to the cubs and walked between them.

We're here at last! Lusa's tiredness melted away and excitement fizzed beneath her pelt. As she reached the top, the view rolled out before her. The lake stretched, sparkling and blue, between pine-wooded hills toward the distant horizon. It was just as she remembered.

"It's so big!" The male cub stared, wide-eyed.

Lusa nuzzled her son's ear affectionately. "There, Yogi. I told you it was as big as an ocean."

His sister hopped from paw to paw. "Can we swim in it?"

Miki glanced at Lusa, checking. "Can they?"

"If they're not too tired from the journey," Lusa answered.

"I'm not too tired!" Yogi raced down the hill toward the shore.

"Neither am I!" yelped his sister, hurtling behind him.

"Watch out, Ashia!" Miki bounded after them as their daughter nearly crashed through a thornbush, swerving just in time.

Lusa paused at the top as her family disappeared among the trees. She gazed at the hills where the fire had ravaged the forest. They were green once more. Joy lifted her heart. She'd been sure that they would still be black and charred, just as they had been two—no, *three*—suncircles ago. Had it really been that long?

She searched the shoreline, her heart quickening as she saw brown bears moving over the pebbles, as small as rabbits from this distance. Farther along, white bears flopped on their rocky beach like patches of melting snow. Warmth flooded her heart. She knew how hard the white bears took the burn-sky sun, and yet they still trekked here every suncircle to honor their spirits.

Her paws pricked. *Are they here?* Plunging down the lush slope, she followed Miki, Yogi, and Ashia into the woods. She could hear them barking excitedly and followed their trail.

"Did you see the islands in the lake?" Yogi puffed.

"I'm going to swim to one and sleep on it all night," Ashia announced.

"No, you're not!" Miki told her. "That lake is deep. You're

going to stay in the shallows with me."

"But Lusa said that her friends swam to the islands," Ashia objected.

"Her friends are brown bears and white bears. They're used to swimming far."

As Lusa caught up to Miki, he flashed her an affectionate look. "I haven't seen them this excited since Yogi found his first bees' nest."

Lusa nudged her head against his shoulder. "I'm pretty excited, too."

"Miki! Is that you?" As they reached the black bears' territory, a gruff voice called through the trees. Ossi ambled out, his snout wet with berry juice.

"Ossi!" Miki hurried to greet him, butting him with his head. "How are you?"

"Fine." Ossi glanced over his shoulder. A female bear pushed through the ferns. "This is Yakni." Yakni dipped her head. "These are old friends," Ossi told her.

Lusa stepped toward Ossi and touched her muzzle to his. "It's great to see you again! Is Chula here?"

Yakni nodded toward the ferns. "She's picking berries back there."

"How's her injured paw?" Lusa asked.

"Injured paw?" Yakni looked puzzled. "She doesn't have an injured paw."

Lusa felt a surge of delight. "It must have healed."

"Thanks to you, Lusa," Ossi told her warmly.

Yakni's eyes lit up. "You're Lusa!" She leaned forward and

brushed her nose along Lusa's cheek. "I've heard so much about you."

As she spoke, Rudi padded stiffly up the slope toward them. "There are two young cubs down there, picking a bilberry patch clean," he grunted. "Anyone would think they hadn't eaten in a moon."

"That'll be Yogi and Ashia. They love bilberries." Miki hurried downslope. "They're going to make themselves sick. They had a whole grub nest for breakfast."

Rudi met Lusa's gaze. "Lusa! Are they your cubs?"

"Yes," she told him proudly.

"They're very handsome," Rudi chuffed.

"Thanks." Lusa felt the tug of the shore. "I'll catch up with you later." She followed Miki down the slope.

Rudi called after her. "Issa's here! And Tibik!"

"Great!" Lusa bounded past a bramble.

Miki was shooing Yogi and Ashia away from the bilberry patch. He glanced at Lusa as she hurried past. "We'll catch up!" He knew where she was going.

She burst from the trees and ran along the shore, slowing as she saw the brown bears ahead. She recognized Hattack rolling in the shallows. And there was Shesh, standing on the wide, flat rock where they'd honored the spirits after the fire.

She hurried past them, surprised to see them watching her warily. Had they forgotten Anarteq's words? *We should remember the power of friendship. We cannot live our lives separate from all the other living things—either prey or bears.*

A large female glared at her as Lusa nosed her way between

two more groups. Suddenly, she felt nervous. Perhaps she shouldn't have come here alone. Slowing, she looked around, meeting only puzzled and hostile stares. Then she saw Toklo.

He was padding from the trees. His pelt was sleek and dark. Was he broader across the shoulders? His gaze still carried a trace of darkness, as though he was concentrating hard.

"Toklo?" Lusa called.

He jerked his muzzle around, his eyes puzzled.

"Toklo! It's me!"

Toklo bounded over to her, scattering stones under his feet. "Lusa! You came!"

She yelped in surprise as he tumbled her over, pummeling her with his great soft paws like they were cubs. Snorting with laughter, Lusa rolled over and stood up. She shook out her pelt, aware that the other brown bears were staring at them.

"Take no notice of them!" Toklo grunted as he got up. "They have no idea how good it is to see you." He walked along the shore to where Aiyanna was playing tag with a cub.

"Toklo!" Lusa gasped. "Is she yours?"

Toklo nodded. "She's called Oka." He blocked Oka's path as she hurtled toward him and, scooping her up into a hug, nuzzled her lovingly.

Lusa recognized Aiyanna's face in the she-cub's, as well as Toklo's solemn gaze. "I'm an old friend of your father," she explained as Toklo let the cub slither to the ground.

"You're Lusa," Oka murmured shyly.

"We told her all about you," Toklo told her. "And Kallik and Yakone."

Lusa swung her head toward the white bears' shore. "Are they here?"

"I don't know yet," Toklo admitted. "We've only just arrived."

Aiyanna came to greet her, rubbing her muzzle against Lusa's cheek. "Where's Miki?"

Lusa glanced back. Miki was herding Yogi and Ashia through the shallows, carefully skirting the crowd of brown bears. "He's coming," she told Aiyanna. "That's Yogi and Ashia with them. They're our cubs."

"How lovely!" Aiyanna trotted to meet them, Oka at her heels.

Lusa glanced at Toklo. "Should we go find Kallik and Yakone?"

"Of course!" Toklo bounded past her, racing for the white bears' shore.

Pebbles clattered as she pelted after him, overtaking him as they reached the rocky stretch of beach.

A white female glared at them as they approached. "What are you doing here?" she growled.

Lusa pulled up. Had the white bears forgotten Anarteq's words, too?

"Nukka!" a familiar voice called from behind. "Don't you recognize them? It's Lusa and Toklo!" Shila moved toward them. She called over her shoulder. "Yakone! Kallik! They're here!"

Lusa stared at the crowd of white bears, her heart leaping as Yakone pushed between them. Kallik followed with two white cubs at her flank.

"You have cubs, too!" Lusa gasped. She bounded over and pressed herself against the huge white she-bear, letting the fishy smell of her old friend wash over her. Beside them, Toklo greeted Yakone by butting his head against the white bear's shoulder.

Lusa felt a wet muzzle in her ear. One of the cubs was sniffing her. She pulled away, twitching with amusement.

"That's Chulyin," Kallik told her. She nosed the other cub forward. "And this is his brother, Suka."

Chulyin didn't look at Lusa. His gaze was on Yogi, Ashia, and Oka. "What are they doing on our shore?"

"Yogi and Ashia are my cubs," Lusa explained.

"Oka's my daughter," Toklo added.

Chulyin's eyes widened. "Can we play with them?" He didn't wait for a reply but rushed toward them, calling to his brother, "Come on, Suka! We can teach them our new game."

Kallik watched them go. "They are so full of energy."

Lusa chuffed happily. "So are Yogi and Ashia."

Kallik blinked at her. "What lovely names." She turned to Toklo. "And you've named your daughter after your mother!"

Lusa gazed at Toklo, Kallik, and Yakone. "We're all here," she breathed.

"We hoped you'd come this year," Toklo told her. "We were starting to worry about you."

"It's been hard to leave my new home." Lusa's thoughts flashed to her first seasons in the forest with Miki. She was so happy. And now she was with her old friends again. Memories flooded her like sunshine: finding Taqqiq; losing Ujurak and then Chenoa; meeting Yakone; rescuing the trapped black bear spirits from the logjam in the river; riding on the back of a firesnake.

"How is Star Island?" she asked Kallik.

"It's great. The hunting has been good these past seasons. It feels wonderful to have nothing but ice beneath my paws." She gazed fondly at Yakone. "I can't imagine living anywhere else."

Lusa turned to Toklo. "And the forest?"

Toklo grunted. "Not bad. I chased Chogan off again, just as I'd promised, and we made his territory ours." For a moment satisfaction sharpened his gaze, but then it drifted to Aiyanna and Oka and softened. "Now I have the home I've always wanted."

Lusa reached up to run her cheek along his. "You deserve it."

"Do you ever see Ujurak?" Kallik asked quietly.

Lusa's heart clenched with familiar grief. "Sometimes." She never stopped searching for him, her heart quickening every time she saw an elk wandering alone or an owl swooping through the twilight. "I think I see him, but I'm never sure."

"I look for him in the stars every night," Toklo murmured.

"I dream of him," Kallik confessed. "But I don't think I've seen him for real, not since the fire."

Toklo shifted on the warm, rocky beach. "He is always with us."

"We'll never forget him," Kallik agreed.

Lusa felt the wind ruffle her fur. "We'll never forget any of it." She gazed around at her friends. "You taught me how to be a wild bear."

"You found me a home!" Toklo exclaimed.

"You gave me a family." Kallik blinked at them lovingly.

Yakone lifted his muzzle. "We should hunt together, one last time."

Lusa flinched. "It won't be the last! There will be more Longest Days. This isn't the end. And we'll always be together, in spirit."

"Oh, Lusa." Kallik leaned forward and touched her nose to Lusa's ear. "So much has changed, and there's still so much change to come. But you're right. Wherever our paths lead us, we'll always be together."

Yakone padded toward the lake. "Let's see who can catch the biggest fish."

"That's not fair!" Lusa bounded after him. "You can swim deeper than me."

Kallik caught up to her. "Then we'll catch the fish and you can decide whose is best."

They passed Aiyanna and Miki, who were sunning themselves while the cubs splashed one another in the shallows.

Toklo broke into a run and plunged into the lake. As Kallik and Yakone waded in after him, Lusa paused at the edge and watched. She saw the three of them reach deep blue water and dive beneath the surface. Sunshine glittered where they'd disappeared. Relishing the warmth on her pelt and the cold water washing around her paws, Lusa leaned forward expectantly, waiting for her friends to come back.

FOLLOW THE ADVENTURES!

WARRIORS: THE PROPHECIES BEGIN

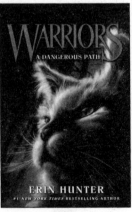

In the first series, sinister perils threaten the four warrior Clans. Into the midst of this turmoil comes Rusty, an ordinary housecat, who may just be the bravest of them all.

HARPER
'An Imprint of HarperCollinsPublishers

www.warriorcats.com

WARRIORS: THE NEW PROPHECY

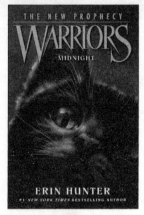

1

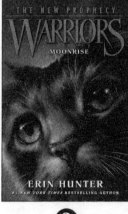

2

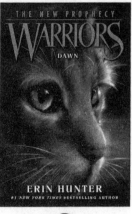

3

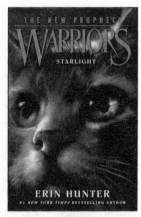

4

5

6

In the second series, follow the next generation of heroic cats as they set off on a quest to save the Clans from destruction.

HARPER
An Imprint of HarperCollinsPublishers

www.warriorcats.com

WARRIORS: POWER OF THREE

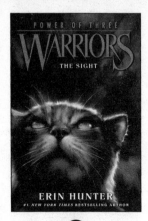

1

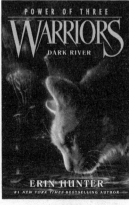

2

3

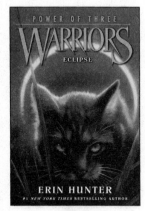

4

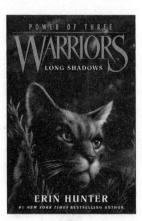

5

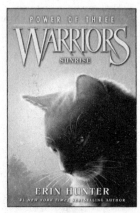

6

In the third series, Firestar's grandchildren begin their training as warrior cats. Prophecy foretells that they will hold more power than any cats before them.

HARPER
An Imprint of HarperCollinsPublishers

www.warriorcats.com

WARRIORS: OMEN OF THE STARS

OMEN OF THE STARS

WARRIORS
THE FOURTH APPRENTICE

ERIN HUNTER
#1 NEW YORK TIMES BESTSELLING AUTHOR

OMEN OF THE STARS

WARRIORS
FADING ECHOES

ERIN HUNTER
#1 NEW YORK TIMES BESTSELLING AUTHOR

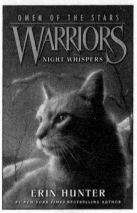

OMEN OF THE STARS

WARRIORS
NIGHT WHISPERS

ERIN HUNTER
#1 NEW YORK TIMES BESTSELLING AUTHOR

OMEN OF THE STARS

WARRIORS
SIGN OF THE MOON

ERIN HUNTER
#1 NEW YORK TIMES BESTSELLING AUTHOR

OMEN OF THE STARS

WARRIORS
THE FORGOTTEN WARRIOR

ERIN HUNTER
#1 NEW YORK TIMES BESTSELLING AUTHOR

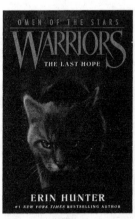

OMEN OF THE STARS

WARRIORS
THE LAST HOPE

ERIN HUNTER
#1 NEW YORK TIMES BESTSELLING AUTHOR

In the fourth series, find out which ThunderClan apprentice will complete the prophecy.

HARPER
An Imprint of HarperCollinsPublishers

www.warriorcats.com

WARRIORS : DAWN OF THE CLANS

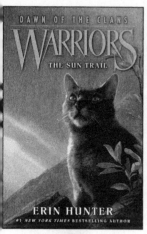

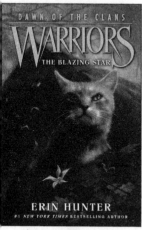

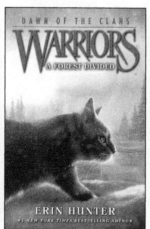

COMING SOON

In this prequel series,
discover how the warrior Clans came to be.

HARPER
An Imprint of HarperCollinsPublishers

www.warriorcats.com

WARRIORS: SUPER EDITIONS

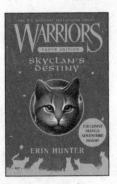

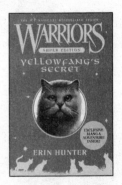

These extra-long, stand-alone adventures will take you deep inside each of the Clans with thrilling adventures featuring the most legendary warrior cats.

WARRIORS: BONUS STORIES

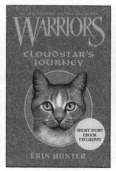

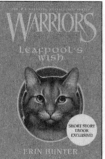

Discover the untold stories of the warrior cats and Clans when you download the separate ebook novellas—or read them in two paperback bind-ups!

HARPER
An Imprint of HarperCollinsPublishers

www.warriorcats.com

WARRIORS: FIELD GUIDES

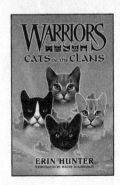

FOR THE ULTIMATE FAN!

Delve deeper into the Clans with these Warriors field guides.

HARPER
An Imprint of HarperCollinsPublishers

www.warriorcats.com

ALSO BY ERIN HUNTER:

SURVIVORS

SURVIVORS: THE ORIGINAL SERIES

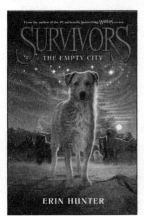  

The time has come for dogs to rule the wild.

HARPER
An Imprint of HarperCollinsPublishers

www.survivorsdogs.com

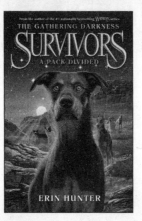